"Perfect pitch . . . incredible pacing . . . Leonard may write the best dialogue of any contemporary writer; his ear is unerring, he doesn't miss a nuance."

—*The Plain Dealer* (Cleveland)

PRAISE FOR
"THE BEST WRITER IN CRIME FICTION TODAY."
—*USA Today*

ELMORE LEONARD

and his magnificent national best seller

RUM PUNCH

"The most loathsome of Elmore Leonard's villains can arouse our pity and amusement even as his ambiguous heroes and heroines may startle us with an act of cold-blooded cruelty."

—*San Francisco Chronicle*

"Breathtaking . . . brilliantly realized . . . like the title says, it's a heady brew."

—*Kirkus Reviews*

"Elmore Leonard is at his best when it comes to portraying the workings of the criminal mind. Nowhere is that talent more evidenced than within the pages of *Rum Punch*."

—*Pasadena Star-Tribune*

"VINTAGE LEONARD . . . the dialogue is as authentic as conversations overheard."

—*Publishers Weekly*

Please turn the page for more extraordinary acclaim . . .

ALSO BY ELMORE LEONARD

ELMORE LEONARD

RUM PUNCH

A DELL BOOK

Published by
Dell Publishing
a division of
Bantam Doubleday Dell Publishing Group, Inc.
1540 Broadway
New York, New York 10036

ISBN: 0-440-21415-7

Reprinted by arrangement with Delacorte Press

Printed in the United States of America

Published simultaneously in Canada

August 1993

10 9 8 7 6 5 4

OPM

For Jackie, Carole, and Larry

1

Sunday morning, Ordell took Louis to watch the white-power demonstration in downtown Palm Beach.

"Young skinhead Nazis," Ordell said. "Look, even little Nazigirls marching down Worth Avenue. You believe it? Coming now you have the Klan, not too many here today. Some in green, must be the coneheads' new spring shade. Behind them it looks like some Bikers for Racism, better known as the Dixie Knights. We gonna move on ahead, fight through the crowd here," Ordell said, bringing Louis along.

"There's a man I want to show you. See who he reminds you of. He told me they're gonna march up South County and have their show on the steps of the fountain by city hall. You ever see so many police? Yeah, I expect you have. But not all these different uniforms at one time. They mean business too, got their helmets on, their riot ba-tons. Stay on the sidewalk or they liable to hit you over the head. They keeping the street safe for the Nazis."

People would turn to look at Ordell.

"Man, all the photographers, TV cameras. This shit is big news, has everybody over here to see it. Otherwise, Sunday, what you have mostly are rich ladies come out with their little doggies to make wee-wee. I mean the doggies, not the ladies." A girl in front of them smiled over her shoulder and Ordell said, "How you doing, baby? You making it all right?" He looked past her now, glanced at Louis to say, "I think I see him," and pushed through the crowd to get closer to the street. "Yeah, there he is. Black shirt and tie? A grown-up skinhead Nazi. I call him Big Guy. He likes that."

"It's Richard," Louis said. "Jesus."

"Looks just like him, huh? Remember how Richard tripped on all that Nazi shit he had in his house? All his guns? Big Guy's got more of everything."

Louis said, "He's serious. Look at him."

"Wants power. He's a gun freak," Ordell said. "You know where you see different ones like him? At the gun shows."

Ordell let it hang. Louis was supposed to ask Ordell what he was doing at gun shows, but didn't bother. He was busy watching the Nazigirls, all of them skinny rednecks, their hair cut short as boys'.

Ordell said, "I got something would straighten them out, make their eyes shine."

He had people looking at him again. Some of them grinned. Louis moved out of the crowd and Ordell had to hurry to catch him. Louis bigger in the shoulders than he used to be, from working out in prison.

"This way," Ordell said, and they started up South County ahead of the parade, couple of old buddies: Ordell Robbie and Louis Gara, a light-skinned black guy and a dark-skinned white guy, both from Detroit originally where they met in a bar, started talking, and found out they'd both been to Southern Ohio Correctional and had some attitudes in common. Not long after that Louis went to Texas, where he took another fall. Came home and Ordell had a proposition for him: a million-dollar idea to kidnap the wife of a guy making money illegally and hiding it in the Bahamas. Louis said okay. The scheme blew up in their face and Louis said never again. Thirteen years ago . . .

And now Ordell had another scheme. Louis could feel it. The reason they were here watching skinheads and coneheads marching up the street.

Ordell said, "Remember when you come out of Huntsville and I introduced you to Richard?"

Starting to lay it on him. Louis was positive now.

"That's what today reminds me of," Ordell said. "I think it's fate working. This time you come out of FSP and I show you Big Guy, like Richard back from the dead."

"What I remember from that time," Louis said, "is wishing I never met Richard. What is it with you and Nazis?"

"They fun to watch," Ordell said. "Look at the flag they got, with the boogied-up lightning flash on it. You can't tell if it's suppose to be SS or Captain Marvel."

Louis said, "You got another million-dollar idea to try on me?"

Ordell turned from the parade with a cool look, serious. "You rode in my car. That ain't just an idea, man, it cost real money."

"What're you showing me this Nazi for?"

"Big Guy? His real name's Gerald. I called him Jerry one time, he about lifted me off the ground, said, 'That's not my name, boy.' I told him I'm for segregation of the races, so he thinks I'm okay. Met him one time, was at a gun show."

Throwing that one at Louis again.

Louis said, "You didn't answer my question. What're we doing here?"

"I told you. See who Big Guy reminds you of. Listen, there's somebody else you won't believe who's down here. This one a woman. Guess who it is."

Louis shook his head. "I don't know."

Ordell grinned. "Melanie."

"You're kidding."

Another one from that time thirteen years ago.

"Yeah, we kep' in touch. Melanie phone me one day . . . She's in a place I have up at Palm Beach Shores. You want to see her?"

"She lives with you?"

"I'm there on and off, you might say. We can drop by this afternoon, you want. Melanie's still a fine big

---

girl, only bigger. Man, I'm telling you, fate's been working its ass off, getting us all together here. What I'm thinking of doing, introduce Big Guy to Melanie.''

Leading up to something. Louis could feel it.

"For what?"

"Just see what happens. I think it'd be a kick. You know Melanie, she hasn't changed any. Can you see her with this asshole Nazi?''

Ordell acting like a kid with a secret, dying to tell it, but wanting to be asked.

He said to Louis, "You don't know where in the fuck you're at, do you? Keep coming out of prison and starting over. I see you got rid of your mustache, have some gray in your curly hair. You staying in shape, that's good.''

"What'd you do," Louis said, "get your hair straightened? You used to have a 'fro.''

"Got to keep in style, man.''

Ordell ran his hand carefully over his hair, feeling the hard set, ran it back to his pigtail braid and curled it between his fingers, fooling with it as he said, "No, I don't imagine you know what you want.''

Louis said, "You don't, huh?''

"Giving me the convict stare. Well, you learned *some*thing in the joint," Ordell said. "Otherwise, Louis, that shirt you have on, you look like you pump more gas than iron. Ought to have 'Lou' on the pocket there. Clean the windshield, check the oil. . . .''

Smiled then to show he was kidding. Ordell in

---

linen and gold, orange crew-neck sweater and white slacks, the gold shining on his neck, his wrist, and two of his fingers.

He said, "Come on, let's go see the show."

Louis said, "You're the show."

Ordell smiled and moved his shoulders like a fighter. They walked up behind the crowd that was held back by yellow police tape cordoning off the steps in front of the fountain. A young Nazi up there was speaking as the others stood facing the crowd in their supremacy outfits. Ordell started to push through to get closer and Louis took hold of his arm.

"I'm not going in there."

Ordell turned to look at him. "It ain't the same as on the yard, man. Nobody has a shank on them."

"I'm not going in there with *you*."

"Well, that's cool," Ordell said. "We don't have to."

They found a place where they could see enough of the young Nazi. He was shouting, "What do we want?" And his buddies and the Nazigirls and the rest of the cuckoos up there would shout back, "White power!" They kept it up until the young Nazi finished and shouted, "One day the world will know Adolf Hitler was right!" That got voices from the crowd shouting back at him, calling him stupid and a retard. He yelled at the crowd, "We're going to re-claim this land for our people!" his young Nazi voice cracking. And they yelled back, what people was he talking about, assholes like him? A black woman in the crowd said, "Come on up to Riv'era Beach and say those things, you be dead." The young skinhead Nazi began screaming "Sieg heil!" as loud as he could, over and over, and the cuckoos joined in with him, giving the Nazi salute. Now young guys in the crowd were calling them racist motherfuckers, telling them to go home, go on, get out of here, and it looked like the show was over.

Ordell said, "Let's go."

They walked over to Ocean Boulevard where they'd left his car, a black Mercedes convertible, with the top down. The time on the meter had run out and a parking ticket was stuck beneath the windshield wiper on the driver's side. Ordell pulled the ticket out and dropped it in the street. Louis was watching but didn't comment. Didn't say much of anything until they were on the middle bridge heading back to West Palm. Then he started.

"Why'd you want to show me that guy? He call you a nigger and you want his legs broken?"

"That payback shit," Ordell said, "you must get that from hanging out with the Eyetalians. Ain't nothing they like better than paying back. Swear an oath to it."

"You want to see where I hang out?" Louis said. "You come to Olive, take a right. Go up to Banyan, used to be First Street, and hang a left." The next thing Louis was telling him, on Olive now, "That's the court building up on the right."

"I know where the courts are at," Ordell said. He turned onto Banyan and was heading toward Dixie

Highway now. Halfway up the block Louis told him to stop.

"Right there, the white building," Louis said, "that's where I hang out."

Ordell turned his head to look across the street at a one-story building, a storefront with MAX CHERRY BAIL BONDS printed on the window.

"You work for a *bail* bondsman? You told me you with some funky insurance company the Eyetalians got hold of."

"Glades Mutual in Miami," Louis said. "Max Cherry writes their bonds. I sit in the office—some guy misses his court date, I go get him."

"Yeah?" That sounded a little better, like Louis was a bounty hunter, went after bad guys on the run.

"What they want me for mainly, see if I can bring in some of those big drug-trafficking bonds, hundred and fifty grand and up."

Ordell said, "Yeah, I 'magine you made some good contacts in the joint. That why the company hired you?"

"It was my cellmate, guy was in for killing his wife. He told me to look up these friends of his when I got out. I go to see them, they ask me if I know any Colombians. I said yeah, a few. Some guys I met through a con named J.J. I told you about him, the one that got picked up again? I'm staying in his house." Louis lifted a cigarette from the pocket of his work shirt. "So what I do is look up these Colombians, down in South Beach, and hand out Max Cherry business cards. 'If you ever go to jail, I'm your bail.'

He's got another one that says 'Gentlemen prefer bonds' with his name under it, phone number, all that.'' Louis went into the pocket again for a kitchen match.

Ordell waited. ''Yeah?''

''That's it. Most of the time I sit there.''

''You get along with the Colombians?''

''Why not? They know where I came from.'' Louis struck the match with his thumbnail. ''They play that cha-cha music so loud you can't hardly talk anyway.''

Ordell got his own brand out and Louis gave him a light in his cupped hands.

''You don't sound happy, Louis.''

He said, ''Whatever you're into, I don't want any part of it, okay? Once was enough.''

Ordell sat back with his cigarette.

''Like you Steady Eddie, huh? I'm the one fucked up that kidnap deal?''

''You're the one brought Richard in.''

''What's that have to do with it?''

''You knew he'd try to rape her.''

''Yeah, and you helped her out of that mess. But that ain't what blew the deal, Louis. You know what it was. We tell the man, pay up or you never see your wife again—'cause that's how you do it, right? Then find out he don't *want* to see her again, even for five minutes? Down there in his Bahama love nest with Melanie? If you can't negotiate with the man, Louis, or threaten him, then you don't have even a chance of making a deal.''

9

"It would've come apart anyway," Louis said. "We didn't know what we were doing."

"I see you the expert now. Tell me who's been in prison three times and who's been in once? Listen, I got people working for me now. I got brothers do the heavy work. I got a man over in Freeport—you remember Mr. Walker? I got a Jamaican can do figures in his head. Can add up numbers, can multiply what things cost times how many"—Ordell snapped his fingers—"like that."

"You got an accountant," Louis said. "I'm happy for you."

"Have I asked you to come work for me?"

"Not yet you haven't."

"You know what a M-60 machine gun is?"

"A big one, a military weapon."

"I sold three of them for twenty grand each and bought this automobile," Ordell said. "What do I need you for?"

2

Monday afternoon, Renee called Max at his office to say she needed eight hundred twenty dollars right away and wanted him to bring her a check. Renee was at her gallery in The Gardens Mall on PGA Boulevard. It would take Max a half hour at least to drive up there.

He said, "Renee, even if I wanted to, I can't. I'm waiting to hear from a guy. I just spoke to the judge about him." He had to listen then while she told how she had been trying to get hold of him. "That's where I was, at court. I got your message on the beeper. . . . I just got back, I haven't had time. . . . Renee, I'm working, for Christ sake." Max paused, holding the phone to his ear, not able to say anything. He looked up to see a black guy in a yellow sport coat standing in his office. A black guy with shiny hair holding a Miami Dolphins athletic bag. Max said,

"Renee, listen a minute, okay? I got a kid's gonna do ten fucking years if I don't get hold of him and take him in and you want me to . . . Renee?"

Max replaced the phone.

The black guy said, "Hung up on you, huh? I bet that was your wife."

The guy smiling at him.

Max came close to saying, yeah, and you know what she said to me? He wanted to. Except that it wouldn't make sense to tell this guy he didn't know, had never seen before . . .

The black guy saying, "There was nobody in the front office, so I walked in. I got some business."

The phone rang. Max picked it up, pointing to a chair with his other hand, and said, "Bail Bonds."

Ordell heard him say, "It doesn't matter where you were, Reggie, you missed your hearing. Now I have to . . . Reg, listen to me, okay?" This Max Cherry speaking in a quieter voice than he used on his wife. Talking to her had sounded painful. Ordell placed his athletic bag on an empty desk that faced the one Max Cherry was at and got out a cigarette.

This looked more like the man's den than a bail bond office: a whole wall of shelves behind where Max Cherry sat with books on it, all kinds of books, some wood-carved birds, some beer mugs. It was too neat and homey for this kind of scummy business. The man himself appeared neat, clean-shaved, had his blue shirt open, no tie, good size shoulders on him. That dark, tough-looking type of guy like Louis, dark hair, only Max Cherry was losing his on top. Up in his fifties somewhere. He could be Eyetalian, except Ordell had never met a bail bondsman wasn't Jewish. Max was telling the guy now the judge was ready to habitualize him. "That what you want, Reg? Look at ten years instead of six months and probation? I said, 'Your Honor, Reggie has always been an outstanding client. I know I can find him right now . . .'"

Ordell, lighting the cigarette, paused as Max paused.

"'. . . out standing on the corner by his house.'"

Listen to him. Doing standup.

"I can have the capias set aside, Reg. . . . The fugitive warrant, they're gonna be looking for you, man. But it means I'll have to pick you up."

Ordell blew out smoke and looked around for an ashtray. He saw the NO SMOKING sign above the door to what looked like a meeting room, a long table in there, what looked like a refrigerator, a coffee maker.

"Stay at your mom's till I come for you. You'll have to go back in. . . . Overnight, that's all. Tomorrow you'll be out, I promise." Ordell watched Max hang up the phone saying, "He's home when I get there or I have a five-thousand-dollar problem. What's yours?"

"I don't see an ashtray," Ordell said, holding up his cigarette. "The other thing, I need a bond for ten thousand."

"What've you got for collateral?"

"Gonna have to put up cash."

"You have it with you?"

"In my bag."

"Use that coffee mug on the desk."

Ordell moved around the desk, clean, nothing on it but his athletic bag, a telephone, and the coffee mug with still some in it. He flicked his ash and sat down in the swivel chair to face Max Cherry again, over behind his desk.

"You have cash," Max said, "what do you need me for?"

"Come on," Ordell said, "you know how they do. Want to know where you got it, then keep out a big chunk, say it's for court costs. Pull all kind of shit on you."

"It'll cost you a thousand for the bond."

"I know that."

"Who's it for, a relative?"

"Fella name Beaumont. They have him up at the Gun Club jail."

Max Cherry kept staring from his desk, hunched over some. He had a computer there and a typewriter and a stack of file folders, one of them open.

"Was sheriff deputies picked him up Saturday night," Ordell said. "It started out drunk driving, but they wrote it 'possession of a concealed weapon.' Had a pistol on him."

"Ten thousand sounds high."

"They ran his name and got a hit, saw he's been in before. Or they don't like it he's Jamaican. You know what I'm saying? They afraid he might take off."

"If he does and I have to go to Jamaica after him, you cover the expenses."

This was interesting. Ordell said, "You think you could pick him up down there? Put him on a plane, bring him back?"

"I've done it. What's his full name?"

"Beaumont. That's the only name I know."

Max Cherry, getting papers out of his drawer, looked over this way again, the man no doubt thinking, You putting that kind of money up and you don't even know his name? Ordell got a kick out of people wondering about him, this man—look at him—holding back from asking the question. Ordell said, "I have people do favors for me don't even have names outside of like Zulu, Cujo, one they call Wa-wa. Street names. You know what they call me sometime? Whitebread, account of my shade. Or they say just 'Bread' for short. It's okay, they not disrespecting me." See what the man thought of that.

He didn't say. He picked up his phone.

Ordell smoked his cigarette, watching as the man punched numbers, and heard him ask for the Records Office, then ask somebody if they'd look up the Booking Card and Rough Arrest on a defendant named Beaumont, saying he believed it was the surname but wasn't sure, check the ones came in Saturday night. He had to wait before getting what he wanted, asking questions and filling out a form on his desk. When he was done and had hung up the phone he said, "Beaumont Livingston."

"Livingston, huh?"

"On his prior," Max Cherry said, "he did nine months and is working out four years probation. For possession of unregistered machine guns."

"You don't tell me."

"So he's violated his probation. He's looking at ten years plus the concealed weapon."

"Man, he won't like that," Ordell said. He drew on his cigarette and dropped it in the coffee mug. "Beaumont don't have the disposition for doing time."

Now Max Cherry was staring again before he said, "You ever been to prison?"

"Long time ago in my youth I did a bit in Ohio. Wasn't anything, stealing cars."

"I need your name too, and your address."

Ordell told him it was Ordell Robbie, spelled it for him when the man asked, and said where he lived.

"That a Jamaican name?"

"Hey, do I sound like one of them? You hear them talking that island potwah to each other, it's like a different language. No, man, I'm African-American. I used to be Neegro, I was cullud, I was black, but now I'm African-American. What're you, Jewish, huh?"

"You're African-American, I guess I'm French-American," Max Cherry said. "With maybe some New Orleans Creole in there, going way back." Now he was shuffling through papers on his desk to find the ones he wanted. "You'll have to fill out an Application for Appearance Bond, an Indemnity Agreement, a Contingent Promissory Note . . . It's the one, if Beaumont skips and I go after him, you pay the expenses."

"Beaumont ain't going nowhere," Ordell said. "You gonna have to figure out some other way to skim, make more than your ten percent. I'm surprised you don't try to double the fee account of he's Jamaican. . . ."

"It's against the law."

"Yeah, but it's done, huh? You people have your ways. Like not refunding the collateral." Ordell got up, went over to the man's desk with the athletic bag he bought at the airport souvenir shop, and took a bundle of currency out of it, old bills held together with a rubber band. "Hundred times a hundred," Ordell said, "and ten more for your cut. You do all right, huh? What I like to know is where you keeping my money till I get it back. In your drawer?"

"Across the street at First Union," Max Cherry said, taking the bills and working the rubber bands off. "It goes in a trust account."

"So you gonna make some money extra on the interest, huh? I knew it."

The man didn't say yes or no, busy counting hundred-dollar bills now. When he was done and Ordell was signing the different papers, the man asked if he was going out to the jail with him. Ordell straightened up and thought about it before shaking his head.

"Not if I don't need to. Tell Beaumont I'll be in touch." Ordell buttoned his double-breasted sport jacket, his canary one he wore over the black T-shirt and black silk trousers this afternoon. He wondered how tall this Max Cherry was, so he said, "Nice doing business with you," and stuck out his hand without reaching toward him. Max Cherry rose up to stand six feet and some, a speck taller than Ordell, with a big mitt on him Ordell shook and let go. The man nodded, that was it, and stood waiting for him to leave.

Ordell said, "You know why I come here, not someplace else? Friend of mine I understand does some work for you."

"You mean Winston?"

"Another fella, Louis Gara. He's my white friend," Ordell said, and smiled.

Max Cherry didn't. He said, "I haven't seen him today."

"Yeah, well, I'll catch him sometime." Ordell picked up his bag and started for the door. He stopped and looked back. "I got one other question. What if, I was just thinking, what if before the court date gets here Beaumont gets hit by a car or something and dies? I get the money back, don't I?"

What he was saying was, he *knew* he'd get it back. The kind of guy who worked at being cool, but was dying to tell you things about himself. He knew the system, knew the main county lockup was called the Gun Club jail, after the road it was on. He'd served time, knew Louis Gara, and drove off in a Mercedes convertible. What else you want to know? Ordell Robbie. Max was surprised he'd never heard of him.

He turned away from the front window, went back to his office to type up bail forms.

The first one, the Power of Attorney. Max rolled it into his typewriter and paused, looking at his problem. It would hit him in the eye every time he filled out a form that had GLADES MUTUAL CASUALTY COMPANY printed across the top.

The Power of Attorney verified Max Cherry as the insurance company's licensed surety-bond representative, here, in the matter of Beaumont Livingston. The way it worked, the insurance company would get one third of the ten percent premium and put a third of it into a buildup fund to cover forfeitures.

If Max wrote fifty thousand dollars' worth of bail bonds a week, he'd clear five grand less expenses and the one third that went to Glades Mutual in Miami. It was a grind, but good money if you put in the hours.

The problem was that after representing Glades for the past nineteen years, no complaints either way, the company was now under new management, taken over by guys with organized crime connections. Max was sure of it. They'd even placed an ex-con in his office, Ordell Robbie's friend Louis Gara. "To help out," this thug from Glades Mutual said, a guy who didn't know shit about the business. "Go after some of those big drug-trafficking bonds."

"What those people do," Max told the guy, "is skip as soon as they're bonded."

The guy said, "So what? We got the premium."

"I don't write people who I know are gonna forfeit."

The guy said, "If they don't want to show up in court, that's their business."

"And it's my business who I write," Max told him.

The guy from Glades said, "You got an attitude problem," and gave him Louis to hang around the office, a convicted bank robber just out of prison.

Winston came in while Max was preparing the forms. Winston Willie Powell, a licensed bondsman following a 39 and 10 record as a middleweight. He was light heavy in retirement, short and thick, with a bearded black face so dark it was hard to make out his features. Max watched him, at the other desk now, unlock the right-hand drawer and take out a snub-nosed .38 before he looked over.

"Have to pick up that little Puerto Rican house-breaker thinks he's Zorro. Has the swords on his wall? Man lies to his probation officer, she violates him, we bond him, and then he don't show up for his hearing. I called Delray PD, said I might need some backup, depending how it goes. They say to me, 'He's your problem, man.' They don't want to mess with those women live there. Touch Zorro, they try to scratch your eyes out."

"You want help? Get Louis."

Winston said, "I rather do it myself," shoving the .38 into his waistband and smoothing his ribbed knit T-shirt over it. "Who you writing?"

"Concealed weapon. Ten thousand."

"That's high."

"Not for Beaumont Livingston. They caught him one time with machine guns."

"Beaumont—he's Jamaican he's gone."

"This African-American gent who put up cash says no."

"We know him?"

"Ordell Robbie," Max said and waited.

Winston shook his head. "Where's he live?"

"On Thirty-first right off Greenwood. You know that neighborhood? It's kept up. People have bars on their windows."

"You want, I'll check him out."

"He knows Louis. They're old buddies."

"Then you know the man's dirty," Winston said. "Where's Beaumont live?"

"Riviera Beach. He's hired help but worth ten grand to Mr. Robbie."

"Wants his man sprung 'fore he gets squeezed and cops to a deal. I can bring him out when I take Zorro."

"I'm going up anyway. I have to deliver Reggie."

"Missed his hearing again? They beauties, aren't they?"

"He says it was his mother's birthday, he forgot."

"And you believe that shit. I swear, there times you act like these people are no different than anybody else."

"I'm glad we're having this talk," Max said.

"Yeah, well, I'm enough irritated the way you act," Winston said, "you better not get smart with me. Like nothing bothers you. Like not even Mr. Louis Gara, the way you let him waste your time. Let him smoke his cigarettes in here."

"No, Louis bothers me," Max said.

"Then throw his ass out and lock the door. Then call that crooked insurance company and tell them you're through. You don't, they gonna eat you up or get you in trouble with the state commission, and you know it."

"Right," Max said. He turned to his typewriter.

"Listen to me. All you got to do is stop writing their bonds."

"You mean quit the business."

"For a while. What's wrong with that?"

"If you haven't looked at the books lately," Max said, "we've got close to a million bucks out there."

"It don't mean you have to work. Ride it out. See, then when it's all off the books you start over."

"I got bills to pay, like everybody else."

"Yeah, but you could do it if you wanted; there ways. What I think is, you tired of the business."

"You're right again," Max said, tired of talking about it.

"But you don't see a way to get out, so you act like nothing bothers you."

Max didn't argue. Nine years together, Winston knew him. It was quiet and then Winston said, "How's Renee doing?" Coming at him from another direction. "She making it yet?"

"You want to know if I'm still paying her bills?"

"Don't tell me what you don't want to."

"Okay, the latest," Max said. He turned from his

typewriter. "I walk in, I just got back from seeing the judge about Reggie, she calls."

He paused as Winston sat down and hunched over the desk on his arms, Winston staring at him now, waiting.

"She's at the mall. Something she ordered, three olive pots, arrived COD and she needs eight twenty right away. That's eight hundred and twenty."

"What's a olive pot?"

"How should I know? What she wanted was for me to drop whatever I was doing and bring her a check."

Winston sat there staring at him, his head down in those heavy shoulders. "For these olive pots."

"I said, 'Renee, I'm working. I'm trying to save a young man from doing ten years and I'm waiting for him to call.' I try to explain it to her in a nice way. You know what she said? She said, 'Well, I'm working too.'"

Winston seemed to smile. It was hard to tell. He said, "I was out there one time. Renee act like she didn't see me and I'm the only person in there."

"That's what I mean," Max said. "She says she's working—doing what? You never see anybody unless she's got the wine and cheese out. You know what I mean? For a show. Then you have all the freeloaders. You see these guys, they look like they live in cardboard boxes under the freeway, they're eating everything, drinking the wine . . . You know who they are? The artists and their crowd. I've even recognized guys I've written. Renee's playing like she's Peter Pan, has her hair cut real short, and all these assholes are the Lost Boys. The place clears out, she hasn't sold one fucking painting."

"So what you're telling me," Winston said, "you're still supporting her habit."

"She's got a Cuban guy now, David, I mean Daveed, she says is gonna be discovered and make it big, any day now. The guy's a busboy at Chuck and Harold's."

"See, what I don't understand," Winston said, "you let a woman don't weigh a hundred pounds beat up on you. It's the same as how you treat some of these lowlife assholes we dealing with. They give you all kind of shit and you go along with it. Then I see you pick up a guy that skipped, some mean-drunk motherfucker and you cuff him, no problem, and take him in. You understand what I'm saying? Why don't you tell the woman to pay her own bills or you gonna divorce her? Or go ahead and divorce her anyway. You don't live together. What're you getting out of being married? Nothing. Am I right? 'Less you still going to bed with her."

"When you're separated," Max said, "you don't get to do that. You don't want to."

"Yeah, well, I imagine you do all right with the ladies. But where she getting hers, off the artists? This Cuban busboy, Da-veed? If she is, that's a good reason to divorce her. Catch her going out on you."

"You're getting personal now," Max said.

Winston looked surprised. "Man, we been getting nothing *but* personal. It's your personal life has you messed up, one problem pressing on another. The way Renee has hold of your balls, you don't have the strength to get the insurance company off your back. All the money you put in her picture store, paying her bills, you could shut down here and live on it till you start up again clean, with a different insurance company. You know I'm right too, so I'm not gonna say another word."

"Good," Max said. He turned to the Power of Attorney form in his typewriter. ·

"You take her the check she wanted?"

"No, I didn't."

"She call back?"

"Not yet."

"She cry and carry on like she does?"

"She hung up on me," Max said. "Look, I have to finish this and get out of here."

"Don't let me disturb you."

Max started typing again.

He heard Winston say, "Hey, shit—" and looked over to see him standing at the desk now holding his coffee mug.

"That goddamn Louis, you see what he done? Put his cigarette butt in here. I'm gonna punch him right in his smokin' mouth."

Max turned back to the form, GLADES MUTUAL CASUALTY printed across the top. He said, "I know how you feel. But when you hit an ex-con who's done three falls, they say you better kill him."

3

Ordell asked one of his jackboys to get him a car with keys in it and leave it in the Ocean Mall parking lot over by the beach. The jackboy asked him what kind of car he wanted. Ordell said, "One has a big trunk with a shotgun in it."

He liked jackboys because they were crazy. They made their living ripping off street dealers for their blow and change and busting into crack houses with assault weapons. Jackboys liked Ordell because he was cool, not some homey everybody knew; the man was big-time from Detroit, had different women he stayed with as it suited him, and could deliver you a full-automatic weapon on two days notice. So now some of the jackboys worked for Ordell, picking up special kinds of guns he needed to fill orders. The one who was getting him the car, Cujo, called him that Tuesday evening where he was staying with one of his women to say it was there waiting, an Olds Ninety-Eight, 12-gauge in the trunk.

Ordell said, "The car, if it's clean now it won't be after."

Cujo said, "It don't matter, Bread, it's stole. Was a brother had it that's dead from the other night. You hear of it? Policeman shot him both in the front and in the back. We try to get him from the house, but he bled out on us so we left him."

"I saw it in the paper," Ordell said. "The cop told them yeah, when a man is shot sometimes he'll spin around on you, it ain't unusual, and that's what happened. But where did he shoot him first, in the front or in the back?"

Cujo said, "Yeaaah . . . that's right, huh?"

You could mess with a jackboy's head, get him to think what you wanted, their brains cooked from doing crack.

Ordell thanked him for the car and Cujo said, "Bread? They's a piece underneath with the keys, case you want it. Belonged to the brother was shot dead."

Ordell had three women he kept in three different homes.

He had Sheronda living in the house on 31st Street off Greenwood Avenue, in West Palm. Sheronda, a young woman he'd picked up coming through Fort Valley, Georgia, one time on his way back from Detroit. There she was, standing at the side of the road, no shoes on, sunlight showing her body in the wornout dress. Sheronda cooked good collards with salt pork, black-eyed peas, chicken-fried steak, cleaned the house, and provided Ordell with grateful pussy, anytime day or night, for taking her out of the peanut fields. There was nothing in this little red-brick ranch that told what Ordell did for a living. About once a week he'd have to explain to Sheronda how to set the alarm system. She was afraid of getting trapped in the house, not able to get out with grillwork covering the windows.

Simone, a cute woman for her age, sixty-three years old, was from Detroit and knew all about alarm systems and liked the bars on her windows. Ordell had her living in a stucco Spanish-looking house on 30th Street near Windsor Avenue, not two blocks from Sheronda's, but without them knowing about each other. Simone put weaves in her hair and believed she resembled Diana Ross. Her pleasure was to sing along with Motown recordings and do the steps and gestures accompanying the Supremes, Martha and the Vandellas, Gladys Knight and the Pips, Syreeta Wright, all the oldies. Whenever Ordell let Simone take him to bed, it was ten times better than he thought it would be. Simone could write a book on the different ways to please a man. Ordell would store guns temporarily in this house, semiautomatic weapons like TEC-9s purchased legally by "straw buyers" that Simone hired to do it, mostly retired people. Give an old woman the cash plus twenty bucks to buy an assault rifle. None of the straw buyers knew about Ordell, at least not by name.

He had his white woman, Melanie, living in the apartment in Palm Beach Shores, located at the south end of Singer Island, only two blocks from the public beach. Melanie was the fine big girl Ordell had met in the Bahamas when he went there to see the husband of the woman he and Louis had kidnapped. Melanie was only about twenty-one then, making her thirty-four or so now, but had hustled her tail all over the world taking up with rich guys. She had been with the husband of the kidnapped woman, but when Ordell looked for him he was hiding and she wouldn't tell where he was. So Ordell, what he did was have his friend Mr. Walker take them out in the ocean in his boat and Ordell threw Melanie over the side. They went off a ways, circled around back to where Melanie's blond head was bobbing in the water, and Ordell asked her, "You want to tell me where the man's at?" She was a show. Told Ordell after she would help him score off the husband of the kidnapped woman 'cause she liked him, Ordell, better. She said also 'cause she didn't want to end up in the fucking ocean.

So here was Melanie after keeping in touch, running into her in Miami . . . Melanie still up for a hustle anytime. She didn't cook or clean too good and, for all her talk and acting sexual, was only average in the bed. (Ordell wondered should he send her over to Simone's for some lessons.) The fine big girl had in thirteen years become bigger, show tits grown to circus tits but still okay, tan, always tanning her body out on the apartment balcony facing the ocean. Ordell used this place sometimes for business, would have his big blond woman get off her butt and serve drinks while he showed his gun movie to buyers from Detroit and New York City. Mr. Walker, over in Freeport, had a print he showed to buyers from Colombia.

The jackboy, Cujo, had called here a few moments ago to say the Olds Ninety-Eight was waiting. Ordell still had the phone in his hand. He punched a number in Freeport, Grand Bahama.

"Mr. Walker, how you this evening?"

Melanie looked up from *Vanity Fair*, the magazine she was reading on the sofa. She went around in cut-offs and had her fine brown legs tucked under her.

"I got Beaumont out. Cost me ten thousand. I get it back, but don't like having it out of my sight." Ordell listened and said, "Was yesterday. I had to do some thinking, reason I didn't call you right away."

Melanie was still watching him. Ordell looked over and she lowered her eyes to the magazine like she wasn't interested. She'd be listening though, and that was fine. He wanted her to know some things without knowing everything.

"You way ahead of me, Mr. Walker. I had the same thought." Cedric Walker had been a two-bit fishing guide with a whaler till Ordell showed him where the money was. Now the man had a thirty-six-foot Carver with all kinds of navigational shit on it. "You understand, the drunk driving alone violates Beaumont's probation. It wouldn't matter he had the pistol on him . . . That's right, they bring up the machine gun charge again. Means he'll be facing ten years and what he gets for the concealed weapon on top of it. That's what the bail-bond man said. . . . No, I let him put up the bond. Max Cherry . . . Yeah, that's the man's name. Sounds like one a calypso singer would have, huh? Maximilian Cherry and his Oil Can Boppers . . . What? No, I can't see it either. They keep him overnight he's pulling his hair out. I'd send him home to Montego if it didn't cost me the ten. . . . No, there's nothing to talk about. Mr. Walker? Melanie says hi." Ordell listened again and said, "She'll love you for it, man. I'll tell her. You be good now, hear?" and hung up the phone.

Melanie, the magazine on her lap, said, "Tell me what?"

"He's sending you a present. Be in the next delivery."

"He's a sweetie. I'd love to see him again."

"We could fly over sometime. Go out in his boat. Would you like that?"

"No, thanks," Melanie said. She picked up her magazine.

Ordell watched her. He said, "But you know the boat's always there."

Two A.M., Ordell left the apartment and walked up to Ocean Mall, a bar named Casey's where people went to dance, a restaurant, Portofino, some stores, some fast-food places, not much else in this block-long strip facing the public beach. The parking lot was back of the mall, only a few cars left in the rows, all the places closed. He got in the black Olds Ninety-Eight, found the keys and a .38 snubby under the seat, fooled with the instruments to find the lights and the air, and drove out of there, over the hump-back bridge to Riviera Beach, a two-minute trip.

Ordell believed if you didn't know Beaumont's house you could ease down these dark streets off Blue Heron till you heard West Indian reggae filling the night, music to get high by, and follow the beat to the little stucco dump where Beaumont lived with a bunch of Jamaicans all packed in there. They'd keep the music on high volume while they maintained their crack binge—only this evening, peeking in, they appeared to be doing reefer, crowded in the room like happy refugees, having some sweet wine and dark rum with the weed. Go in there, start to breathe, and be stoned. It most always smelled of cooking too. A messy place—Ordell had wanted to use the bathroom one time, took one look, and went outside to relieve himself among trash barrels and bright clothes hanging on the line.

From the doorway he caught Beaumont's eye, Beaumont the one with slicked-down almost regular hair among the beards and dreadlocks, and waved at him in the haze of smoke to step outside.

Ordell said, "Dot ganja, mon, mek everyone smile to show their teet, uh?" bringing Beaumont out through wild fern and a tangle of shrubs to the big

Olds parked in the street. "You the most relaxed people I ever met."

Except now Beaumont was rubbing a hand over his jaw, looking at the car he knew wasn't Ordell's.

"There's a man," Ordell said, "I never dealt with before, wants to buy some goods. I want to test him out. You understand?" Ordell unlocked the trunk. Raising the lid he said, "When I open this to show my wares, you gonna be inside pointing a gun at him."

Beaumont frowned. "You want me to shoot him?"

Beaumont was no jackboy. He was Ordell's front man on some deals, figuring prices in his head, and his backup man other times. Mr. Walker set up deliveries, received the payments, and arranged for getting the funds from Grand Bahama to West Palm Beach. Right now Beaumont was peering into the trunk, dark in there.

"I have to be inside how long?"

"We just going over to the beach, mon."

Beaumont kept looking in the trunk, his hands flat in the tight pockets of his pants, no shirt, skinny shoulders hunched up some.

"What's the matter?"

"I don't like to be in there."

"I put up ten thousand," Ordell said, "to get your skinny ass out of jail. Now you gonna take a stand on me? Man, I don't believe this shit." Sounding surprised, hurt. "Nothing's going to happen, it's just in case."

Beaumont took his time to think about it, Ordell

listening to the reggae beat coming from the house, moving just a little bit with it, till Beaumont said, "Okay, but I have to dress."

"You look crisp, mon, you fine. We be right back."

"What do I use?"

"Look in there. See the trash bag?"

He watched Beaumont hunch in to bring it out unwrapping the brown plastic from a 12-gauge, no stock, the barrel sawed off at the pump.

"No, don't rack it, man, not yet. Not till we there and I open the trunk. Right then you can rack it, dig? Get the man's attention."

Ordell drove back Blue Heron Boulevard to the bridge that humped over Lake Worth and followed the curve north past Ocean Mall, past hotels and high-priced condos with gates, until his headlights showed a solid wall of trees behind a wire fence on his side of the road, MacArthur State Park, and what looked more like jungle on the other side. Ordell picked a sandy place to pull off on the left, all mangrove along here and scraggly palm trees growing wild. No headlights showed in either direction. He got out and unlocked the trunk. A light went on inside as the lid came up, and there was Beaumont hunched on his side with the shotgun, ducking his head to see who was here.

Ordell said, "It's just me, babe." He said, "I was wondering did any federal people come visit you in jail and I should be watching my ass."

Beaumont bent his head some more to see out, frowning.

"You wouldn't tell me if they did, and I wouldn't blame you," Ordell said, unbuttoning his double-breasted sport jacket, the yellow one. He had a Targa on him that fired .22 longs, okay for this kind of close work. Or he could use the one Cujo left him—and decided, yeah, he would.

So now Beaumont was looking at the five-shot .38 snubby Ordell slipped from his waist. Beaumont quick racked the pump shotgun, pulled the trigger, and there was that click you get from an empty weapon. Beaumont had a pitiful look on his face racking the pump again, hard. *Click.* Racked it again, but didn't get to click it this time. Ordell shot him in his bare chest. Beaumont seemed to cave in like the air was let out of him and Ordell put one in his head. Loud. Man, but it was a nasty gun the way it jumped and felt like it stung your hand, Ordell wishing he had used the Targa now. He wiped the piece clean with his T-shirt pulled out of his pants, threw it in the trunk with Beaumont, and closed the lid.

The digital clock on the dash read 2:48 as he pulled into the parking lot behind the mall. He used napkins he found on the ground by a trash bin to wipe off the steering wheel, the door handle, trunk lid, any part of the car he might have touched. Walking home along the beach, dark out in the Atlantic Ocean, quiet, nobody around, he could hear the surf coming in and the wind blowing, that was all. It felt good on his face.

* * *

Ordell got home, all the lights were off in the apartment, Melanie asleep, girlish little snores coming from the bedroom. She was hard to wake up if you wanted anything. Simone snored louder, but would stop if you made any noise and say in her sleepy voice, "Come on in the bed, baby." Sheronda would hear him unlocking the door, turning off the alarm, and would come out of the bedroom with her big eyes asking what he wanted, wide awake.

Melanie had slowed down some in thirteen years. Had become a blowhead and wasn't as spunky as she used to be. That was too bad. But she wasn't as apt to surprise you either. As close as Ordell was to realizing his dream of becoming a wealthy retiree, he didn't need any surprises.

What he needed was somebody to take Beaumont's place. Not a jackboy. Somebody smarter, but not too smart. Like Louis. He was the one. You could talk to Louis. You could kid around with him and act foolish if you wanted to. Man, they had laughed picking out masks to wear when they kidnapped the woman. He seemed more serious now. Looked meaner than he used to. He could use some more meanness. Maybe prison had done him some good. Louis said he didn't want any part of whatever it was. But Louis, you pin him down, he didn't know what he wanted.

Maybe a way to get him, put Melanie on him.

Then put her on Big Guy at the right time. The Nazi.

4

They watched Jackie Burke come off the Bahamas shuttle in her tan Islands Air uniform, then watched her walk through Customs and Immigration without opening her bag, a brown nylon case she pulled along behind her on wheels, the kind flight attendants used.

It didn't surprise either of the casual young guys who had Ms. Burke under surveillance: Ray Nicolet and Faron Tyler, in sport coats and neckties with their jeans this Wednesday afternoon at Palm Beach International. Jackie Burke came through here five days a week flying West Palm to Nassau, West Palm to Freeport and back.

"She's cool," Nicolet said. "You notice?"

"She ain't bad either," Tyler said, "for a woman her age. She's forty?"

"Forty-four," Nicolet said. "She's been flying nineteen years. Some other airlines before this one."

"Where you want to take her, here or outside?"

"When she gets in her car. It's upstairs."

They watched her from a glass-partitioned office in this remote wing of the terminal, Ray Nicolet commenting on Jackie Burke's legs, her neat rear end in the tan skirt, Faron Tyler saying she surely didn't look forty-four, at least not from here. They watched her bring a pair of sunglasses out of her shoulder bag and lay them in her hair that was dark blond, loose, not too long. It did surprise them when Jackie Burke took the escalator up to the main concourse. They watched her go into the Ladies' rest room, come out after about five minutes not looking any different, and pull her cart into the snack bar. Now they watched her sit down with a cup of coffee and light a cigarette. What was she doing? Ray Nicolet and Faron Tyler slipped into the souvenir shop, directly across the way, to stand among racks of pastel-colored Palm Beach T-shirts.

Tyler said, "You think she made us?"

Nicolet wondered the same thing without saying it.

"You don't come off a flight and have a cup of coffee, you go home," Tyler said. "She doesn't act nervous though."

"She's cool," Nicolet said.

"Who's here besides us?"

"Nobody. This one came up in a hurry." Nicolet fingered the material of a pink T-shirt that had green and white seagulls on it, then raised his gaze to the snack bar again. "You make the bust, okay?"

Tyler looked at him. "It's your case. I thought I was just helping out."

"I want to keep it simple. A state charge, she won't have as much trouble bonding out. I mean if we have to take it that far. You badge her, lay it on—you know. Then I'll ease into the conversation."

"Where, here?"

"How about your office? Mine," Nicolet said, "I don't have enough chairs. Your place is neater."

"But if all she's carrying is money . . ."

"The guy said fifty grand this trip."

"Yeah, what's the charge? She didn't declare it? That's federal."

"You can use it if you want, hold Customs over her head. I'd still like it to be a state bust, some kind of trafficking. Otherwise, if I bring her up," Nicolet said, "and she has to bond out of federal court—man, they make it hard. I don't want her mad at me, I just want to see her sweat a little."

Tyler said, "If you know who she's taking it to . . ."

"I don't. I said we have an idea. The guy kept holding out, wouldn't give us the name. He was afraid it could fuck up his life worse than prison."

"I guess it did," Tyler said. "So how about if we follow her, see who she gives it to."

"If we had a few more people. We lose her," Nicolet said, "we have to come here and start all over. No, I think if we sit her down and give her dirty looks she'll tell us what we want to know. Whatever that is."

"She sure looks good for her age," Tyler said.

They were a couple of South Florida boys, both thirty-one, buddies since meeting at FSU. They liked guns, beer, cowboy boots, air boats, hunting in the Everglades, and chasing bad guys. They'd spent a few years with the Palm Beach County Sheriff's Office before splitting up: Ray Nicolet going to ATF, the Treasury Department's Bureau of Alcohol, Tobacco, and Firearms; Faron Tyler to FDLE, The Florida Department of Law Enforcement, Division of Criminal Investigation. Every once in a while they got a chance to work together. Right now the ATF office was busy working a sting operation out of a pawnshop they'd taken over, buying a lot of hot guns on camera. So Nicolet had called FDLE and got his buddy to help out on an investigation. One they believed had to do with the illegal sale of firearms.

"She's leaving," Tyler said.

One of the two guys Jackie Burke first noticed in the Customs office got on the elevator with her, the dark-haired one. He asked what floor she wanted. Jackie said, "I'm going all the way."

He grinned saying, "Me too," pushed the button, and then touched his hair. The kind of guy who was used to women coming on to him. Almost a hunk, but not quite. Jackie was pretty sure if she asked if his partner was already on the top level he wouldn't act too surprised. Maybe grin at her again. Both were young, but with that lazy confidence of pro athletes or guys who carried badges and guns. She hoped she was wrong, felt the urge to light a cigarette, and thought of leaving her flight bag on the elevator.

The door opened. The dark-haired one said, "After you," and Jackie walked off pulling her wheels into the dim parking structure. She moved past rows of cars expecting the other one, more boyish-looking, short brown hair down on his forehead, to step out in front of her. He didn't though. She had the trunk of her gray Honda open and was lifting the aluminum frame to put it inside before she heard him and looked over her shoulder. He came holding open his ID case.

"Hi, I'm Special Agent Faron Tyler, Florida Department of Law Enforcement?"

Not sounding too sure about it. The case held a badge and an ID that had FDLE printed on it in bold letters.

Jackie said, "Fiddle? I've never heard of it."

"Yeah, but there it is," Tyler said. "Can I ask what you have in that bag?"

Giving her that official deadpan delivery. His voice soft, though, kind of Southern. Jackie had a good idea what was going to happen, but wanted to be absolutely sure and said, "The usual things, clothes, hair curlers. I'm a flight attendant with Islands Air."

Tyler said, "And your name's Jackie Burke?"

It was going to happen.

She felt the urge again to have a cigarette and lowered the frame to rest on its wheels. The dark-haired one appeared behind Tyler, coming out of the row of cars, as she was getting her cigarettes from her shoulder bag.

The dark-haired one said, "Excuse me, I couldn't help but observe your plight. Can I be of assistance?"

Jackie said, "Gimme a break," and held her Bic lighter to a cigarette.

Now Tyler, the FDLE guy, was introducing him. "This is Special Agent Ray Nicolet, with Alcohol, Tobacco, and Firearms. Would you mind if we looked in that bag?"

"Would I *mind?* Do I have a choice?"

"You can say no," Tyler said, "and wait here with him while I go get a warrant. Or we can take you in on suspicion."

"Of what?"

"All he wants to do is peek in your bag," Nicolet said. "I'll watch he doesn't take anything."

"It's just a routine spot check," Tyler said. "Okay?"

Jackie drew on the cigarette, let her breath out, shrugged. "Go ahead."

She watched Tyler hunch down to unhook the elastic straps and lay the flight bag on the pavement. Nicolet lifted the cart out of the way, placed it in her trunk. Tyler had the bag open now and was feeling through her things, a soiled blouse, uniform skirt, bringing out a manila envelope, a fat one, nine by twelve. Jackie watched him straighten the clasp, open it, and look inside. Nicolet stepped closer as Tyler pulled out several packets of one-hundred-dollar bills secured with rubber bands, and Nicolet whistled, a sound that was like a sigh. Tyler looked up at her.

"I'd say there's, oh, fifty thousand dollars in here. What would you say?"

Jackie wasn't saying anything at the moment. They knew how much was in the envelope. Without counting it.

Tyler said, "This is your money?"

Jackie said, "If I were to tell you, no, it isn't . . ."

She saw Tyler start to grin.

"That I was supposed to wait in the cafeteria and a man I don't know would come by and pick it up . . ." Without looking at the other one she knew he was grinning too. It made her mad. "And I saw you cowboys looking at T-shirts and thought one of you might be the person . . . Listen, if it's yours, take it." She glanced at Nicolet.

He was grinning. Both of them having fun.

Tyler said, "You should know if you bring in anything over ten thousand you have to declare it. You forgot or what? You could get a two-hundred-and-fifty-thousand-dollar fine and two years in prison. You want to talk to us about it, or you want to talk to Customs?"

Jackie said, "I'm not saying another fucking word."

Mad. At these guys, their attitude, and at herself for being so dumb.

Nicolet said to Tyler, "You tried," and put his hand on her shoulder. He said, "Those Customs guys, all

day they see people coming back from their vaca-
tions, trips to Europe, the Caribbean, while they have
to sit there working. You can understand it makes
them hard to get along with. You want to talk to them
or a couple of good-natured guys like us? Someplace
quiet we can sit down and take it easy."

"I don't have to talk to anybody," Jackie said.

"No, you don't," Nicolet said. "But would you ex-
tend us the courtesy of listening to what we have to
say? Help you get this straightened out?"

Florida Department of Law Enforcement was on
the eighth floor of a glassy gray-blue building on Cen-
trepark Boulevard in West Palm. They were in an office Faron Tyler shared with another agent, gone for
the day: two clean desks, a wide expanse of windows
looking east, a calendar on the wall, and a sign that
read: "Bad planning on your part does not automati-
cally constitute an emergency on my part."

Jackie Burke thought it might be true, but so what?

She stood at the windows. With a slight turn of her
head to the left she could see Ray Nicolet's legs ex-
tending toward her, his cowboy boots resting on the
corner of the desk. He said, "You see that canal right
below us? I was up here one time, I saw an osprey
circle around, dive down there, and pick up a bass, a
pretty good-size one. Faron, you remember that?"

"Last summer."

Faron Tyler was somewhere behind her.

She heard Nicolet say, "It's starting to get dark,

huh? Rush-hour traffic on the freeway picking up, everybody going home . . ."

"I want a lawyer," Jackie said. She got her cigarettes out of the shoulder bag, feeling only about four or five left in the pack. She wondered if she should save them.

But then Tyler's voice said, "There's no smoking here."

So Jackie lit the cigarette, using the tan Bic that matched her uniform, and dropped it back in the bag. Without looking at Tyler she said, "Arrest me."

"It can happen," Tyler said. His voice closer this time. "Or we can work out what's called a Substantial Assistance Agreement. That's if you're willing to cooperate, tell us who gave you the money and who you're giving it to."

There was a silence.

It was a game to them. Nicolet playing the good guy, out of character but having fun. Tyler, though, came off as a decent guy and wasn't too convincing as the heavy. Jackie was fairly sure they didn't want to charge her. Cooperate, name a few names, and they'd give her a break. About all she could do was try keeping her mouth shut. Maybe send out for cigarettes.

When Nicolet said, "You have a good lawyer?" she didn't answer.

"Can she afford a good one," Tyler's voice said, "is the question."

He had a point.

"Otherwise she'll be in the Stockade three weeks,

easy, before a public defender gets around to her. In there with all those bad girls . . . I don't know, maybe they pay her enough she can afford a high-priced defense."

"Jackie, you have an apartment in Palm Beach Gardens?" Nicolet said, the ATF agent getting into it now. "That's a pretty nice neighborhood."

"Considering," Tyler said, "she works for a little shuttle airline."

There was a silence again, Jackie looking at downtown West Palm Beach in the distance, the sky still blue but fading. She heard a drawer open. Nicolet said, "Here," offering her an ashtray. "I brought this myself, to have when I visit, and I used to smoke." The good guy again, saying now, "That parking lot you see right there? Behind the hotel? You can sit here and watch drug deals go down. By the time you get over there everybody's split."

Jackie placed the ashtray on the windowsill. "Is that what you think I'm into?"

Behind her, Tyler said, "I notice you have a prior. Wasn't that about drugs?"

"I was carrying money."

"Four years ago," Tyler said. "With another airline then and they fired you. But you didn't answer my question. Wasn't it money for a drug payoff? Taking it out of the country?"

"I think," Nicolet said, "Jackie was carrying it for one of the pilots. Guy that happened to be her husband at the time. They found her guilty of conspiring . . ."

"I entered a plea," Jackie said.

"You mean they offered you a deal and you grabbed it. A year's probation and your hubby drew five to ten. He must be out by now."

"I think so," Jackie said.

"That's right, you got a divorce. You remarried—what about your present husband?"

"He died last year."

"You go through 'em," Nicolet said. "What kind of work did he do?"

"He drank," Jackie said.

They let it go and she heard Tyler's voice say, "Now you're in a different kind of business, coming the other way with a payoff, selling instead of buying. Wasn't this money given to you by a Bahamian named Walker? I believe it's Cedric Walker. Lives in Freeport?"

Jackie didn't answer, watching her reflection in the glass raise the cigarette.

"Name doesn't ring a bell? How about a guy named Beaumont Livingston?"

Beaumont—she had met him only once, with Mr. Walker. No, she had *seen* him that time and was told later who he was. She could say she had never met him; but made up her mind not to say anything.

"You don't know Beaumont?"

Not a word—staring through her reflection at a dark strip on the horizon she believed was the ocean.

"He knows you," Nicolet said. "Beaumont's Jamaican. That is, he was. Beaumont ain't no more."

Jackie could feel them waiting. She didn't move.

"He used to fly over to Freeport a couple of times a month," Nicolet said. "Maybe you'd recognize him. Faron, we could arrange for Ms. Burke to look at the body, couldn't we?"

Tyler's voice said, "No problem."

She turned her head enough to see Ray Nicolet reaching into his cowboy boot, the left one crossed over the right. He drew out a snub-nosed revolver, laid it on the desk, and slipped his hand into the boot again to rub his ankle.

He said, "They found Beaumont yesterday morning in the trunk of a car, a brand-new Olds registered to a guy in Ocean Ridge. He'd reported it stolen. I had a chance to speak to Beaumont just the day before, about his future. He was in jail at the time, not too sure he wanted to do ten years." There was a pause before Nicolet said, "Beaumont was bonded out and got popped before I could talk to him again." There was another pause. Nicolet said, "You may not know Beaumont, but what if the guy who popped him knows you?"

There was a silence.

Jackie drew on the cigarette. Beaumont—she had listened to him talking to Mr. Walker. He left and Mr. Walker told her Beaumont could do tricks with numbers, add columns of figures in his head.

Tyler's voice said, "If you don't want to talk to us, I guess we'll have to hand you over to Customs."

She stubbed out the cigarette, intent on it for several moments, staring at the black plastic ashtray before turning now to face Tyler.

She said, "Okay, let's go."

He stood by the other desk in the office, where they had placed her flight bag, an open file folder in his hands.

"Now you're gonna get him mad," Nicolet said. "You know Faron could bring you up on a RICO violation? That fifty grand suggesting you're mixed up in some kind of racketeering activity. And if I know Faron he'll file a Probable Cause affidavit and take it all the way to the wall."

Tyler was staring at her. She watched him lay the folder on the desk and place his hand on the flight bag. He said, "I'd like your permission to open this again. Is that okay? So we'll know exactly how much we're talking about here."

Jackie walked over to the desk and unzipped the bag. She brought out the manila envelope, dropped it on the desk, and said, "Help yourself."

"While you're at it," Tyler said, "let's see what else is in there. You mind?"

Jackie looked at him for a moment.

She brought out a leather kit. "My toothbrush and bathroom stuff." Next, a plastic travel case. "My curlers. You want me to open it?"

"Let's see what else's in there first," Tyler said.

Jackie picked up the flight bag with both hands, turned it upside down, and shook it. A white blouse, a skirt, underwear, a bra, and pantyhose fell to the desk on top of the manila envelope. She set the bag aside. Tyler picked up the envelope and she watched him open it and shake out the packets of currency.

She watched him look in the envelope and then at her and saw his look of surprise become a grin. His hand went into the envelope and he said, "Well, what have we here?"

Jackie said, "Now wait a minute," as Tyler's hand came out and she heard Nicolet's boots hit the floor.

He approached them saying, "Is that Sweet'n Low or what I think it is?"

Tyler was holding a clear cellophane sandwich bag that showed a rounded half inch or so of white powder inside. He raised it toward the overhead light saying, "Is it to sell or get stoned with? That's the question."

"It's not mine," Jackie said.

It *wasn't*.

"Listen, okay? Really . . ."

"It isn't enough for trafficking," Nicolet said. "How about possession with intent to distribute?"

"Considering all the cash," Tyler said, "I think I could go with conspiracy to traffic."

A couple of happy guys.

Jackie was shaking her head. She said, "I don't believe this."

Nicolet pulled the chair out from the desk. He said, "Why don't we sit down and start over," giving Jackie a nice smile. "What do you say."

5

Louis Gara could sound like a decent guy, an ex-con with possibilities. It came through, Max thought, in the way Louis played down his career as a bank robber.

He said what he'd do was hand the teller a note that read: *Take it easy. This is a holdup. Get out your 50s and 100s right now. I will tell you what to do next.* Louis said he wrote the note on a typewriter in an office supply store and made copies. Max asked him how many, to see how optimistic the guy was. "Twenty," Louis said. "I could always have some more run off." The first seven banks he did okay, making a little over twenty grand, total. He said people thought banks were always big scores. No, the bank robbers he'd met at Starke were amateurs, mostly crackheads. "On the next one I got seventeen hundred loose and five hundred in a strap the teller handed me I should never've taken. It was a dye pack. I get out in the street it pops and there's this red dye on my hands, my arms, all down the front of my clothes. I got away though." Max asked if the dye washed off. Louis said, "Yeah, it washes off, but some of the bills I didn't do a good job on and were kinda pink. You try and pass a pink twenty, which I should never've done, they have an idea how it got that way. The next thing I know the police are at my door. I got eight years and did forty-six months. Came back to Miami and got picked up for violating my probation on a fraud charge, using somebody else's credit card I found. See, I did the bank while I was on probation and would've done two and a half on the violation, but the judge was a good guy. He counted the time served on the bank conviction and I walked."

How about that? Told in a quiet manner with what seemed a reasonable attitude, get caught for the crime, you do the time.

He said he worked in auto repair at Florida State Prison—referring to it as Starke or FSP—the food wasn't too bad, and he got along with his cellmate, an older guy from Miami who had put away his wife. According to the cellmate his wife never shut up, was always nagging him about something until finally he had enough.

Max said, "How did he do it?" Renee had called earlier and he listened to her for twenty minutes before he could get off the phone.

Louis said the guy smothered her with a pillow. "He'd lift it off. 'You gonna shut up?' She'd start yapping at him and he'd push the pillow down over her face, hold it, lift it off. 'You gonna shut up?' No, she kept yapping until the last time he lifted it off she had shut up.''

Max believed it could happen, you lose control for a minute and it's done. What bothered him about Louis, the guy was a repeat offender. Grand theft auto in Ohio, felonious assault in Texas, fraud and bank robbery here in Florida. Louis was forty-seven with a hard, weathered look to him, dark curly hair showing some gray; he had a pretty good build from working out with weights at FSP. The three falls had only taken seven years out of his life, which Louis said didn't set him back too much. Actually six years and ten months. That sounded like a positive-thinking guy, didn't it? Louis never complained or acted resentful.

It was his eyes that gave him away.

Max saw it. Those dull eyes that didn't seem to have life in them but didn't miss anything. Three falls, you don't come out, put on a new suit of clothes, and become a normal person again. That life changed you. Max said to Winston, "Watch him."

Winston said, "I know who he is." Winston asked Louis had he ever boxed in the slam. Louis said, a little; but would never put the gloves on with Winston.

Max said, "He isn't stupid."

Winston said, "One round, I could bust him up good. We wouldn't see him for a while."

Max said, "But he'd get you if you did. Don't you

know how that works? Don't you see that in his eyes?"

He had told Glades Mutual Casualty he didn't need Louis or want him; a convicted felon, Louis would never be able to apply for a surety license. The guy at Glades Mutual told Max to "use him for heavy work," like picking up guys that failed to appear. So Max had Louis helping out with some of the more violent FTAs, guys that were likely to give them trouble. Louis could carry a pair of cuffs, that's all. They'd never let him pack a gun or even touch the ones they had in the office: revolvers and a nickel-plated Mossberg 500 12-gauge, a short-barreled shotgun with a pistol grip and a laser scope. They kept the guns locked in a cabinet in the meeting room. They didn't give Louis even a key to the office.

Thursday, right after Max got back from lunch, he let Louis go with Winston to pick up Zorro, the Puerto Rican burglar with the swords and hyper women. The other day when Winston had gone to get him, Zorro wasn't home.

Ten past three they were back.

Winston came in shaking his head at Max, Winston followed by Louis Gara and Ordell Robbie, Ordell with a grin saying, "I'm coming to see you, I run into Louis out front. Let me talk to my friend a minute, then I want to collect the money you owe and have you write me another bond."

Max, sitting at his desk, didn't say a word.

Neither did Louis Gara. He didn't speak or look at

Max as he picked up the coffee mug from Max's desk. Louis motioned with a nod of his head and Ordell followed him into the meeting room, Ordell saying, "Man, I been calling and calling you . . ." Winston followed them to the door and slammed it closed.

He turned to Max saying, "What'd you send him with me for?"

Max said, "What?" preoccupied, trying to make sense of Louis taking his coffee mug, not asking if it was okay. He said to Winston, "They just happen to run into each other outside?"

Now Winston had to shift gears in his head. "Who? You mean those two? I guess so."

Max said, "It was Louis's idea to go with you."

"Well, he ain't ever again."

"He's a different guy today," Max said.

Winston stood close to the desk. He touched his face saying, "Lookit here. You see these scratches?" He held his arm out to show the sleeve of his sport shirt torn and bloodstained. "You see this?"

Max straightened in his chair. "Jesus, what happened?"

"I told Louis I'd do the talking, he was along to back me up was all. I reminded him how you never *ever* try to handcuff a Cuban, a Puerto Rican, any those Latin people, in front of their women. They won't allow it, their manhood won't, have women see them submit like that. You have to bring the man outside first, get him by the car. I asked Louis, you understand that? Yeah, he knows, says he does. We get to the house, Zorro lets us in. The man knows he's going in but has to wave his arms around first, make a speech how somebody snitched him out and it ain't his fault, the situation he's in. Louis is standing there—you say you think he's *dif*ferent? He looks at me, says, 'Fuck this,' and takes Zorro by the arm, goes to cuff him. Zorro's woman, his two sisters, they all come at us hitting and scratching, screaming their heads off. His mother come out of the kitchen with a butcher knife. . . . Lookit here." Winston pushed up his torn sleeve to show a bloody handkerchief wrapped around his forearm. "You know how Zorro's got the swords on the wall? He tries to get one and Louis hits him with his fist, hard, kept hitting him while I'm defending myself from this old woman with the butcher knife. We get outside I say to Louis, 'You pretty good with a little PR stoned on acid. How 'bout trying me?' I mean I was mad how he fucked it up. Louis gives me that sleepy look, says he'll think about it and let me know. The first time he ever said anything like that, like he might put on the gloves with me. You think the man's different, I think it could be his real self coming out."

Max watched Winston unwrap the handkerchief to look at his wound. "Zorro's still home?"

"I saw I wasn't gonna take him without killing somebody. Yeah, so we left."

"I'll get him," Max said. "You take care of your arm."

"It'll be all right, I get some stitches." Winston raised his arm to his face and sniffed. "I think that old woman was chopping onions."

* * *

"I got another one for you," Ordell said to Max, "friend of mine, she's an airline stewardess. Got caught coming back from Freeport with some blow. See, I'm thinking what you could do is use the ten you owe me left over from Beaumont. It's what they set the stew's bond at this afternoon, ten thousand, for possession. They say Jackie had forty-two grams on her. Not even two ounces. Shit."

"The bond for possession's only a thousand," Max said.

"They calling it possession with in*tent*."

"It's still high."

"She had, I believe it was, fifty grand on her too," Ordell said. "There was a cop at the hearing, young guy with FDLE, wanted the bond set at twenty-five saying there was risk of flight here, Jackie could get on a airplane and take off anytime she wanted. Being, you understand, a stewardess."

They were alone in the office. Winston had gone to Good Samaritan; Louis had told Ordell he'd see him later and left, not saying where he was going. Ordell, sitting against Winston's desk, wore that same yellow sport jacket with a silky rust-colored shirt today. Max noticed he didn't have his Dolphins athletic bag with him, his money sack. He said, "Let's get Beaumont out of the way first," and saw Ordell's expression change to almost a grin.

"Somebody already did. Police came to see me about it. Must've found out was me put up his bond. They speak to you?"

Max shook his head. "What police?"

"Riv'era Beach, some detectives, look like they got dressed from the Salvation Army. They scared my woman, Sheronda. She thought they was gonna take me away. I told them I didn't even know Beaumont's last name till the other day. They want to know then why did I pay his bail? I told them his mama use to take care of my mama when I brought her down here to live? Took care of her till she passed on. Nice woman name Rosemary, Beaumont's mama. You know it's funny, I never knew Rosemary's last name either. She went back to Jamaica, I think lives in the country. So now, you keep the money you owe me and use it to get Jackie out of the Stockade. Jackie Burke's her name, fine-looking woman, has kinda blond hair."

Max said, "What did her mother do for you?"

Ordell let his grin come this time. "Man, Jackie's a friend of mine, met her flying. My friends get in trouble, I like to help them out."

"Didn't Beaumont work for you?"

Ordell shook his head. "That's what the police thought. I told them I'm unemployed, how could I have anybody working for me? Now I bail out Jackie, I'm liable to have the police on me again, huh? Wanting to know was she doing things for me, was she bringing me that money . . ."

Max said, "Was she?"

Ordell looked one way and then the other, a gesture. He said, "Is this, me and you, like a lawyer-client relationship? The lawyer can't tell nothing he hears?''

Max shook his head. "You're not my client until you get busted and I bond you out."

"You sound like you think it could happen."

Max gave him a shrug.

"If there's no—what do you call it—confidentiality between us? Why would I tell you anything?''

"Because you want me to know what a slick guy you are," Max said, "have a stewardess bringing you fifty grand."

"Why would she?"

"Now you want me to speculate on what you do. I'd say you're in the drug business, Ordell, except the money's moving in the wrong direction. I could call the Sheriff's office, have you checked out . . ."

"Go ahead. They look me up on the computer they won't find nothing but that bust in Ohio I mentioned to you and that was a long time ago, man. It might not even still be on the screen."

Max said, "Ordell, you're a shifty guy. You must be getting away with whatever you're into. Okay, you want another bond and you want to move the ten thousand you put down on Beaumont over to the stewardess. That means paperwork. I have to get a death certificate, present it to the court, fill out a Receipt for Return of Bond Collateral, then type up another application, an Indemnity Agreement . . ."

"You know it's *there*," Ordell said. "You have my cash."

"I'm telling you what I have to do," Max said.

"What you have to do, in case you forgot, is come up with the premium, a thousand bucks."

"Yeah, well, I won't have that for a couple of days," Ordell said, "but you can go ahead, write the bond."

Max sat back in his chair. "Couple of days? I can wait."

"Man, you know I'm good for it."

"Something happens to you before you pay me . . ."

"Ain't nothing could happen. Man, I lead a clean life."

"You could get shot. Beaumont did."

Ordell was shaking his head. "I *got* money. I don't have any with me's all. Thousand bucks is nothing."

"You're right there, if I don't see it in front of me."

"Look," Ordell said, coming over to plant his hands on the desk, putting himself square in Max's face. "This fine-looking woman is out at the Stockade among all those bitches they have in there. Jackie spent the night with 'em and was at First Appearance this afternoon, that courtroom by the Gun Club jail? She didn't see me, had her head down—I was in the back. But, man, she looked bad. Couple more days, it could kill her."

"If she can't hack the Stockade," Max said to the face close in front of him, "how's she going to do state time?"

Ordell stared. He raised one hand from the desk, reached into the open neck of his silky shirt and came out with a gold chain hooked on his thumb. "I paid twenty-five hundred for it."

"I don't wear jewelry," Max said.

Ordell let go of the chain and thrust his arm in Max's face. "Rolex watch. Look at it. Worth five thousand, easy. Come on, write the fucking bond."

Max said, "I don't run a pawnshop. Hock the watch if you want, come back when you have the thousand bucks. That's all I can tell you."

"Look at it again," Ordell said, turning his wrist, gold flashing in the overhead light. "She a beauty?"

6

Max sat talking to Zorro in a living room done in a mix of scarred oak furniture from another time, bright plastic patio chairs, framed holy pictures, and swords. They both had drinks, rum and Pepsi Cola. Zorro sat in a lounge chair holding ice cubes wrapped in a dish towel to the side of his face. The women were in the kitchen. Max could hear them, voices in Spanish blending with voices from the television in English. There were four sets in the living room; only the one in the kitchen was playing. He said to Zorro, "This hits the spot," raised his glass, and was looking at bullfight swords in leather scabbards crossed beneath the Sacred Heart of Jesus. There were other mail-order swords on the walls, sabers, a cutlass, a scimitar, several pictures of the Blessed Mother, St. Joseph, different saints; Max recognized one as St. Sebastian, pierced with arrows.

He said to Zorro, "If we leave now you can be there in time for supper. Don't they eat around five? Or you can have your dinner here, that's fine. I'll wait in the car, give you some time with your family."

"You should fire that guy," Zorro said, his mouth against the ice pack, "for what he did to me."

Max nodded. "I'm thinking about it. I don't know what happened to him."

"He went crazy."

Max nodded again, serious about getting rid of Louis. He said, "Listen, tomorrow I'll talk to your probation officer. Karen's a good kid, but she's mad at you because you lied to her. That business about going to your grandmother's funeral."

Zorro took the ice pack away from his face to nod his head, Max looking at all that thick black hair, Christ, more than he needed.

"I went, I did. I took my mother and my sisters."

"But you didn't ask permission. You broke a trust. If you had asked, Karen probably would have let you. In fact I'm sure she would."

"I know," Zorro said, "that's why I went."

"But then you told her you were home."

"Sure, 'cause I didn't ask her could I go."

Maybe it was a language problem. Max let it go. He said, "Anyway, if Karen's willing to reinstate you, the judge might go along. But you have to show up at the hearing for it to happen." Max sipped his drink, comfortable in the plastic chair. "What was the original charge?"

"Burglary from a dwelling," Zorro said. "I got a year and a day and the probation."

"You did what, about three months?"

"A little more."

"You're lucky, you know it? How many burglaries have you done?"

"I don't know." He glanced toward the kitchen. "Maybe two hundred."

"I would think you'd be tired," Max said. He looked over to see Zorro's mother in the kitchen doorway, a squat woman in an apron; she would be about his age but looked a lot older. He said, "It smells good, whatever you're doing in there."

They drove toward a red wash of sky, west on Southern Boulevard toward Gun Club in Max's '89 Seville. He had put away a big soup plate of *asopao de pollo*, chicken fixed with salt pork and ham, with peas, onions, peppers, pimientos in a spicy tomato sauce and served over rice. The woman could be a threat with a butcher knife but cooked like a saint. He'd start his diet again tomorrow, take off ten pounds, most of it around his middle. Lay off beer for a while. He said to Zorro, in the front seat next to him, "Are you clean?"

Zorro, wearing sunglasses, stared straight ahead. Zorro, with his two hundred burglaries and all that hair, being cool. After a moment he reached into his pants, dug all the way to his crotch, and brought out several cellophane squares of blotter acid.

"This is all."

"Get rid of it."

Zorro let them blow from his hand out the window.

"Are you clean now?"

"I think so."

"Come on, are you clean?"

Zorro raised his knee. He reached into his boot and brought out the handle of a toothbrush with a single-edge razor blade fixed to one end, the plastic melted to hold the strip of metal.

"Get rid of it."

"Man, I have to have a weapon in there."

"Get rid of it."

Zorro tossed it out the window.

"You clean now?"

"I'm clean."

"You better be," Max said. "They find anything on you, we're through. You understand? I'll never write you again. I won't speak to you, I won't speak to your mother or your girlfriend when they call. . . ."

What a business. Sit down to dinner with a burglar and his family and then take him to jail. Max moved his hand on the steering wheel to glance at the gold Rolex he was holding for Ordell. Half past six. He'd drop Zorro off and drive out to the Stockade for the stewardess, Jackie Burke. See what she was all about.

The house where Louis was staying, down in the south end of West Palm, might've been somebody's dream thirty years ago. Now it belonged to a guy named J.J. who had gotten his release the same time

Louis did and offered to let him stay if he wanted. J.J. had lasted less than a month on the street and was back in for conspiring to traffic. So Louis had the house to himself—still a mess from when the police banged in and tossed it. He'd replaced the front door with one he'd pried off an abandoned house and put J.J.'s clothes back in the drawers they'd dumped on the floor and cleaned up the kitchen, coffee, sugar, Rice Krispies all over the place. Louis hadn't been home at the time of the raid and was lucky the cops didn't know he was living here, or he'd be up at Gun Club with J.J. waiting on an arraignment. There was no way Max Cherry would have bonded him out. Max kept him at arm's length, didn't want him there, so they hardly ever spoke. Louis could understand how he felt. What was he doing for Max? Once in a while pick up a guy who'd FTAed. He was doing even less for the insurance company. Nothing.

Sunday, when Ordell dropped him off after the white-power demonstration, Ordell sat in his sixty-thousand-dollar car looking at the house. He said, "Louis, you on food stamps?"

Louis said, "It's small, but I don't need a lot of room."

Ordell said, "Size ain't what I'm talking about. This house is the next thing to being condemned. I 'magine it smells bad in there, huh? Any place a junkie lived. You have bugs?"

"Some."

"Some—shit. Nighttime, I bet you can't walk in the kitchen without the roaches crunching under your feet. Turn on the light you see 'em split, gone. That's your car, huh?"

The '85 Toyota Louis was making payments on sat in the carport attached to the house. (The insurance company paid him fifteen hundred a month in cash. They were giving him one more week to bring in some business or he was through.) There was a mattress in the yard the cops had torn up and trash barrels of junk Louis hadn't set out by the street to be picked up.

He said to Ordell, "What do you want—I just got out of the can."

Ordell said, "It ain't what I want, Louis. It's what you want."

The next time they spoke, Wednesday evening, Ordell had come by while it was still light. Louis asked him in the house. Ordell said he was fine sitting in his car; his car was clean, had it washed and vacuumed.

He said, "You know what your trouble is, Louis? Why you ain't ever going to make it less you change?"

Like his father speaking to him from the car, Louis standing there.

"You think you're a good guy," Ordell said, "and it messes you up."

Not like anybody's father after that. Louis relaxed and got out a cigarette.

"You get into a deal, you don't see yourself taking it all the way," Ordell said, "doing whatever has to be done to make the score. You go in looking for a way out. Not 'cause you scared. It's 'cause you think you're a good guy and there things a good guy won't do. What's the most you ever took robbing a bank? Maybe twenty-five hundred? Was me, I decided to do banks? Man, I'd go in and clean the fucking place out. Plan it and do it right. What you stole each time, you couldn't even buy a good used car with it, could you?"

Ordell said, "Listen to what I'm saying to you. Once you decide what you're going after you ride it out, no stops, no getting off. You need to use a gun you use it. Look at the situation. If it's him or you, or if it's him doing time or you doing time? There's nothing to think about, man, you take him out." Ordell said, "Once I pick up the goods and make one more delivery? I won't ever have to work again till I've spent something like a million bucks. You think some dude gets in my way I won't remove him?"

He said, "Listen, I already have so much money in lockboxes, man, in a Freeport bank, it's spilling out. I'm bringing some over a little bit at a time as I need to buy goods and pay different ones work for me. Finding the right kind of help these days is the problem. I have an airline stewardess doing it for me I believe I can trust. She don't ask where the money comes from. I think she don't want to know and that's fine with me, I don't tell her. I could bring it myself, ten grand at a time, but they ever look in my bag once, they be looking in it every time after that.

Ask me all kind of questions, get the IRS on my ass. They don't even look in hers. But she only does it when she feels like it. I said, 'Girl, we have to step it up.' I don't like my funds sitting over there where I can't get at them. I said, 'Bring me like a hundred thousand at a time. How would that be?' She don't want to. Then says okay, but she'll only bring what can fit in a big envelope or she won't do it. It don't make any difference, they catch you with even one buck over the ten-grand limit they got you by the ass. No, has to fit in this manila envelope. You understand? She can live with thinking she's delivering the envelope Mr. Walker gives her. But if it's a big package, like I ask her to bring, say, five hundred thousand at one time? She couldn't do it. It wouldn't be just a manila envelope then. She's afraid her hands would sweat and the Customs people would see it." He said, "You understand how this woman thinks? You do, huh? It even makes sense to you."

Ordell in his Mercedes making a speech, telling how to be bad and become successful. Throwing these numbers around to impress him. One more delivery and he'd be a millionaire.

Ordell was ready to leave when Louis said, "Okay, you're talking about guns. What kind?"

Ordell said, "What do you need? A fifteen-shot Beretta, Colt .45? Shit, name it. You want a MAC-11 converted to full automatic, with a suppressor on it? I'll show you my demo movie, you can take your pick."

"Where do you get them?"

"Buy some, steal the hard-to-get stuff. This is big-time, man. Got brothers working for me love to smash and grab. Jackboys, home-invasion experts. Learned their trade ripping off dope houses. They fearless 'cause they crazy. We got a jump coming up could interest you—seeing how you're asking me my business. It's up to you, you want to look at some real money. I ain't talking you into anything."

Louis said, "What kind of jump?" Feeling himself being drawn in.

"I showed you Big Guy?" Ordell said. "The grown-up skinhead Nazi looks like our old friend Richard? We gonna jump his place and clean him out, all his military type of shit, and sell it. Big Guy ain't as stupid as Richard, but you saw how serious the man is. I know he'll try to protect his property."

Louis said, "You're gonna kill him?"

"Did you listen to what I told you a minute ago? I don't premeditate that kind of business," Ordell said. "I'm gonna get what I need to make a sale. Whatever happens to Big Guy in the process of it, man, it happens."

Louis shook his head. "I don't know."

"What's that?"

"About going with you."

"You don't think you will or you know it?"

Louis shrugged and drew on his cigarette.

"I said before I ain't talking you into anything. But just answer me this, Louis. What does a three-time loser have to lose?" He started to back out of the drive and stopped. He said, "Louis? You only think you're a good guy. You're just like me, only you turned out white."

7

They had booked Jackie at the admitting desk, removed the handcuffs, and brought her to a counter at the end of a narrow hallway where she was searched, photographed, and fingerprinted on six separate cards. She studied a list of bail bondsmen displayed on the wall while they inventoried her property, taking her bag, her watch, jewelry, the gold wings pinned to her uniform jacket. They took her heels and pantyhose and gave her a pair of "slides" to put on that were like shower slippers. They took the razor and mirror from her bathroom kit. They let her keep the rest, her cigarettes—the two she had left—and the change in her purse. They snapped a blue plastic ID bracelet around her wrist and said she was lucky to get processed through early, before they brought in a hooker sweep. The deputies wore dark green. Their holsters were empty. They said she could make her phone call now.

Jackie dialed a number. A young black woman's voice said, "He ain't home," and the line went dead. Jackie dialed the number again. The woman's voice said, "He ain't home," in the same tone. Jackie said, "Wait." But not in time. They told her she could try later, once she was in the dorm.

The dorm. She thought of college.

But it wasn't like college or a fort either, imagining the Stockade on the way here as a stockade fence, pointed logs planted upright. The fences were wire, the one-story buildings seemed to be either cement block or siding. In the dark, driving in, she saw construction equipment, piles of building materials.

They brought her from Administration across the street to Medical where they gave her a questionnaire to fill out, took her temperature, her blood pressure, and examined her for vermin. Outside again walking along the street, the deputy with sergeant stripes said, "That's 'F' Dorm, where you'll be," nodding toward a building enclosed in double fencing: Spotlights reflected on rolls of razor wire strung along the top. Unlocking the gate he smiled at her and said, "Fuels your apprehension, doesn't it?" Jackie looked at him, a young guy, clean-shaved, his hair carefully combed. He said, "After you," and she walked in expecting to see cells with bars.

What she saw were doors to six dormitory rooms, each with an expanse of wire-covered windows across the front, three on one side of a guard post in the open area, three on the other. She saw faces at the windows watching her and heard faint sounds, voices. A woman deputy stood inside the waist-high enclosure, the guard post: a tall, broad-shouldered woman with pale-blond hair combed up in a pile. She was smoking a cigarillo, the pack stuck in her empty holster. The sergeant said, "Miss Kay, take care of this lady, would you, please?" and handed her a three-by-five inmate status card. Miss Kay said, "Why certainly, Terry," looked at the card for a moment and then at Jackie. "Would you believe you're my first flight attendant in about, I'd say, three years?"

Jackie didn't say anything, wondering if they were putting her on. She caught the aroma of Miss Kay's cigarillo. That was real.

With two bed sheets under her arm she scuffed along in the slides to the first room on the left, the holding dorm, Miss Kay told her, for prisoners awaiting court appearances. Faces moved away from the wire-mesh windows as Miss Kay unlocked the door and stood holding it open. Jackie stepped inside to see women at two of the four picnic tables in the front part of the dorm. Black women, one or two Hispanic. All watching her, paying no attention to the television set that was on. The double bunks in the rear area all looked empty. Miss Kay told Jackie she could have any bunk that wasn't occupied. She said, "If anyone asks you to pay for a bunk, tell me." Toilets and showers were back there. The two phones on the wall—one was a hot line to the Public Defender's office, the other a pay phone, but you could only make collect calls out of the area. You were allowed to have six dollars in change. The television set was showing a movie, Mel Gibson . . . And the women were still watching her, waiting. Miss Kay let them. She said the dorm held sixteen, but there were only seven in here now. Two dorms were for misdemeanants, two for drug offenders, one for violent prisoners. Miss Kay turned to the women at the picnic tables, all wearing street clothes, slacks, a few in dresses, and said, "This is Jackie."

A black woman wearing a shiny black wig said, "What is she, a general? Got her uniform on?"

The other women laughed, some with screams of appreciation, to please the woman in the wig or to let go and hear the sound of their own voices, loud inside the cement-block walls, until Miss Kay said, "Zip it," and they shut up. Now she looked at the black woman who had spoken and said, "Ramona, I'm only going to tell you once. Stay away from her."

Jackie dialed the number she'd tried before. The young woman's voice said, "He ain't—" and Jackie said over it, "Tell him Jackie called." There was a silence. "Tell him I'm in jail, the Stockade. Have you got that?" There was a silence again before the line went dead.

She picked up her bed sheets from the picnic table, the women still watching her, and scuffed her way back to the eight double bunks in two rows. There were no overhead lights here but the ones in front,

Jackie imagined, would be left on all night. So take a lower bunk. Five already had sheets on them. A radio was playing now along with the television set, the movie. She chose a bunk wondering if she'd be able to sleep and bent over, one hand on the rail of the upper bunk, to look at the mattress. Something behind her moved in front of the light. Jackie knew who it would be as she straightened and turned to look over her shoulder at Ramona.

Heavyset, her skin dark, her black wig highlighted from behind. She said, "You gonna talk to me?"

"If you want," Jackie said. "Just don't give me a hard time, okay? I've got enough problems."

"You a stewardess, huh? Work for the airlines?" Jackie nodded and Ramona said, "What I was wondering, they pay pretty good?"

She would sleep and wake up to stare at criss-crossed springs and the mattress close above her in faint light and would hear voices and a radio playing. She would feel the plastic ID bracelet, turning it on her wrist. She would hear the sergeant saying, "Fuels your apprehension, doesn't it?" and remember looking at him, not sure it was what he said.

A few times she thought of crying.

But changed her mind, replaying parts of her conversation with Ramona, here pending a charge of felonious assault for, Ramona said, busting a man's head open when he wouldn't leave her house. Assault, or it could be some kind of manslaughter if he didn't come out of Good Samaritan. But, hey, what about working for the airlines? . . . Jackie told her you could make thirty-five to forty thousand after ten years, never fly more than seventy hours a month, and choose the runs you wanted out of your home base. Her own experience, she was three years with TWA, fourteen with Delta and got fired. With Islands Air she was making less than half what she used to. Getting personal now. It didn't begin to cover rent, clothes, car payments, insurance, and now Islands Air would drop her as soon as they found out she was in jail. Ramona said, "If you not happy there, what do you care if they fire you?" She said she cleaned houses for fifty dollars a day when she could get it, but only three, four days a week, all the people there was doing it now, the Haitians taking work from the regular people. She asked Jackie if she had someone doing her apartment.

Before long Jackie was describing her situation to Ramona, seeking the advice of a cleaning woman in a forty-nine-dollar wig who didn't smoke.

Ramona said, "Possession with what, intent? I don't see you have a problem. The way you look? The kind of hair you got? If I done it I'd go to jail, see, but you won't. They slap your hand and say, 'Girl, don't do it again.' No, if the man you work for has money to pay a good lawyer, you have nothing to worry about. If he don't choose to, that's when you think about making a deal with the law, get your charge dismissed if you help them, not just reduced. Hear what I'm saying?"

They got mad, Jackie told her, when she wouldn't

talk to them, cooperate. Ramona said, "They ain't
your worry. What you need to think about is if you
put it on the man, you want to know he don't have
friends he can set after you. That's the tricky part.
You have to put it on him without him knowing it.
The worse thing that can happen, say you don't tell
on the man *or* cop to the deal? You might do, oh,
three months county time, something like that. Six at
the most and that's nothing."

Jackie said, "Terrific. I'll be starting my life over at
forty-five."

She remembered Ramona, who she thought was
old enough to be her mother, smiling at her with gold
crowns, saying that's how old she was and asking,
"When's your birthday, dear?"

She would sleep and wake up and remember looking out Tyler's office window at West Palm fading in
the dusk and remember Nicolet's boots on the desk
and the sound of his voice, Nicolet telling about the
Jamaican found in the trunk of an Oldsmobile.

At noon the next day, Thursday, Jackie was hand-
cuffed to a chain with Ramona and four other
women from the holding dorm. They were brought
outside and marched past a crew of male prisoners
on a cleanup detail to board the Corrections bus.
Jackie stared at the pavement, at bare heels in front
of her. A prisoner leaning on his push broom said,
"The ladies from the slut hut." Jackie looked up as
Ramona said, "Watch your mouth, boy." The prisoner with the broom said, "Come over here, I let you

sit on it." Ramona said, "Now you talking." They laughed and the women on the chain with Jackie came to life, moving their hips with the shuffle step, turning to grin at the men watching them. One of them cupped his crotch and said, "Check this out." Jackie glanced at him—a white guy, shirt off sweating in the sun, twenty years younger than she was, at least—and looked away. She heard him say, "Gimme that blond-haired one, I'll stay here forever," and Ramona, next to her, say, "Listen to that sweet boy, he's talking about you."

The First Appearance courtroom reminded her of a church with its wide center aisle and benches that were like pews. Male prisoners in dark blue outfits like scrubs, brought over from the county jail, sat in the first few rows. The women were unshackled, directed to sit behind them, and the men turned to look and make remarks until a deputy told them to shut up and face the front. When the judge entered they rose and sat down again. Still nothing happened. Court personnel and police officers would approach the judge and exchange words with him, hand him papers to be signed. Jackie said, "How long do we have to wait?"

Ramona said, "Long as they want us to. It's what you do in jail, dear, you wait."

From the time the bailiff began calling defendants, an hour and a half went by before Jackie was brought up to the public defender's table. He turned to her looking at a case file and asked how she wanted to plead.

"What are my choices?"

"Guilty, not guilty, or stand mute."

Nicolet and Tyler were here, off to one side. They lounged against the wall watching her.

Jackie said to the public defender, "I'm not sure what I should do."

He was young, in his early thirties, clean-cut, moderately attractive, wearing a pleasant after shave. . . . For some reason it gave her hope, a guy who appeared to have it together.

He said, "I can get it down to simple possession if you're willing to tell FDLE what they want to know."

And hope vanished.

Jackie said, "My cleaning woman can get me a better deal than that," and saw her public defender's startled look. Not a good sign. "Tell those guys they'll have to do a lot better before I'll even say hi to them."

Nicolet and Tyler, over there acting like innocent bystanders.

"Well, that's the state's offer," the public defender said. "If you plead to possession your bond will be set at one thousand dollars. If you don't, FDLE will request one at twenty-five thousand, based on your prior record and risk of flight. If you don't post it or you don't know anyone who can, you'll spend six to eight weeks in the Stockade before your arraignment comes up."

She said, "Whose side are you on?"

He said, "I beg your pardon?"

"What happens if I plead guilty?"

"And cooperate? You might get probation."

"If I don't cooperate."

"With the prior? You could get anywhere from a year to five, depending on the judge." He said, "You want to think about it? You've got about two minutes before we're up."

It was his attitude that hooked her, the bored tone of voice. And the way Nicolet and Tyler posed against the wall with their innocent, deadpan expressions. Jackie said, "I'm standing mute. After that I'm not saying another word."

Her public defender said, "If that's what you want."

Jackie said, "What I want is a fucking lawyer."

That got his startled expression again.

"I didn't mean that," Jackie said. She paused to glance around before saying to him, "You wouldn't happen to have a pack of cigarettes you could let me have."

He said, "I don't smoke."

She said, "I didn't think so."

8

Thursday night, Max waited at the admitting desk while deputies went to get Jackie Burke. He had read her Booking Card and Rough Arrest report and produced the forms required for her release, Appearance Bond and Power of Attorney. Now he was making small talk with the sergeant, a young guy named Terry Boland. Max had worked under his dad, Harry Boland, when Harry ran the Detective Bureau at the Sheriff's office. He was a colonel now, head of the Tactical Unit, Max's buddy and his source of information.

"I see they've finally started on the new dorms."

Terry said yeah, and by the time they were finished they'd need a few more.

"It's too bad," Max said, "you can't invest money in jails, like land development. It's the one business that keeps growing." Terry didn't seem to know if he should agree with that or not, and Max said, "How'd Ms. Burke do? She get along okay?"

"She wasn't any trouble."

"You didn't expect her to cause any, did you?"

"I mean she didn't break down," Terry said. "Some of them, you know, it's a shock coming in here from the civilized world."

"She's done it before," Max said. "That helps."

What surprised him, reading the Booking Card, was Jackie Burke's age. He had been picturing a fairly young airline stewardess. Now, the revised image was a forty-four-year-old woman who showed some wear and tear. But then, when the two deputies brought her in the front entrance, from outside dark into fluorescent light, Max saw he was still way off.

This was a good-looking woman. If he didn't know her age he'd say she was somewhere in her mid-thirties. Nice figure in the uniform skirt, five five, one fifteen—he liked her type, the way she moved, scuffing the slides on the vinyl floor, the way she raised her hand to brush her hair from her face. . . . Max said, "Ms. Burke?" and handed her his business card as he introduced himself. She nodded, glancing at the card. There were women who sobbed with relief. Some men too. There were women who came up and kissed him. This one nodded. They brought out her personal property and inventoried it back to her. As she was signing for it Max said, "I can give you a lift home if you'd like."

She looked up and nodded again saying, "Okay," and then, "No, wait. My car's at the airport."

"I can drop you off there."

She said, "Would you?" and seemed to look at him for the first time.

Right at him, not the least self-conscious, smiling a little with her eyes, a warm green that showed glints of light. He watched her step out of the slides and turn to press her hip against the wall, one and then the other, to slip her heels on. When she straightened, brushing her hair aside with the tips of her fingers, she smiled for the first time, a tired one, and seemed to shrug. Neither of them spoke again until they were outside and he asked if she was okay. Jackie Burke said, "I'm not sure," in no hurry walking to the car. Usually they were anxious to get out of here.

Now they were in the car ready to go and he felt her staring at him.

She said, "Are you really a bail bondsman?"

He looked at her. "What do you think I am?"

She didn't answer.

"I gave you my card in there."

She said, "Can I see your ID?"

"You serious?"

She waited.

Max dug the case out of his pocket, handed it to her, and opened the door so the inside light would go on. He watched her read every word from SURETY AGENT LICENSED BY STATE OF FLORIDA down to his date of birth and the color of his eyes.

She handed it back to him saying, "Who put up my bond, Ordell?"

"In cash," Max said, "the whole ten thousand."

She turned to look straight ahead.

Now they were both silent until the car reached the front gate and Max lowered his window. A deputy came out of the gatehouse with Max's .38 revolver, the cylinder open. Max handed the deputy his pass in exchange for the gun, thanked him, and snapped the cylinder closed before reaching over to put the revolver in the glove box. The gate opened. He said, "Ordinarily you have to go inside, but they know me. I'm out here a lot." Leaving the Stockade he turned on his brights and headed in the direction of Southern Boulevard, telling Ms. Burke for something to say that no one entered with a weapon, not even the deputies; telling her the office trailer next to the gatehouse was full of guns. He looked over as she flicked her lighter on and saw her face, cheeks drawn to inhale a thin cigarillo in the glow of the flame.

"You smoke cigars?"

"If I have to. Can we stop for cigarettes?"

He tried to picture a store out this way on Southern.

"The closest place I can think of," Max said, "would be the Polo Lounge. You ever been there?"

"I don't think so."

"It's okay, it's a cop hangout."

"I'd just as soon wait."

"I thought you might want a drink."

"I'd love one, but not there."

"We could stop at the Hilton."

"Is it dark?"

"Yeah, it's nice."

"We need a lounge that's dark."

He glanced at her, surprised.

She said, "I look like I just got out of jail," and blew a stream of cigar smoke at the windshield.

Dinner with a burglar, drinks with a flight attendant who did coke and delivered large sums of money. Cocktail piano in the background.

She looked different now, her eyes seemed more alive. Green eyes that moved and gleamed, reflecting the room's rose-colored light. Max watched her open a pack of cigarettes and light one before taking a sip of Scotch and glancing toward the cocktail piano.

"He shouldn't be allowed to do 'Light My Fire.'"

"Not here," Max said, "in a tux."

"Not anywhere." She pushed the pack toward him.

Max shook his head. "I quit three years ago."

"You gain weight?"

"Ten pounds. I lose it and put it back on."

"That's why I don't quit. One of the reasons. I was locked up yesterday with two cigarettes. And spent half the night getting advice from a cleaning woman named Ramona, who doesn't smoke."

Not sounding too upset.

"Ramona Williams," Max said, "she dips snuff. I've written her a few times. She has a tendency, she gets mad when she's drinking, to hit people with hammers, baseball bats. . . . You get along okay?"

"She offered to clean my apartment for forty dollars and do the windows on the inside."

Sounding serious now.

Max shifted around in his chair. "She was advising you, huh? . . . To do what?"

"I don't know—I guess what I need is a lawyer. Find out what my options are. So far, I can cooperate and get probation, *may*be. Or I can stand mute and get as much as five years. Does that sound right?"

"You mean just, or accurate? I'd say if you're tried and found guilty you won't get more than a year and a day. That's state time, prison."

"Great."

"But they won't want to take you to trial. They'll offer you simple possession, a few months county time, and a year or two probation." Max took a sip of his drink, bourbon over crushed ice. "You were brought up once before. Didn't that tell you anything? You ever get hooked on that stuff . . . I wrote a woman last year, a crack addict. I saw her again the other day in court. She looked like she'd had a face transplant."

"I don't do drugs," Jackie said. "I haven't even smoked grass in years."

"You were carrying the forty-two grams for somebody else."

"Apparently. I knew I had the money, but not the coke."

"Who packs your suitcase, the maid?"

She said, "You're as much fun as the cops."

In her quiet tone, looking right at him in cocktail

lounge half-light with those sparkly green eyes, and he said, "Okay, you don't know how it got in your bag."

It wasn't good enough. She sipped her drink, not seeming to care if he believed her or not.

So he started over. He said, "I figured out the other day I've written something like fifteen thousand bonds since I've been in business. About eighty percent of them for drug offenses or you could say were drug-related. I know how the system works. If you want, I can help you look at your options."

She surprised him.

"You're not tired of it?"

"I am, as a matter of fact." Max let it go at that; he didn't need to hear himself talk. "What about you? You spend half your life up in the air?"

"Even when I'm not flying," Jackie said. "I think I'm having trouble mid-lifing. At this point, with no idea where I'm going." She looked up at him, stubbing her cigarette out. "I know where I *don't* want to go."

Able to say things like that because he was older than she was by a dozen years. That was the feeling he got. He said, "Let's see if we can figure out what you should do. You want another drink?"

Jackie nodded, lighting a cigarette. One after another. Max gestured to the waitress to do it again. Jackie was looking at the piano player now, a middle-aged guy in a tux and an obvious rug working over the theme from *Rocky*.

She said, "The poor guy."

Max looked over. "He uses every one of those keys, doesn't he?" And looked at Jackie again. "You know who put the dope in your bag?"

She looked at him for a moment before nodding. "But that's not what this is about. They were waiting for me."

"It wasn't a random search?"

"They knew I was carrying money. They even knew the amount. The one who searched my bag, Tyler, didn't do much more than look at the money. 'Oh, I'd say there's fifty thousand here. What would you say?' Not the least bit surprised. But all they could do was threaten to hand me over to Customs, and I could see they didn't want to do that."

"Get tied up in federal court," Max said. "They were hoping you'd tell them about it."

"What they did was stall, till they lucked out and found the coke." She raised her glass and then held it. "You have to understand, they were as surprised as I was. But now they had something to use as leverage."

"What'd they ask you?"

"If I knew a man named Walker, in Freeport. They mentioned a Jamaican . . ."

The waitress came with their drinks.

"Beaumont Livingston," Max said.

Jackie stared at him while the waitress picked up their empty glasses and placed the drinks on fresh napkins, while the waitress asked if they'd care for some mixed nuts, and shook her head when Max looked at her and waited until he told her no thanks and the waitress walked off.

"How do you know Beaumont?"

"I wrote him on Monday," Max said. "Yesterday morning they found him in the trunk of a car."

She said, "Ordell put up his bond?"

"Ten thousand, the same as yours."

She said, "Shit," and picked up her drink. "They told me what happened to him. . . . The federal agent, the way he put it, Beaumont got popped."

Max hunched over the table. "You didn't mention that. One of the guys was federal? What, DEA?"

"Ray Nicolet, he's with Alcohol, Tobacco, and Fire-arms. I thought I told you." Jackie's gaze moved to the piano player. "Now it's 'The Sound of Music.' He likes big production numbers."

"When he starts to do 'Climb Every Mountain,' " Max said, "we're going someplace else." He felt ani-mated and could have smiled, beginning to under-stand what this was about. He said, "Ray Nicolet—I don't know him, but I've seen his name on arrest reports. He's the one who wants you. He uses you to get a line on Ordell, makes a case, and takes him federal."

Max was pleased with himself.

Until Jackie said, "They never mentioned his name."

And it stopped him. "You're kidding."

"I don't think they know anything about him."

"They talked to Beaumont."

"Yeah, and what did he tell them?"

"Well, you know what Ordell's into, don't you?"

"I have a pretty good idea," Jackie said. "If it isn't alcohol or tobacco, what's left that would get an ATF guy after me?"

Max said, "He never told you he sells guns?"

"I never asked."

"That wouldn't stop him."

She said, "You want to argue about it?"

Max shook his head and watched as she leaned in closer, over her arms on the edge of the table, that gleam in her eyes.

"What kind of guns are we talking about?"

It gave him the feeling they were into something together here and he liked it and if she was putting him on, using him, so what.

He said, "You name it. We're living in the arms capital of America, South Florida. You can buy an assault rifle here in less time than it takes to get a library card. Last summer I wrote a guy on a dope charge. While he's out on bond they get him trying to move thirty AK-47s, the Chinese version, through Miami International going to Bolivia. You know what gun I'm talking about?" She shrugged, maybe nodding, and Max said, "It's a copy of the Russian military weapon. Couple of weeks ago there was a story in the paper, how the cops pulled a sting on a guy who was buying TEC-9s in Martin County, no waiting, and selling them to drug dealers in West Palm, Lake Worth, all convicted felons. There's a guy in Coral Springs sold cluster bombs to the Iraqis, he says before we went to war in the Gulf. I don't see

Ordell into military hardware, but you never know. What amazes me about him, he's a bad guy, there's no doubt in my mind, but he's only had one conviction and that was twenty years ago."

"He told you that?"

"A friend of mine at the Sheriff's office ran his name. And Ordell's the kind of guy loves to talk about himself."

"Not to me," Jackie said. "When I first met him he was flying over to Freeport a lot, he said to gamble. He'd tell me how much he won, or lost. How much he paid for clothes . . ."

"He hints around," Max said, "wants you to guess what he does. Tell him you think he deals in guns and watch his face, he'll give it away. Gets paid in the Bahamas, so he's dealing out of the country. You bring the payoff here on one of your flights . . ." Max waited.

So did Jackie.

After a moment she said, "I used to bring over ten thousand at a time. Never more than that or any of my own money. I'd have to keep enough in my car for parking, to get out of the airport."

"How many trips did you make?"

"Nine, with ten thousand."

"He's got that kind of money?"

"He wanted me to start bringing over a hundred thousand at a time."

Max said, "Jesus," in a whisper.

"He kept after me until I said okay, I'll bring whatever fits in a nine-by-twelve manila envelope and I want five hundred dollars. He said fine and arranged it. His friend Mr. Walker in Freeport gave me the envelope. . . ."

"You didn't look inside to check?"

"For what? Walker said he put in fifty thousand. Fine. It could've been any amount. What he didn't mention was the baggie with forty-two grams in it."

Max said, "If you knew bringing in anything over ten thousand was risky, why not pack a hundred grand? What's the difference?"

"Whatever the amount, it had to fit in my flight bag and not hit you in the face if the bag was opened. That was the idea."

"Even ten thousand at a time," Max said, "you don't have to ask what he does to know he came by it illegally."

"You're right," Jackie said, "I don't have to ask, since I'm not with the IRS." She paused, still looking at him. "Every once in a while you sound like one of them. Not so much Tyler as Nicolet."

"I have trouble being myself with you," Max said. "At the Stockade you weren't sure I was a bail bondsman. You thought I might be a cop, didn't you? Trying to pull something sneaky."

"It crossed my mind," Jackie said.

"I spent ten years in law enforcement," Max said, "with the Sheriff's office. Maybe it still shows. Or the business I'm in, you tend to speak the same language."

She said, "You aren't by any chance hiring? I haven't missed work yet, I was off today. But if I can't leave the country I'm out of a job. And if I can't work I won't be able to hire a lawyer."

"Ask, they might give you permission."

"If I cooperate."

"Well, you have to give them *some*thing. You want to stay out of jail, don't you?"

"Yeah, but not as much as I want to stay out of the trunk of a car."

"I'm pretty sure," Max said, "whether you give them anything or not, they're gonna be watching you."

She hunched over the table again, intent. "I've been thinking, if all I can give them is a name, nothing about what he does, I don't have much to bargain with, do I?"

"Offer to help," Max said, "short of wearing a wire. That's all you have to do, show a willingness. Once they get him, and that's all they really care about, they're not gonna say, well, you didn't do enough, too bad. No, once they have Ordell, they'll get the state attorney to nolle pros your case and you'll be off the hook. That means they can refile in thirty to sixty days, but they won't. If they get him before you're arraigned, they'll let you off on an A-99, a no-file."

She said, "You're sure?"

"I can't guarantee it, no. But what else have you got?"

"Walk in and offer to help."

"Tell them who gives you the money, who you take it to, how much you get paid, all that."

"Name names."

"Your Mr. Walker, you'll have to give him up."

"Act contrite?"

"Play it straight."

He watched her now, Jackie staring at her cigarette as she rolled the tip of it in the ashtray, and he kept quiet, giving her time. But moments passed, Max felt himself running out of patience and said, "Where are you?"

She raised her head and he saw her eyes, that gleam, that look that could change his life if he let it.

She said, "You know something?" The gleam becoming a smile. "I might have more options than I thought."

9

Louis walked into a liquor store on Dixie Highway in Lake Worth that Thursday evening. They had vodka now that was imported from Russia, from Poland, Sweden, fifteen to twenty bucks a fifth. They might've had it before he did his forty-six months at Starke, but Louis couldn't recall having seen any. He had always drunk the cheaper stuff.

Not anymore.

An older guy behind the counter came over to him saying, "What can I do you for?" Older but bigger than Louis, with a gray brush cut. The guy looked like a boozer; he hadn't shaved in a few days and was wearing a T-shirt with GOD BLESS AMERICA on it, the kind that was popular during the Persian Gulf War. The guy's belly had AMERICA stretched out of shape.

Louis said, "Let me have two fifths of that Absolut."

The guy reached to get them from the shelf and Louis stuck his right hand in the pocket of the dark blue suit coat he'd found in the closet and was wearing as a sporty jacket with his white T-shirt and khakis. As the guy turned with the bottles and placed them on the counter, Louis said, "And all the money you have in the till."

Now the guy was looking at Louis holding the pocket of the suit coat pointed at him. He didn't seem surprised by it. He rubbed a hand over the salt-and-pepper beard stubble on his jaw and said, "Why don't you take your finger out of there and stick it in your ass while I go get my shotgun." Shaking his head as he started for the back of the store. Louis got out of there.

So much for his new start.

He drove to Max Cherry's office and let himself in with the key he'd taken from Max's desk this morning. Optimistic then, feeling close to making his move. What he had to do now was put his mind to it, get serious. Ordell was right, he had nothing to lose. Louis went out to his car and got the tire iron from the trunk.

This afternoon he had driven all the way down to South Miami Beach, two and a half hours, to the Santa Marta on Ocean Drive near Sixth. The hotel was owned by Colombians and some of them hung out in the bar off the lobby. Louis walked in, saw four of them down the bar, one guy showing the others a dance step, shoulders hunched, hips moving to Latin riffs screaming out of hidden speakers. They looked up to see Louis and back to the guy dancing. That was it. Louis could put on a grin and walk up to them, hand out Max Cherry bail-bond cards. . . . He had come to make sure he was right, that he couldn't fake it with these people.

What he did, he turned around and walked up the street of art deco hotels, *Miami Vice* country, to the Cardozo and sat at a table on the sidewalk to have a vodka tonic. It was no more Louis's scene than the hotel where the Colombians hung out, but the show was better: all the tank tops and hundred-dollar pump-up basketball shoes. Louis had lived here ten years ago when old retired people from New York sat on the hotel porches wearing hats, their noses painted white, and boat-lift Cubans worked their hustles down the street. Five years ago when it was beginning to change he had returned to rob a bank not ten blocks from here, up by Wolfie's Deli. Now it was the hip place to be in South Florida. Guys with sunglasses in their hair posed skinny girls on the beach and photographed them. There was no place to park anymore on Ocean Drive. Louis had a couple more vodka tonics. He watched a dark-haired girl in leotards and heels coming along the sidewalk, a winner, and was about to put his hand out, ask if she wanted a drink, when he realized she was a guy wearing makeup and tits. That's how trendy it was now. What was he doing here? He wasn't a salesman who handed out bail-bond cards. If anyone asked him what he did he would have to say he robbed banks, even though the last one was almost five years ago.

What if, while he was in the neighborhood, he stopped by that bank on Collins again? It was the one where the girl handed him the dye pack.

Louis had another vodka tonic and wrote a note on a cocktail napkin. *This is a stickup. Do not panic. . . .* He used another napkin to write *or press a button . . .* He saw he would have to write much smaller to get in *or I will blow your head off* and something about the money, wanting only hundred-dollar bills and fifties. He started over with a clean napkin opened up and put down what he wanted to say. Perfect.

But by the time he paid his check, walked several blocks to his car, and drove up Collins Avenue to the bank, it was closed.

Last week he might have given up. Not today; he was making his move. Looking stupid to the guy in the liquor store didn't even set him back. It told him to, goddamn it, do it right. Liquor stores, he *knew,* were never as easy as banks.

Louis used the tire iron to pry the lock off Max's gun cabinet in the meeting room with the office refrigerator and the coffee maker. Inside were four handguns and the nickel-plated Mossberg 500, the pistol-grip shotgun with the battery-operated laser scope. Louis felt his image changing as he got serious and chose the chromed Colt Python he knew was Winston's, a 357 Mag with an eight-inch barrel, big and showy. That should do it, and a couple of boxes of hollow points. But then thought, if he was going for show he might as well go all the way and took the Mossberg 500 too. Even with the laser scope the shotgun would fit under the coat he was wearing as a sporty jacket. Buttoned, the coat was snug on him and had the widest lapels Louis had ever seen. All J.J.'s clothes were like new but out of style, hanging twenty years in closets or packed in trunks while J.J. was in and out of the system. Ordell would never see this coat. Tomorrow he'd go to Burdine's or Macy's and get some new outfits. Nothing too bright, like Ordell's yellow sport coat, he wasn't feeling that showy. Something in light blue might be nice.

When Louis walked in the liquor store the second time, the guy with GOD BLESS AMERICA on his T-shirt rubbed his hand over his jaw and said, "Jesus Christ, don't tell me you're back."

Louis said, "Let me have two fifths of that Absolut," this time bringing the Mossberg out of the coat from under his left arm, the nickel plate gleaming in the overhead light, the red dot of the laser scope showing the bottles he wanted as he squeezed the grip.

The liquor store guy said, "You swipe that toy gun offa some kid?"

Louis said, "See the red dot?" He moved it off the Absolut, squeezed the trigger, and blew out three rows of the cheap stuff. Louis said, "It's real," Christ, with his ears ringing. "That's two fifths of Absolut, whatever you have in the till, and that wad in your hip pocket."

He felt good and had some vodka out of the bottle driving up Dixie, on his way to finding a motel, through living at J.J.'s, through hanging around the bail-bond office. . . . And realized, Christ, he had to go back there right now. Put the key in Max's desk and make it look like a break-in, or Max would know he did it. He should've taken all the guns. Max still might figure it out. Four years locked up, he was rusty, that's all. At least he knew what he had to do. Then keep going, ride it out. No stopping or getting off once you start. Wasn't that how Ordell said it?

Something like that.

Ordell had tried showing his jackboys how to use a tension tool with a feeler pick or what was called a rake—none of these gadgets more than five inches long, they fit right in your pocket—to open most any locked door to a house. See? It was easy once you practiced and got the feel. No, jackboys liked to bust into places. They liked to smash windows or blow the lock out with a shotgun. Their trip was driving a big pickup truck through the front door of a pawnshop or a hardware store: drive in, load up, and drive out again in the stolen truck with some company name on the side. Gun shops put iron posts in the concrete outside the door so you couldn't drive in. What they would do juiced up was walk in when the gun shop was open, pull their pieces, and go for the assault weapons they loved. It didn't matter they could get shot doing it, they were crazy motherfuckers. Ordell gave up on teaching them subtle ways to gain entry.

He brought out his tools only when he needed to use them himself.

Like this evening, getting into Jackie Burke's apartment.

Max drove home seeing her across the table in bar-room light, Jackie looking at him the way she did with those sparkly green eyes, looking off at the piano and saying he shouldn't be allowed to play "Light My Fire." Saying "Great," in that same dry tone of voice when he told her she might do a year and a day. Saying "You're as much fun as the cops," when he didn't believe her at first. But pretty soon she was confiding in him and he could feel them getting closer, like they were in this together and she needed him. It was a good feeling. He had watched her eyes to sense her mood. Watched the way she smoked cigarettes and wanted one for the first time in a couple of years. Before they'd left the cocktail lounge he knew something could happen between them if he wanted it to.

He hadn't had this feeling in a long time. Never with a defendant.

Once, during the past two years living alone, he had almost told a woman he loved her. A waitress named Cricket with a Georgia accent. Got that tender feeling one night lying in bed with her, stirred by the way the light from the window softened her hollow cheeks and lay across her small pale breasts. Except the shine was from a streetlight outside, not the moonlight of "Moonlight Becomes You" or "That

Old Devil Moon," and realizing this might have stopped him if good sense didn't. Cricket sang Reba McEntire numbers with gestures. She sang that old Tammy Wynette song "D.I.V.O.R.C.E.," would give him a look and say, "Hint, hint." Cricket made him feel good. The trouble was finding something to talk about. It was the same way with Renee. All those years of not talking. He had tried reading poetry to her when they were first married. If she said anything at all after it was, "What's that suppose to mean?"

He hadn't told Renee he loved her in about ten years. He told her a few times when he knew he didn't love her and then quit. What was the point? She never told him. Not even that much in the beginning when he told her all the time, because he did. She was tiny, she was cute as a bug, and he wanted to eat her up. She never said a word making love. She was afraid of getting pregnant; she said a doctor had told her she was too small and it would kill her, or her uterus was tipped or she was afraid of hydrogen bombs; take your pick. It was okay if she didn't appreciate his reading to her. It wasn't romantic poetry anyway, it was mostly Ginsberg and Corso, those guys. He liked them even though he had to face demonstrators in those days with a riot baton, out in the streets being called a pig, and he'd wonder, Wait a minute. What am I doing here? This was before he made detective and liked Homicide so much he was willing to die there. One time he finished reading a poem and Renee said, "You should see yourself."

Meaning a uniformed deputy in dark green reciting poetry, but missing the point entirely that it was one of the Beats.

He remembered a poem more recently by a guy named Gifford called "To Terry Moore" that ended with the lines,

> Tell me, Terry
> when you were young
> were your lovers ever gentle?

He remembered it because he had been in love with Terry Moore in the fifties, right after being in love with Jane Greer and just before he fell in love with Diane Baker. This year he had passed on Jodie Foster, only because he was old enough to be her dad, and fallen in love with Annette Bening. He didn't care how old Annette was.

Jackie Burke had made him think of the poem to Terry Moore. The last part, "were your lovers ever gentle?" On the way to dropping her off to get her car. Jackie telling him she had been flying nearly twenty years and married twice. Once to an airline pilot "who went to prison with a two hundred-dollar-a-day habit." And once to a Brit in Freeport, floorman at a hotel casino, "who decided one evening it was time to die." And that was all she said about them. He thought of the poem because he could imagine guys coming on to her as a matter of course, before those marriages and in between and maybe during, thirty thousand feet in the air.

She asked in the car as they were coming to the airport if he was married. He told her yes and how long and she said, "Twenty-seven *years?*"

Almost raising her voice. He remembered that. Making it an unimaginable period of time.

He said, "It seems longer," and in the dark, staring at his headlight beams, tried to explain his situation.

"We started out, I was already with the Sheriff's Office, but Renee didn't like being married to a cop. She said she was worried sick all the time something would happen to me. Also, she said, I put the job first."

"Did you?"

"You have to. So I quit. She didn't like being married to a cop—she *hates* being married to a bail bondsman. Nineteen years she's been telling people I sell insurance."

Jackie said, "You don't look like a bail bondsman."

Meaning it, he assumed, as a compliment. She didn't say what a bail bondsman was supposed to look like. He imagined she meant a sleazy type, fat little guy in a rumpled suit who chewed his cigar. A lot of people had that picture.

"Renee moved out of the house. She opened an art gallery and has these guys, they look like gay heroin addicts, hanging around her. Twice before, we separated. This time it's been almost two years."

Jackie said, "Why haven't you gotten a divorce?"

"I'm seriously thinking about it."

"I mean before this. If you don't get along."

"It always seemed like too much trouble."

It didn't now, driving home, putting up pictures of Jackie Burke in his mind. The ones where she had that gleam in her eyes, the look saying, *We could have fun.*

Unless she was appraising him with the look, making a judgment, and what it said was, *I could use you.*

Maybe.

Either way it was a turn-on.

Max pulled into the drive of the house he and Renee had bought twenty-two years ago, when she was coming out of her decoupage period and getting into macramé, or the other way around. The house was an old-Florida frame bungalow being eaten by termites and almost obscured from the street by cabbage palms and banana trees. Renee had moved to an apartment in Palm Beach Gardens, not far from where Jackie Burke lived—according to her Rough Arrest report. He'd leave the car in the drive while he went in the house, planning to go back to the office later. He was surprised his beeper hadn't gone off while he was with Jackie. Prime time for a bail bondsman was six to nine.

He opened the glove box to get his .38 Airweight. Whenever it was out of his hands for a period of time he liked to check it; this evening, make sure it was his gun the guard at the Stockade had handed him. He felt inside, then leaned across the seat to take a look. The gun wasn't there. No one had touched the car while they were in the hotel cocktail lounge or the alarm would have gone off. They came out, he opened the door for Jackie. She got in, he closed the door and walked around to the other side. . . .

Maybe the look said, *I can take care of myself.*

10

It was the kind of building had all outside doors on balconies and at night you'd see these orange lights on every floor up and across the front of the building. Jackie's apartment was on the fourth level you got to by elevator, then *in*to using the thin little tension tool and feeling around with the feeler pick until you heard the click. Nothing to it. Ordell had checked the kind of lock it was the first time he came here. . . .

Through a little hallway that went past the kitchen into the living room and dining-L. The bedroom and bath were to the left. He remembered she had it fixed up nice but kind of bare-looking, mostly white, drapes over the glass door to the balcony. Ordell pulled the drapes open and could see better, light coming from outside. He sat down on the sofa to wait. Sat there in the dark calculating how long it would take Max Cherry to drive out to the Stockade and bond her out, give her a ride home. . . . Unless she had to get her car. He felt like smiling at the way Max Cherry had accepted the watch as his take for the bond. This place looked cold. Fixed nice, but like she could move out in about ten minutes. Not like a place you called home, with all kinds of shit laying around. He reached over and turned the lamp on.

No sense frightening the woman, come in and see a man sitting in the dark, maybe scream. Best to keep her calm, not expecting harm. See how she behaves first, if she was nervous talking to him. Man, who could you trust these days? Outside of Louis. See? Thinking of Louis right away coming to mind. Knowing him twenty years as a man would never tell nothing on you. Had that old-time pro sense of keeping his mouth shut. Even thinking of himself as a good guy basically, Louis would never snitch you out. Louis could be worth a cut of the score. Not a big cut, more like a nick.

Ordell waited.

Got tired of it and went to the kitchen, found the Scotch, and put some in a glass with ice from the refrigerator. Hardly any food in there, the woman getting by day to day. Orange juice, Perrier, half a loaf of bread. Some cheese turning green. Some of those little cups of nonfat yogurt with fruit in it, the woman watching her weight. He didn't see she needed to worry about getting fat, she had a fine body on her. One he'd wanted to see but couldn't ever get her in a mood to show to him. He'd touch her, tell her, man, she was fine and she'd look at him like . . . not stuck-up exactly, more like it was too much trouble to get it on and she had her laundry to do. Maybe tonight if she came in scared and saw she had to please him . . .

Yeah, it should be dark. Ordell turned the light out in the kitchen, took his drink to the living room to sit down on the sofa again, and switched off the lamp.

He waited.

Finished the drink and waited some more.

At least it was comfortable. He felt himself starting to doze off, eyelids getting heavy . . . eyes opening then, quick, Ordell full awake hearing her key in the lock, Jackie home at last. There she was now in the light coming through from the balcony, her bag hanging from her shoulders, trying to remember—look at her—if she had closed the drapes or left them open. Slipping her keys in the bag now . . .

Ordell said, "How you doing, Ms. Jackie?"

She didn't move, so he got up and went over to her, seeing her face now, no color to it in this light. He came up close and put his hands on the round part of her arms below her shoulders. "You looking fine this evening. You gonna thank me?"

"For what?"

"Who you think got you out of jail?"

"The same guy who put me in. Thanks a lot."

"Hey, you get caught with blow, that's your business."

"It wasn't mine."

Not sounding mean, looking straight in his eyes, like to say it was his fault. Ordell had to stop and think. He said, "Hey, shit, I bet it was the present Mr. Walker was sending Melanie. Yeaaah, he's the one musta put it in there if you didn't. Hey, I'm sorry that happened. I 'magine they asked you all kind of questions about it, huh? And about all that money? Want to know where you got it?"

She didn't answer him.

"Who you giving it to? All that, huh?"

"They asked."

"And what did you tell them?"

"I said I wanted a lawyer."

"Didn't let nothing slip?"

She said to his face, "You're not asking the right question."

Ordell's hands moved up to rest on her shoulders. He said, "I'm not?" feeling her body there under her jacket and the strap of her bag, thin little bones he rubbed with his fingers.

She said to him, "Ask why I was picked up."

"Dog didn't sniff your bag?"

"They didn't need a dog. They knew about the money, the exact amount."

"They tell you how they found out?"

"They asked if I knew Mr. Walker."

"Yeah? . . ."

"I didn't tell them anything."

"My name come up?"

He watched her head go side to side but didn't feel the bones move. His thumbs brushed her collarbone, the tips of his fingers touched her neck, caressed the skin, Ordell seeing how lightly he could touch her, not wanting her to move, try to run, and maybe scream. Her eyes never blinked.

"Say they know about Mr. Walker. Who else?"

It made her hesitate before she said, "The Jamaican, Beaumont."

"What'd they say about him?"

"They'd spoken to him in jail."

Ordell nodded. He'd had that right. "You know what happen to him?"

"They told me."

"Yeah, somebody musta been mad at Beaumont, or got worried about him facing time. You understand what I'm saying? Somebody knowing what he might tell not to get sent away. I suppose they give you all kind of shit then about what they know. Get you thinking you may as well tell what *you* know, huh?"

Her head went just a little bit side to side.

He brought his thumbs from her collarbone up to her throat and her shoulder with the strap on it moved like she meant to twist away from him, but he held on to her and felt the shoulder ease back. He liked the way she was trying to act cool, staring at him. He liked the way she looked too, her face pure white in the dark, whiter than Melanie's face or any white face he had been this close to, thinking he could put her down on the floor, or he could take her in the bedroom, and after they were done put the pillow over her face and aim the pistol he had with him into the pillow. . . . Man, it was a shame to have to do it. . . . He said, "You scared of me?"

Her head went side to side without her eyes leaving his.

He *knew* she was scared, man, she had to be, but wasn't acting like she was and it made him press his thumbs into her soft skin and tighten up on his fingers, wanting to know what she'd told them and knowing he'd have to take her close to the edge to find out. He said, "Baby, you got a reason to be nervous with me?" He saw her eyes close and open. . . .

And felt what must be her hand down there touch his thigh, brush across it, and move on up and had to admire her using a female way of getting to him, liking it, yeaaah, till something else besides a hand, something *hard*, dug into him.

She said, "You feel it."

Ordell said, "Yes, I do," wanting to grin, let her know he wasn't serious and she shouldn't be either. He said, "I believe that's a gun pressing against my bone."

Jackie said, "You're right. You want to lose it or let go of me?"

If either Max or Winston phoned the other from the office and said, "Get dressed," it meant come right away, armed.

This time it was Max who phoned and Winston arrived while the sheriff's people were still there, blue lights turning on their radio cars. Somebody had shattered the glass in the front door and reached in through the bars to unlock it. Max, in the office with the two uniforms taking notes, looked up at Winston. He said, "These guys were here inside of two minutes from the time the alarm started to blow." Max seemed impressed.

Winston said, "They get him?" Knowing they hadn't. He saw Max motion with his head to the meeting room and went in there to see the gun cabinet broken into, two pieces missing, three still hanging on pegs. Now he watched from the doorway to the office while the uniforms finished their report, left, and Max came over.

"What'd I get dressed for," Winston said, "if he's gone?"

" 'Cause we know who did it," Max said, moving past him to the gun cabinet.

"We talking about Louis?"

Watching as Max chose the Browning 380 auto, took it from its peg, and checked the slide.

"How you know it's him?"

"He wouldn't have time to break in," Max said, "come in here, bust into the cabinet—all the time the alarm's making a racket. You know how loud it is? He doesn't clean us out, he takes only the Python and the Mossberg, and does it all inside of two minutes. I think he broke the glass on the way out, make it look like a B and E."

"Then how'd he get in?"

"Lifted a spare key out of my drawer, had one made, and put it back. Planning something like this. That's why I think it's Louis."

"You don't know for sure."

"Let's go ask him. Your arm okay?" Max reached out as if to touch Winston's sleeve.

"It's all right; they put in some stitches. What's that you got, a new watch?"

"Rolex," Max said, turning his arm to let the gold catch the light, the way Ordell had shown it to him. "I took it on a bond till I get the premium."

Winston said, "Lemme see," putting his hand under Max's arm to look at the watch up close. He said, "I hate to tell you, but it ain't a Rolex. I know, 'cause I have a real one at home. This decoration here don't look right."

Max took his arm back. "This's a different model."

"I'm talking about this one. How much was the premium it's for?"

"Don't worry about it, okay?"

"Was gonna say, if it's over two-fifty . . ."

Max said, "Let's get outta here," sticking the Browning in the waist of his pants. He picked up his jacket from a chair and Winston followed after him.

"How come you're taking the Browning? Don't you have that little Airweight in your car?"

Max stopped dead at the busted front door and turned around. He said, "I forgot, one of us has to stay here," still with that short tone of voice, edgy. "I called a guy, he's gonna come nail up a sheet of plywood. You wait for him, all right?"

Asking, but actually telling.

Winston said, "That's my punishment, huh, for saying it ain't a Rolex?"

* * *

The pistol Ordell had on him was the little Targa .22 he used for close work. Jackie found it in the side pocket of his coat. Felt him all over with her free hand, the other hand holding the gun pressed against his bone, before she stepped back, shrugged, and let the shoulder bag slip off and drop on the floor. He said, "It looks like we have a misunderstanding here." Not moving, believing she would shoot him with either hand, this two-gun woman he had somehow misjudged.

"You were about to strangle me," Jackie said. "I understood that part."

"Baby, I was playing with you. You on the team. Didn't I get you out of jail?"

She said, "You got Beaumont out too."

Ordell gave her a pained look. "That hurts, what I think you mean to imply there, I could be wrong. . . . Baby, you aren't wearing a wire, are you?"

She didn't answer on that one.

"Listen, I didn't have nothing to do with that dope you brought in, but I'll get you a lawyer, a good one. I had that fifty gees I'd get you F. Lee Bailey himself."

She said, "But you don't have it."

"That's why we should sit down and talk," Ordell said. "Work something out here. Put the lights on, maybe have a drink. . . ." He cocked his head to study this woman, kind of mussed but still looking fine. He had to smile. A two-gun woman turning him on. "Baby, you want to talk or shoot me?" And when she didn't answer right away he said, "Hey now, I don't want to give you ideas. I'm gonna pay you the five hundred too. Even if you didn't deliver. But if we gonna talk about it, girl, you have to show you trust me."

Jackie raised both the guns, putting them dead on him, saying, "I trust you."

He had to smile, appreciating her.

"You felt me," Ordell said. "Now let me feel you and put my mind at ease. See if you might have a wire running around that fine body."

"I'm not wired," Jackie said. "I haven't talked to them yet. If I trust you, you have to trust me."

"Yeah, but you said something there I didn't especially like the sound of. Like you threatening me, saying you haven't talked to them *yet*."

She gave him an easy shrug with her shoulders he liked.

"Sooner or later," Jackie said, "they'll get around to offering me a plea deal if I talk to them. You know that. They might even let me walk. The only thing you and I have to talk about, really, is what you're willing to do for me."

"I told you, baby, I'm gonna get you a lawyer."

Now she was shaking her head at him, still cool, saying, "I don't think that's going to do it. Let's say if I tell on you, I get off. And if I don't, I go to jail."

"Yeah? . . ."

"What's it worth to you if I don't say a word?"

Max opened the trunk of his car, parked down the street from the house where Louis was staying, the place dark. He'd need a flashlight, he got that out. And his stun gun, the best way to throw a punch without hurting your hand. He didn't want to shoot Louis. He wanted to knock him down, handcuff him, and turn him over to the police. The house appeared empty, deserted, trash laying around. Walking up to the side entrance by the carport, he was surprised there weren't broken panes in the windows. Max tried the door, gave it a shoulder, then stepped back and kicked it open.

The place smelled of mildew.

He sat in the living room in the dark, an expert at waiting, a nineteen-year veteran of it, waiting for people who failed to appear, missed court dates because they forgot or didn't care, and took off. Nineteen years of losers, repeat offenders in and out of the system. Another one, that's all Louis was, slipping back into the life.

Is this what you do?

He knew why he was here. Still, he began to wonder about it, thinking not so much of waiting other times in the nineteen years but aware of right now, the mildew smell, seeing himself sitting in the dark with a plastic tube that fired a beanbag full of buckshot.

Really? This is what you do?

Max pointed the stun gun at a window, pushed in the plunger and saw a pane of glass explode.

In the car, driving back to the office, he saw Jackie again and was anxious to tell her something.

He said to Winston, waiting in the front office, "He'll never come back."

Winston said, "That's right."

"So we're out a couple of guns. It's worth it."

Winston said, "You didn't see him."

"I think he's cleared out."

"The man didn't come fix the door."

Max turned to look at it, not saying anything.

"You want me to keep waiting on him?"

Max said, "I'm getting out of the business." Still looking at the door.

Winston began to nod. He said, "That's a good idea."

The way Ordell heard what Jackie was saying: If she kept quiet and did time on his account, she wanted to be paid for it. He asked her was this a threat. She said that would be extortion. It might be, but wasn't an answer to the question. Was she saying if he didn't pay her she'd go talk to the police?

Wait a minute.

He said, "Baby, you don't know any more what my business is than they do."

She said, "Are you sure?"

"You run some money you say is mine. What am I suppose to get convicted of?" Asking what sounded like the key question . . .

She came back saying, "The illegal sale of fire-arms." Like that. "It's true, isn't it? You sell guns?"

Sounding innocent saying it that way, naïve, nice-looking airline stewardess sitting across the room on her white sofa. Except she had the two guns resting on cushions to either side of her, little guns to look at but nothing naïve about them. She had watched him fix drinks—hers on the coffee table in front of her now. From where he sat holding his Scotch it would take him two, three, almost four strides to get to her once he jumped up and if he didn't trip over the coffee table. He believed he would get only about halfway, even with her smoking and drinking, before she picked up most likely the Airweight she'd got hold of somewhere between the Stockade and here and blew him back in the chair. So Ordell was more interested now in their conversation than estimating space and his chance of getting to her. Jackie telling him now:

"Whatever they know, they got from Beaumont, not me. Why did ATF pick me up if it's not about guns? Even if they didn't know you before, they do now. You got us out of jail."

"You don't get convicted for putting up bonds."

"No, but I think you took a chance."

Man, she had that right.

Telling him now, "If they think you're selling guns, they'll keep an eye on you. Won't they? Then what? You're out of business."

"I'm trying to hear what you're saying," Ordell said. "If I pay you to keep quiet and they ask you about guns, then you say you don't know nothing about any. Is that right?"

"I don't, really. You're right, you've never told me."

"Then what do I have to worry about? You saying you *will* tell them if we don't agree on a price here?"

"If I say I won't," Jackie said, "will you take my word for it?"

"You getting me confused now."

"All I'm saying is we have to trust each other."

"Yeah, but what's it gonna cost me?"

She said, "How about a hundred thousand if I'm convicted. That would be for jail time up to a year or if I'm put on probation. If I have to do more than a year, you pay another hundred thousand."

"You be making more in than out, huh?"

She said, "You'd have to put the money in some kind of escrow account in my name. If I get off, you get it back."

"Just like that, huh?"

"It's up to you."

"Even if I agree," Ordell said, "I think you're high. But say I agree. I see two problems. One, you put a hundred grand in cash in the bank, anything over ten, the U.S. government gets told and they want to know where it came from."

She said, "I think we can find a way around that. What's the other problem? I bet I know what it is."

Listen to the woman.

"All my money," Ordell said, "is over in Freeport." Watched her nod and take a sip of her drink.

"What's there now and what will be coming in." Watched her raise her eyebrows at that.

"If ATF's on my ass like you say, how do I get money here to pay you?"

She said, "You're right, it's a problem. I'm pretty sure, though, I can work it out."

"Now that we talking big money it's worth the risk?"

She smiled at him.

"Okay, how you gonna do it if you out on bond and can't go nowhere?"

"There's a way," Jackie said. "Trust me."

11

Friday morning, half-past eight, Tyler and Nicolet had Ordell Robbie's house under surveillance. They were in Tyler's Chevy Caprice parked on Greenwood Avenue, close enough to the corner of 31st to give them a clear view of the third house down on the south side of the street.

At ten to eight they had checked the garage and knocked on the front door. Nothing happened until Tyler held his ID case open to the peephole. That got the sound of locks snapping open and the face of a young black woman peering at them over the chain. She said, "He ain't here," and closed the door. Tyler had to keep knocking and ringing the bell to get the door open again and the woman to tell them no, he hadn't been there all night, and no, she didn't know where he was at. Big eyes in the space that narrowed gradually until the door closed again. They drove around the block and parked on Greenwood to watch the house: a neat little red brick ranch with bursts of pink and white impatiens in the flower beds and bars on the windows. Tyler thought he saw the drapes move and checked with his binoculars. Yeah, the woman was there looking out.

"Waiting for hubby," Nicolet said. "He gets home she's gonna kill him."

Tyler said, "We don't even know it's his wife, or if he's got one."

"We don't know shit," Nicolet said, "except he's into guns, that I'm positive of. Doing big business too, or he wouldn't have stuck his neck out putting up their bonds. He was desperate, had to get them out before either one of them finked on him."

"Or he's stupid," Tyler said.

"He's got one fall that goes back twenty years," Nicolet said. "That's not a guy that fucks up."

"Maybe he's been clean."

"No way—he's into guns big-time. Got Beaumont out as fast as he could and popped him, or had it done. Riviera Beach said they questioned Ordell. Yeah, but they didn't know what to ask. That was the problem there. Same thing with Jackie Burke, he got her out right away. . . . You better call her again."

Tyler picked up the phone and punched her number.

Nicolet saying, "Try and scare her a little."

Tyler waited and then said, "Ms. Burke, how you doing? This is Faron Tyler. . . . Oh, I'm sorry. I was just checking to see if you're okay. We have a man outside your building. . . . Well, just in case. You never know. You have my number. . . ." He listened for several moments and said, "Oh?" And said, "We can do that any time you want, your place or ours. . . . Okay, sounds good. We'll call later and you tell us. So long." He replaced the phone saying to Nicolet, "She wants to talk."

"One night all alone," Nicolet said, "can do that. When?"

"Later sometime today. I woke her up again."

"Man, I like that type," Nicolet said. "Can't get 'em out of bed. They give you that sleepy look, a little puffy, hair all mussed up. Like the broad in that beer ad on TV. She works in this joint out in the desert? You've seen it. The guy comes in, right away she's interested, but you don't see him. You never see him. He asks for the kind of beer they're advertising, I forgot what it is, and she says, 'I was hoping you'd say that,' like he's her kind of guy. She even looks a little sweaty but, man, you know she's ready. That type. Jackie Burke reminds me of her a little."

Tyler said, "So you're gonna look into that?"

"I might, if I can get her to flip, and it sounds like she's ready, huh? Otherwise, no, *sir*, that can get you in serious trouble."

Ray Nicolet was divorced; he went after women assuming they would be attracted to him and enough of them were to keep him happy. Faron Tyler was married to a girl named Cheryl he met at FSU; they had two little boys, four and six. Faron only fooled around once in a while, if he was with Ray and couldn't get out of it. Like if during deer season they were out and happened to run into a couple of friendly girls in a bar. Once Ray started making the moves on the one he wanted, Faron always felt he had to move on the other one so she wouldn't be hurt, feel rejected.

Right now Nicolet was watching a white Cadillac Seville turn onto 31st Street from Greenwood. It crept along like the driver was looking at house numbers, stopped, backed up, and pulled into Ordell Robbie's driveway. Nicolet said, "Well, who have we here?" taking the glasses from Tyler to put them on the guy getting out of the car, a big guy in a short-sleeved shirt. "You want to call it in?"

Tyler said, "Gimme the number," picking up the phone.

Nicolet read it to him off the plate. The guy was at the front door now. Nicolet saw him as a white male in a mostly black neighborhood, mid to late fifties, a little over six foot, and about one eighty. The door opened for a moment and closed. The guy stood there. The door opened again and now the guy was talking to the woman.

Tyler said, "Thanks," and said to Nicolet, "I know him, that's Max Cherry, he's a bail bondsman. You see him eating lunch at Helen Wilkes."

"He must've written them," Nicolet said. "But what's he doing here?"

Tyler took the glasses from him. "Yeah, that's Max. It could be Ordell put his house up as collateral and Max is checking it out. They do that."

"He's still talking to her," Nicolet said. "Now *she's* talking, look. She's opening the door. . . . She's asking him to come *in?*"

"No, he's leaving," Tyler said.

The woman stood in the doorway as Max got in his car. Now she was closing the door, but not all the way, not until the Cadillac backed into the street. It came up to Greenwood and turned south, going away from them.

"That was business," Tyler said. "Max is one of the good ones. He was with the Sheriff's office before we got there. You remember some of the older guys would mention him? Max Cherry?"

"Vaguely," Nicolet said.

"He was in Crimes Persons and worked mostly homicides. One time at Helen Wilkes—Max knew the state attorney I was having lunch with and joined us. We happened to be talking about drive-by shootings, gang stuff, jackboys. . . . I remember Max said, 'Get to know the friends of the victim, talk to them. It could be one of them did the guy and it only looks like a drive-by.' I asked him questions . . ."

Tyler stopped talking. A car shining hot in the sunlight was coming toward them on Greenwood, turned onto 31st Street: a bright red Firebird with dark-tinted windows and chrome duals sticking out of its rear end. It eased to a stop in front of Ordell's house, engine grumbling in idle. Tyler got the plate number and handed over the glasses.

"Trans Am GTA, the expensive one," Nicolet said. Tyler was on the phone now. Through the glasses

Nicolet watched a young black male, eighteen to twenty, five ten, slim build, not much more than one forty, wearing an Atlanta Braves warm-up jacket and clean white pump-up basketball shoes that looked too big for him, walk up the drive to Ordell's garage and look in the window. Nicolet said, "Tell me where this kid got twenty-five grand to buy a car like that?" thinking he knew the answer, drugs. He expected the kid to cross now to the front of the house. No, he was coming back down the drive. . . .

As Tyler replaced the phone saying, "It's not his, it's stolen. The plate was lifted off a Dodge last night in Boca." He took the glasses, wanting to get a look at the guy.

Nicolet said, "You boost a car like that, park it in your fucking neighborhood and nobody's suppose to notice."

"He doesn't give a shit who sees him," Tyler said, lowering the glasses and turning the key to start the Chevy. "He's living dangerously."

Nicolet held up his hand. "Wait. What's he doing?"

"Nothing. He's standing there."

On the sidewalk in front of the house. But looking the other way, staring. Tyler raised the glasses to see the car coming up 31st toward the house.

Nicolet said, "Tell me it's a black Mercedes."

"It sure is," Tyler said. "I believe this's our guy. Mercedes convertible . . ."

The top up, slowing down now, coming past the Firebird and turning into the drive. Now the kid in the Atlanta Braves jacket was approaching the Mercedes, taking his time, as Mr. Ordell Robbie got out and was seen by Tyler and Nicolet for the first time: black male, mid to late forties, six foot maybe, about one seventy, sunglasses, patterned tan silk shirt and tan slacks. Stylish and fairly dressed up, compared to the two law enforcement officers in their Sears sport shirts and Levi's this morning, Nicolet in his cowboy boots, Tyler wearing gray-and-blue jogging shoes. They kept quiet now watching Ordell and the kid standing by the rear deck of the Mercedes talking, couple of cool guys, except for Ordell's gaze moving up and down the street now and again. Tyler took a look through the glasses, saw four, five kids at the far end of the block, all black kids, like they might be waiting for a school bus.

"He just showed him something," Nicolet said. "You see that? Under his jacket."

"I missed it," Tyler said.

"Held the jacket open to give him a peek."

"You think a gun?"

"I'd like to believe it is," Nicolet said. "Felon with a firearm, he's my kind of guy." Ordell was talking now. The kid laughed, shuffling around, and Nicolet said, "Rapping. They love that rap shit. Now they high-five each other. Have these rituals they have to go through."

They watched Ordell walk toward the house, saying something else to the kid who nodded a few times and gave him a lazy wave. The front door opened and they caught a glimpse of the woman. Ordell was inside, the door closed again, by the time the kid reached the Firebird and got in.

"Let's take him," Nicolet said, reaching around to get his attaché case off the back seat. "But I want to see where he goes first."

Tyler had the Chevy in drive. "What for? We got him with the car."

"He's into more than boosting cars. He came here to sell a gun."

"You don't know what he showed him."

"It was a gun," Nicolet said.

They followed the Firebird west on 31st toward Windsor Avenue, Nicolet with the attaché case on his lap. He snapped it open, brought out a Sig Sauer nine-millimeter auto and returned the case to the back seat. He said, "I bet yours's in the trunk, with all that shit you haul around."

"It's in there," Tyler said, looking at the glove box.

Nicolet opened it, drew a Beretta nine from a black holster, and handed it to Tyler. "I don't see your flak jacket in there."

Tyler said, "Fuck you," wedging the pistol between his thighs.

They drove north on Windsor, over 36th Street west to Australian Avenue and north again, still in a low-income residential area, light traffic in this direction, trailing a red Firebird on a nice spring morning. No problem.

"You mentioned jackboys before," Nicolet said and then paused and seemed to start over. "Where was Beaumont Livingston found? In a stolen car, a new

Olds. The gun in the trunk with him, a five-shot .38 wiped clean. That is, clean on the outside. They found latents on the three bullets still in the cylinder and on the casings of the two that killed him. They check the registration number, the piece belongs to a guy ran a crack house who right now is facing federal prosecution and no doubt some hard time. This guy will tell you anything you want to know, so you have to be selective in what you ask. He says the gun was stolen last month along with all his cash, his dope, a few other guns. . . . Jackboys, he says, came in shooting and cleaned him out. One of them he identifies, a kid named Bug Eye he used to know in Delray. The latents on the gun that did Beaumont, they find out, belong to a convicted felon named Aurelius Miller. And what's Aurelius's street name, as if he needed one? Bug Eye.''

"The crack-house guy," Tyler said, "I don't see he gave you all that much. I mean it's not like he stuck his neck out and finked on anybody.''

"The point I was making there, he's anxious to please," Nicolet said, "and we're not through yet, are we? Okay, ten days ago Bug Eye was shot dead by a West Palm police officer. It was in the paper. . . .''

"I saw it," Tyler said. "There was some question about the guy being shot both in the chest and the back?''

Nicolet, his gaze on the red car a half block ahead of them, said, "That's the one. There was a shoot-out.''

"He got hit in the chest and spun around," Tyler said, "while the officer was still firing."

"We know that can happen," Nicolet said, the red car now getting bigger. "He's slowing down."

They had reached an industrial area of warehouses and loading docks, a few small businesses, in Riviera Beach now.

"He's pulling off," Tyler said.

Nicolet looked around, saw no cars behind them.

"Keep going."

Now he stared straight ahead as they drove past the Firebird parked off the road in an open area, a trucking company freight yard.

"What's around here?"

"Nothing," Tyler said. "I think he made us."

Nicolet was looking back now. "Place they make patio furniture, a bump and paint shop . . . That could be it."

"A rental storage place," Tyler said, "down the side street."

"What're we coming to?"

"Blue Heron."

"Turn around and go back. You see him?"

Tyler looked at the mirror. "He's still there."

"He's gonna sell the Firebird for parts," Nicolet said. "Drives in the chop shop and you never see it again. You understand why I thought of Bug Eye?"

Tyler nodded. "I'll go through the light and come back."

Nicolet turned to look over his shoulder at the Firebird, way back there now. "Here's a kid in a stolen car who looks like he could be a jackboy, right? He goes to see a gun dealer named Ordell Robbie to sell him a piece. The same Ordell Robbie who bailed out a guy who was popped by somebody using a piece that was ripped off a crack dealer by a known jackboy named Bug Eye, now deceased."

"So you want to talk to this guy," Tyler said, anxious now, making an abrupt U-turn and starting back.

"See what he has to say," Nicolet said, holding the chunky Sig Sauer auto in his lap. "Citizen cooperation can sure make our work a lot easier, can't it?"

"I'll come around behind him," Tyler said. "You think he has a gun, huh?"

Nicolet raised his pistol enough to rack the slide.

"Bet your life on it."

What Cujo showed Bread in his driveway was the big stainless .44 Mag Bread had him get for one of his customers. How it worked was once Bread found out who owned such a weapon and where the man lived, Cujo or one of the others would break in the house and get it, take the weapon and whatever he saw he liked or could sell. In the driveway Bread wanted to know was it the right gun, asking him how long was the barrel. Cujo told him looong, man, they go in the house he could show him. Unh-unh, Bread never let people in this house, having, Cujo believed, a woman in there he didn't want nobody to see. Or it was where he kept the million dollars he must have made by now on guns. Bread said the Mag his customer wanted had a seven and a half-inch full lug barrel on it, whatever the fuck that meant. Was this the one? Cujo asked was he suppose to bring a ruler with him breaking in a house to measure the weapon with? Bread said, "No, man, you don't need a ruler." He said, "You know how long your bone is, don't you? You take it out, lay the piece alongside your bone, and figure the difference." He'd crack you up saying things like that with his serious look he put on. Man could be on TV, fun-ny, but had his rules. Wouldn't put the gun in his trunk, right there, or take it in the house. Said it had to go out to where the guns were kept. No bullshit about that. Then lightened up saying be ready in a few days for the Turkey Shoot. Meaning when they'd go jump the Nazi had all the guns at his place. There was a name he gave for everything they did. Rum Punch was the deal he had going in the Bahamas, Open House was what he called the places he lined up for them to break in. When they jumped the Nazi it would be like a combination Open House, Bread said, and a Turkey Shoot. Jump him early in the morning. . . .

When he stopped here to make sure nobody was on him, Cujo had taken the big hunk of .44 Mag out of his pants and laid it on the floor under him. He'd watched this one car come up behind him when there was no other traffic, the car easing along. It became a white Chev Caprice going past. Two white guys in the white car. Cujo waited some more to make sure, watching cars in the mirror come up on him and through the smoked windshield as they went past, on up to Blue Heron. When he saw the white Chev coming back from there, going past the other way and then U-turning to come back toward him, it became an unmarked police car and not a couple of guys looking for a street they might have missed. See, coming off the road now to ease up behind him. He watched both front doors open in his mirror and thought of taking off soon as they were out of the car.

Except that high-speed shit could kill you. He'd tried it one time and got pulled from the wreck, a big cut in his head.

Be better to look the motherfuckers in the eye. Call the play.

"He's getting out," Tyler said.

Nicolet thought the kid was going to come back to their car with some kind of bullshit story. The kid knew who they were. But what he did was stand by the Firebird showing how cool he was, right arm on the open door, his left arm on the roof of the car. Waiting for them. About thirty feet away.

"Keep your door in front of you," Nicolet said, "till I cover him."

"You sure he has a gun?"

"I'm positive."

"What if he doesn't?"

"Then don't fucking shoot him."

He watched Tyler slide out of the car to stand behind the door and lay his Beretta on the sill of the open window. Nicolet got out and started toward the right side of the Firebird, moving a few steps away from the cars to get a cross-fire angle, his pistol held against his leg.

The kid looked over the low roof at them.

Tyler said, "Keep your hands up where I can see 'em."

The kid, posed against the door, turned his palms up. Too cool. Maybe high.

Tyler said, "Step away from the car."

The kid said, "You police? What'd I do?"

"I said step away from the car."

Nicolet saw the kid glance this way and then back to Tyler, saying, "You want to look at my driver's license? Lemme get it for you," and ducked his head into the Firebird.

Nicolet was moving. Heard Tyler yelling again to get away from the car. Saw the kid's head and shoulders come up and saw bright metal flash in the sunlight, the kid firing what looked like a Magnum at Tyler, firing again, coming around now to put the gun on the car roof, and Nicolet brought up the Sig and squeezed off three at him fast. Saw the kid duck down maybe hit, maybe not. Nicolet moved. Got to the off side of the Firebird crouched, looking straight at that fucking smoked glass you couldn't see through, and blew it out firing three quick ones and three more, catching a glimpse of the kid through the shattered window and heard him scream. Nicolet went over the hood, rolled over it, and hit the door as the kid was getting to his knees and he screamed again, wedged against the front seat, his shiny .44 Mag on the ground. Nicolet kicked it under the car and put the barrel of the Sig Sauer against the kid's head, the kid's eyes dazed looking up at him, the kid saying, "Man, I'm shot."

Nicolet turned his head to look toward the Chevy. He saw two bullet holes in the door and Tyler lying on the ground on his side, holding himself.

12

Max had that effortless feeling of a natural high. He couldn't wait to see her. But the moment Jackie opened the door, looked at him and said, "Oh," he felt his high begin to nose over.

All right, she was surprised, no question about it. He said, "You're expecting someone."

She said, "No . . ." not sounding too sure. She said, "Well, yes and no, but come on in."

At this point there was still hope. She looked great. "It's okay?"

"Yeah, really."

But then closing the door she said, "You want your gun, don't you?" and the good feeling sunk all the way to hit bottom as she went to the bedroom in her loose T-shirt and tight jeans saying, "Let me get it."

Like going to get change for the paper boy.

No apology or acting sheepish about it, wanting to

explain. No—you want your gun? And goes to get it. He had come here prepared to treat it lightly. "You get a chance to use that gun you stole on anybody?" Like that, with a straight face. Well, no fun and games now. It pissed him off, this act she put on, so fucking casual about it. Ask her how she'd like to go back to the Stockade, since Ordell hadn't paid the bond premium. See how casual she was then.

Jackie came out of the bedroom with his gun in her hand and kind of a sad smile, saying, "Max, I'm sorry," and he felt his mood begin to swing up again, hope stirring in him. "I was afraid if I asked to borrow it you'd say no, and you'd have every right to. Would you like some coffee?"

Just like that, back in the game.

He said, "I wouldn't mind," following Jackie to the kitchen. "You get to use it?"

She gave him the smile again. "I felt a lot safer having it. I hope you don't take milk. It turned sour while I was in jail."

"No, black's fine."

He watched her lay the Airweight on the kitchen table, bare except for an ashtray, and go to the range. She looked even slimmer in the jeans than she did last night. Not slim exactly, just right.

"You want to hang on to it for a while? It wouldn't be legal but, you know, if it makes you feel better to have it . . ."

She said, "Thanks," pouring their coffee, "but I have my own now." She came over to the table with two ceramic cups, plain white. "Do you take sugar?"

Max said, "No, thanks. You went out this morning and bought a gun?" It was possible if she drove up to Martin County; here, there was a three-day wait to buy a handgun, a cooling-off period.

"Let's just say I have one," Jackie said, "okay? I don't want you to be concerned about it."

"Somebody loaned it to you."

"Right," Jackie said, leaving the kitchen.

Max pulled a chair out from the table and sat down, wondering what kind of gun it was and if she knew how to use it. He thought of asking as Jackie came back in with cigarettes and the tan lighter and sat down across from him.

She said, "I couldn't wait last night to get in the shower and wash my hair."

And he forgot about the gun.

"It looks nice."

"I called in sick. As far as the airline knows, I'm still available."

"Are you?"

"I don't know yet. I'm going to see Tyler, and I suppose Nicolet, later on today and ask them." She paused to light a cigarette. "Do what you suggested. Offer to help and see what happens."

"What I meant," Max said, "was have a lawyer do the negotiating for you. If you can't afford one there's a good friend of mine, semiretired, I think would do it as a favor. He doesn't need the fee as much as you need a lawyer."

She was staring at him over her coffee mug and it reminded him of last night.

She said, "Maybe not. Let me talk to them first, about Ordell's money."

"That'll interest them, but only up to a point."

"All of it in Freeport. I mean a lot. Like a half million in safe-deposit boxes and more coming in."

"How'd you find that out?"

"He told me last night."

"Ordell called you?"

"He was here when I got home."

Max said, "Jesus Christ," and lowered his coffee mug to the table. "He broke in?"

"He picked the lock."

"You call the police?"

"We talked," Jackie said. "He had some doubts at first. But he's always trusted me and wants more than anything to believe he still can. You know why? Because he needs me. Because without me all that money is going to sit in Freeport. There may be other ways to get it out, but I'm the only one he's ever used, and all the other people he deals with are crooks. Put yourself in his place."

Max stared at her. "How do you get it out?"

"The same way I've been doing it. But first they have to let me go back to work."

"You're offering to set him up."

"If they let me off. Otherwise no deal."

"You understand the risk involved?"

"I'm not going to prison or do that probation thing again."

He watched her studying her cigarette, carefully

turning the tip of it in the ashtray. "Well, you said you might have more options than you thought."

Jackie was concentrating on the cigarette, bringing the ash to a point. She said, "You know how many miles I've flown?" and looked up at him.

Max shook his head. "How many?"

"About seven million, jetway to jetway. I've been waiting on people for almost twenty years. You know what I make now, starting over? Sixteen thousand, with retirement benefits you can stick in your ear. How do you feel about getting old?"

"You're not old—you look great."

"I'm asking how *you* feel. Does it bother you?"

"It's not something I think about. I look in the mirror, I'm the same person I was thirty years ago. I see a photograph of myself—that's different. But who's taking my picture?"

She said, "It's different with guys. Women get older at an earlier age."

He said, "I guess they worry about it more. Some women, all they have is their looks. They lose that . . . But you've got way more than looks."

"I have? What?"

"You want to argue about getting old? What's the point?"

"I feel like I'm always starting over," Jackie said, "and before I know it I won't have any options left. I'll be stuck with whatever I can get." She said, "I told you last night I've been married twice? Actually I've had three husbands, but two of them I think of as the same guy, at age twenty, and then a much older version. Their names were even the same. So I say I've been married twice. I was nineteen with the first one, going to school in Miami, U of M. He raced dirt bikes, did the hill climb?"

"That's pretty young to get married."

"I wouldn't live with him otherwise. That's how smart I was then."

"Times change," Max said, "but that's generally the custom."

"We were married five months . . . he was killed racing a drawbridge going up, trying to jump his bike across the opening. Like in the movies. Only he was drunk and didn't make it."

Max kept his mouth shut.

"My second husband was hooked on drugs, started dealing to pay for his habit and went to prison. Before he got the airline job he was a fighter pilot in Vietnam. Are you getting the picture? The last one was fifteen years older than I am, about your age. I thought, Ah, here's one with some maturity. Not knowing he was the dirt biker come back to life."

Max said, "I'm only twelve years older than you are."

She seemed to smile—for whatever reason, he wasn't sure—and then was serious again.

"It bothered him being older, or getting old. So he'd run I don't know how many miles every day. He'd swim out into the ocean alone, until you couldn't see him. He drove too fast, got drunk every night. . . . He was funny, he was very bright, but, boy, did he drink. One evening we were sitting out on the balcony, he hopped up on the cement railing and started walking it, his arms out, one foot in front of the other. . . . We were on the sixth floor. I said, 'You don't have to prove anything to me.' I remember I said, 'I'm not watching, so you might as well get down.' I turned my head, I couldn't watch.'' Jackie stopped for a moment. "When I looked up again he was gone. I don't know if he fell or stepped off. He didn't make a sound.''

It was quiet in the kitchen.

She said, "That's my history. I've logged seven million miles married to two drunks and a junkie.''

Max cleared his throat. "You know, you didn't refer to any of them by name.''

"Mike, Davey, and Michael," Jackie said. "What difference does it make?" But then she said, "They were nice guys, really, most of the time, and yet I wasn't surprised. . . . You know what I mean? My big mistake, I let myself get into situations I *know* can be trouble, my eyes wide open, and then have to figure a way out." She paused, stubbing her cigarette in the ashtray. "But you know what I'm more tired of than anything?"

"Tell me," Max said.

"Smiling. Acting pleasant."

"Now you're talking about your job."

" 'Have a wonderful time in the Bahamas and thank you for flying Islands Air.' Or thank you for flying Delta, or TWA. 'Sir, would you like another cup of TWA coffee?' "

Max grinned at her, seeing it coming. An old one.

" 'Or would you prefer TWAT?' "

"You like it though, don't you? Flying?"

"Not anymore."

"You get a lot of guys hitting on you?"

"Enough."

"How about when you were a young girl," Max said, "were the boys rough with you?"

She looked at him over the coffee mug with that gleam of fun in her eyes.

"How did you know?"

13

Ray Nicolet called at four in the afternoon. By this time she had already tried to get hold of Tyler. The FDLE office told her he was on the street, and when she dialed his beeper number and waited there was no response.

"I'd like you to drop whatever you're doing and come to Good Samaritan," Nicolet said, his voice quiet and, she felt, grim. Maybe putting it on. "If you want I'll send a car for you. What do you say?"

"Why do you want me to come?"

"See what one of Ordell's guys did to Faron. Then I want you to look at the guy and tell me if you know him."

"Where are you?"

He told her the third floor, east wing.

And was standing by the nurse's station when she walked up to him less than forty minutes later, wearing a man's white shirt with her jeans now, tan bag hanging from her shoulder.

"Thanks for coming," Nicolet said.

It surprised her.

He stared for a moment not saying a word, then walked off, and she trailed after him along the hallway to where two deputies in dark green stood by the open door to a room. The deputies stepped aside, looking her over as Nicolet gave them a nod and Jackie followed him in, past the first bed, empty, to a young black guy lying in the second bed, his eyes closed. There were tubes in his arms, one coming out of his nose, another from under the sheet to a catheter bag hooked to the side of the bed.

"What happened to him?"

"I shot him," Nicolet said, "after he shot Faron."

Jackie turned from the young guy in the bed to the ATF agent. "How is he?"

"Which one?"

"Tyler. Is he all right?"

"I want you to look at this guy first. You know him?"

Jackie stepped closer. "No."

"Have you ever seen him before?"

"I don't think so."

"Maybe one time with Ordell?"

She shook her head. "No."

"I wonder," Nicolet said, "if this is another one of those times you don't know him but he knows you. Like with Beaumont."

"Is he Jamaican?"

"No, this one's a homey," Nicolet said. "His street name, according to one of the deputies outside, is Cujo. And Cujo, I find out, is fairly well known in criminal court. His driver's license says he's Hulon Miller, Jr., but I doubt if there's anyone outside of his mother calls him Hulon." Nicolet put his hand on Cujo's shoulder and gave it a shake. "Isn't that right? Open your eyes, I want you to look at somebody here's come to visit you."

Jackie watched the young guy scowl as Nicolet shook him again and his eyes opened.

"The fuck you doing to me?"

"You in pain, Cujo? I hope to Christ you are," Nicolet said. "I want you to look at this lady here, tell me who she is."

She watched Cujo squint at her saying, "Man, how would I know? You the one brought her."

Nicolet took a handful of Cujo's hair and yanked his head back, Cujo saying, "Hey, shit, lemme go," looking into Nicolet's face.

Jackie watched them. Nicolet seemed calm. He said, "Somebody could come in here and rip your tubes out. Have you thought of that? People die in hospitals, man." He gave Cujo a pat on the head and turned to her with his deadpan cop expression. Time to leave. In the hallway, walking back toward the nurse's station, he took hold of her arm above the elbow.

"I shot him in the groin area and it messed up his plumbing, but not too bad. He might need more surgery, they don't know yet, or he could be out in a couple of days. I have mixed feelings about it. I was hoping he'd die." Jackie glanced at him and he said, "But I want him alive too, so we can use him."

"He works for Ordell?"

"We're pretty sure. I know he sells him guns."

"What if he won't tell you anything?"

"He will. He's twenty years old and has been arrested seventeen times. We can do business with a fella like that. His quality of life is based on how much time he can get out of doing."

"What about Tyler," Jackie said, "am I going to see him?"

"Right now. His wife's with him," Nicolet said. "We'll take a peek in there, see how he's doing. . . . Faron was hit twice. One in the thigh fractured the bone, the femur? The other one took a chip out of his ilium." Nicolet's hand slid down to touch her hip. "That bone right there. He's gonna be all right. The slugs went through the door of his car and were slowed down some. One hit his beeper and got deflected."

"I tried to call him," Jackie said.

"That's right, you want to talk to us."

"I need my job."

"We all need something," Nicolet said. "Let's wait'll we see Faron."

He was in a private room. Nicolet approached the bed saying, "Hey, partner, you sleeping?" Jackie watched his eyes open. Head on the pillow, hair mussed, he seemed younger, barely out of his teens.

"Where's Cheryl?"

"I think she went to get some coffee."

"They gave you some good dope, huh?"

Tyler closed and opened his eyes, trying to smile.

"Look who I brought to see you."

Jackie moved closer to the bed. "How're you doing?"

Now he was looking at her and managed to smile. "I'm okay."

It gave her a strange feeling, that she was with friends. Nicolet got her seated and brought over another chair, both with plastic cushions and wooden arms. She kept watching Tyler, his face turned to them with a sleepy look, his right leg raised a few inches beneath the sheet, bare toes sticking out at the foot of the bed. An IV tube ran from his arm to a clear plastic bottle hanging from a stand.

Nicolet leaned on the arm of his chair, close to her.

"Where were we?"

"I need my job."

And a cigarette. She'd love one right now.

"Well, you know what I want."

"If I can work I can help you."

"Or you could fly away."

"It wouldn't be worth it. What am I looking at, a few months?"

"A lot more'n that if I take you federal, which I can do."

Maybe it was okay to smoke in a private room.

"How does your working help me?"

"You want Ordell Robbie, don't you?"

"Oh, now you know him."

"You never asked if I did or not."

"We thought you'd want to surprise us."

"I deliver money for him."

"No kidding. Where's he get it?"

"He sells guns."

"He told you that or you've seen him do it?"

"What I have to have," Jackie said, "if I'm going to help, is permission to leave the country, and immunity."

"You don't want much."

"Yes or no."

"It's possible."

"I show you how to get him and the dope charge is nolle prossed."

"You've been talking to a lawyer."

She got her cigarettes and lighter out of her bag.

"Yes or no."

"You haven't told me what *I* get."

She lit a cigarette.

"Him. You get Ordell."

"You nervous?"

"Of course I am."

"I get him with guns?"

"With money from the sale of guns."

She didn't know what to use for an ashtray.

Nicolet said, "Put it on the floor," and said, "Where's my case? I'm not Customs, I don't give a shit about the money. I need him with guns. In possession of illegal weapons, stolen or unregistered firearms or selling without a license." He looked over at the bed. "Isn't that right, partner? We want us a gift-wrapped gun case."

Tyler said, "Right," in a voice they could barely hear.

"He's sailing on the dope they gave him," Nicolet said, looking at Jackie again. "I don't give a shit about the forty-two grams either. I can get you nolle prossed on that, but only if you get me Ordell Robbie with guns. You understand?"

"All I can do is tell you what I know," Jackie said.

"Like what?"

She hesitated and drew on her cigarette.

"He already has more than a half million dollars sitting in Freeport."

"He does pretty good."

"And more coming in, as soon as he makes another delivery."

"He told you that?"

"He trusts me."

"That's good. It can keep you from getting shot."

"He wants me to help him get the money here."

"Doesn't he know you can't leave the country?"

"I told him I could get permission."

Nicolet said, "Jesus Christ," with a grin. "So if we let you, we'll be helping too, won't we?"

"You follow the money."

"I understand that. We'd mark it before you ever left the airport. Tag along and watch you hand it to him. But where's my gun case?"

"If he's planning a delivery, you know he has guns."

"Where?"

"Right here."

"If I let them go—otherwise he doesn't get paid—we have some more money, but my evidence is gone."

Jackie said, "Excuse me a minute," holding up what was left of her cigarette. "I have to get rid of this." She crossed the room to the lavatory and dropped the cigarette in the toilet. It gave her less than a minute. She was back in the chair before asking, "What if you let him ship out most of the guns, but kept enough to have a case. Would that work?"

"He doesn't make the delivery himself?"

"He hasn't been to Freeport in months."

Nicolet said, "Well, some more money would come in—"

Jackie cut him off. "It's not your main interest, I know. But why let the Bahamian government have it? As soon as he's arrested, won't they confiscate his funds?"

"If they know where they are."

"Your getting the money would be like a bonus," Jackie said. She gave him a weak smile. "I'll admit I'm trying to make it sound as attractive as I can. . . ."

Nicolet smiled back at her. "You aren't doing bad either."

"I just don't want you to think, you know, all that money and no one to claim it, I'm trying to buy you off. . . ."

"Not for a minute," Nicolet said.

"To get you to drop the charge against me."

"I want to," Nicolet said, "honest. But where're the guns? I hate to keep coming back to that."

She thought of having another cigarette, picked up her bag from the floor, then decided to wait.

"Don't you guys ever work undercover?"

"All the time."

"What if you approached him as a buyer, looking for some kind of gun you can't buy in a shop?"

Nicolet glanced at Tyler. "Hey, partner, you hear that?" He said to Jackie, "We've been playing with the same idea, only work the sting the other way. Offer him military hardware, something exotic."

She said, "How do you do that? Just walk up to him?"

"You have to be introduced. And till now we haven't been able to get next to anybody who knows him."

She said, "You don't mean me, do you?"

Nicolet shook his head.

But smiling, she noticed, just a little. Secretive about it. Something in mind that he wasn't going to tell her.

"It's your business," Jackie said. "What do I know."

14

Saturday morning, lying in the sun in her cutoffs and a stringy bra top, Melanie was thinking that for the past seventeen years she had been lying in the sun just about full time, making a living at it as the tan blond California girl. She was thinking that not many of the guys she stayed with spent time lying in the sun. Frank, the one from Detroit she was with when she met Ordell in the Bahamas, almost fourteen years ago, did. He was an asshole but loved the sun. Film-production guys never did. Or Japanese industrialists or Mideast types on Greek islands. She read about movie stars and beautiful people while lying in the sun, about all these young girls no one had ever heard of suddenly making it. But never read anything about what happened to girls who made a living lying in the sun once the sun had fucking ruined their skin and they were down to living with a colored guy who saw no point in ever lying in the sun. This is where Melanie was at thirty-four, in a lounge chair stained with tanning lotion, out on the balcony. She didn't hear them come in.

She didn't know they were in the living room until Ordell said, "Girl? Look who's here."

She turned her head to see Ordell and a guy in a light-blue sport coat and yellow shirt holding a fat shopping bag from Burdine's. Kind of a rough-looking guy, his jacket new, right off the rack. She didn't recognize him until Ordell said, "It's Louis, baby." That got her off the lounge and into the living room, Melanie pinching the sides of the bra top between her fingers to keep it from slipping off her nips. Ordell saying, "She still a fine big girl?"

"Holy shit, it's true," Melanie said, "you're really here. Louis, the last time I saw you . . ."

"He knows," Ordell said. "Louis don't want to talk about that time."

Melanie said, "I can understand why." She released the bra top, let it slip if it wanted to, going up to Louis to give him a kiss on the mouth and didn't back away after.

"At the time, I thought you two guys were the biggest fuckups I'd ever met."

"I just told you," Ordell said, "he don't want to *talk* about it."

She kept looking at Louis. "You were having fun though, weren't you? With your box of masks? You would've kidnapped *me*, if you thought anyone'd pay the ransom."

He smiled, finally.

"Yeah, it was an idea."

"He told me you were here, I couldn't wait to see you."

Ordell said, "What Louis wants to see is my gun movie."

Melanie made them a vodka tonic and sat down to watch Louis while Ordell showed his movie on TV, a video he'd bought at a gun show, Ordell talking on top of the voice in the movie.

"He gives you mostly a lot of technical shit. Yeah, the Beretta—I think he said PM-12S. It don't matter, I don't see too many of those. Listen to it though. Tat-tat-tat-tat. Huh?

"Here the dude is shooting a M-16. You understand you buy these weapons semiautomatic, anybody can. Then I have them converted to full auto and you have a submachine gun. Nothing to it, but costs me a C-note a gun, 'cause it's the man's ass he gets caught. Like the man use to make my suppressors? . . .

"Here, you see one on the MAC-10. Same thing as a silencer. Bup-bup-bup-bup, spittin' 'em out. The man was caught with eighty-seven of 'em in his van, the suppressors. He's looking at thirty years, no bail. I got another guy in Lantana makes 'em for me now. Next trip I deliver an even hundred for thirty grand, my man, three bills apiece." He said, "Baby, I could use some more ice."

Melanie picked up his glass and went into the kitchen.

"MAC-10's the one you see in all the movies. Here, this's the famous Uzi, beautiful weapon. I can get fifteen hundred apiece for the real thing. Jews over in Israel make them.

"Styer AUG, one of the best. Listen to it. Man, that's doing the job. Very expensive, comes from Austria. My customers don't know shit about it so there's no demand."

Melanie came back with his drink as Ordell was going "Bop-bop-bop" and swung into "Ou-bop-ba-da, ba-diddly-a," from guns to the Diz. He did it every time he showed the movie, working his ass off being cool. Louis hadn't said a word since it started. She liked his type, his rough-cut bony features, big hands. . . . Big hands, big schlong.

"AK-47 the best there is. This's the Chinese one. I pay eight fifty and double my money. Comes with three banana clips and a bayonet, man, for stickin'."

The phone rang and Ordell said, "Get that for me, will you, baby?"

Melanie said, "You know it's for you."

Ordell stared at her because she always got up and did what she was told. She might take her time or kid around sounding grouchy, but never gave it to him straight. This was a first.

He said, "What? I didn't catch that."

Louis kept staring at the screen.

Melanie got up, went to the counter that separated the living room from the kitchen, and picked up the phone. She said hello, put the phone down, and said, "It's for you." Ordell stared at her a moment before stopping the video and getting up. Melanie sat down on the sofa with Louis.

"It's boring, isn't it?"

"I can sit through it once," Louis said.

"He thinks he knows what he's talking about."

Louis said, "Where's he keep all these guns?"

"He has a place . . ." She stopped.

Ordell came back saying, "Man in New York wants a Bren-10. Gun's a piece of shit, but it's the one Sonny Crockett used and that makes it worth twelve fifty. Big piece of iron, ten millimeter."

Louis said, "You have one?"

"Not yet. I make one phone call and have it the next day, give the boy two hundred." Ordell pushed a button on his remote box. "Man's firing a TEC-9 here, cheap spray gun made in South Miami. Cost three eighty retail. I get them for two hundred and sell them for eight. Louis, you adding up these numbers? . . . This TEC-9? They advertise it as being 'as tough as your toughest customer.' Say it's the 'most popular gun in American crime.' No lie, they actually say that."

The phone rang again.

"I know they love it down in Medellín."

Melanie looked at Ordell as he stopped the tape and they stared at each other a few moments before she got up and went over to the phone. She said hello, put the phone down, and said, "It's for you."

Ordell was telling Louis how he'd bought all kinds of military shit a man had picked up after the war in Panama and brought over to the Keys in his boat.

Ordell saying it was where he got the M-60 machine guns he's told Louis about. Saying it was like a garage sale with hand grenades and rockets and shit.

"It's a woman," Melanie said.

That shut him up. Ordell went over to the phone.

She said to Louis, "Can I get you anything?"

He raised his empty glass.

She said, "It's not too early?"

"I'm not working," Louis said.

"So you went shopping." She felt the lapel of his jacket between her fingers. Part rayon and something else. "Who picked this out, Ordell?"

"We don't have the same taste," Louis said.

"In clothes."

"Yeah, in clothes."

She went into the kitchen with his glass. Ordell, a few feet away, was saying into the phone, "They might be watching your place. Lemme think a minute. . . . Yeah, go to the public beach. . . . The one over the Blue Heron bridge. Walk up toward Howard Johnson and I'll see you around there. . . . Right now if you want. Get in your car." He hung up and looked across the counter at Melanie.

"I have to go out for a while. Will you be nice to my friend? Try not to assault him? Tear his clothes off? They brand new."

"I wouldn't mind sitting out on the balcony," Louis said. "I could use some sun."

Melanie said, "You aren't kidding."

"You're nice and brown."

She said, "You want to see my tan lines?" and sat up straight on the sofa with her back arched, hooked the bra top with her thumbs, and pushed it down from her breasts.

"You're tan, all right," Louis said. "You don't ever let them out in the sun, huh?"

"I used to. I think they look better natural, though, don't you?"

"Yeah, I think you're right." They were big ones. He kept staring at them, seeing little blue veins like rivers on a map. When he raised his glass to take a sip he found there was only ice left.

Melanie said, "Let me fix you up."

Looking him right in the face rather than at the glass. When she did take it from his hand and went to the kitchen, Louis got up and walked out on the balcony.

The building was kind of tacky, faded light-green paint peeling from the concrete, but had all the view you needed of the Atlantic Ocean, right there out the back door, and a white sandy beach that went clear up to Jacksonville. Tiny people down there. Not too many till he looked toward the public beach, to the left, and saw rows of blue wind shelters, or whatever they were called, more people out of them than in. It was a perfect kind of day, enough wind to raise the surf and blow in a cloud every once in a while to relieve the sun heat. Melanie, next to him now at the concrete rail, said, "Keep watching over that way. You'll see Ordell walking out to the beach."

"He's meeting a woman?"

"That's what he said."

"You don't mind?"

"You're kidding."

"I mean if you're living with him."

"He doesn't live here, he stops in. You know Ordell, he does whatever he wants."

It seemed Melanie did too, still exposing herself handing him the fresh drink.

"You don't want to burn those babies."

"I'll keep my back to the sun," Melanie said. "Why don't you stretch out on the lounge, take your shirt off. Your pants too, if you want."

She held the drink while he got out of the shirt, folded it, laid it on a low metal table, and sat down in the lounge. Melanie saying, "Boy, you really need sun. Where've you been?"

"In jail. Two months shy of four years."

It seemed to brighten her eyes, talking to a convict.

"Really? He didn't tell me that. What did you do?"

"I robbed a bank."

That got her moving, throwing her head to the side to get her blond hair out of her face. She had an awful lot of hair. She said, "I've thought about you a lot, wondering what you've been doing. . . ."

"We only met that one time. Thirteen years ago?"

"Almost fourteen. I know, and when I saw you come in I couldn't believe it. I recognized you right away." She glanced over her shoulder toward the public beach.

He said to her, "What've you been up to?"

Now she was looking at him again, the sun hitting him from directly above her head. He had to squint.

"I lie in the sun."

"That's all?"

"I read."

"You get bored?"

"A lot. You want to fuck?"

Louis said, "Sure," and put his drink on the floor. She was the kind who liked to be on top. She would moan and say Oh God throwing her head back and rubbing her hands in the hair on his chest like it was a washboard, back and forth, or a surface she was scrubbing clean. She had long red nails that scratched him but felt good too. He wanted to get on top and do it right, but the sun got brighter against his closed eyes, red-hot, and it was over before he could get around to it. She hopped off and got into her cutoffs, not wearing any underwear. Louis pulled his pants up, got his drink off the floor, and estimated maybe five minutes had passed.

Melanie said, "Whew, I feel a lot better. How about you?"

Louis nodded. "Yeah, that hit the spot."

"We can relax now," she said, "and get caught up."

Ordell said to Jackie, "I can't hear what you're saying. Come up here and talk to me."

She was facing away from him, standing on wet sand, and letting the surf wash up over her bare feet, the wind blowing her hair. Irritating, this woman could bug you; but still fine to look at this morning in her T-shirt, her long brown legs coming out of those white shorts.

She said over her shoulder at him, "Take your shoes off."

"What do I do with them?" Four-hundred-dollar oxblood-colored alligator loafers with tassels. "I put my shoes down, somebody gonna walk off with them." He had sand inside his shoes and should've known better than to say meet him here. Every time he walked out on the beach he got sand in his shoes. Ordell would never go barefoot, though, like Melanie and Sheronda. He didn't have a reason other than something in his head telling him to keep his shoes on except when he went to bed. He didn't swim, never went in the water. . . . He said, "Girl, you want to be drug over by the hair?"

Look at her. Wasn't mad, wasn't nervous being here. Coming over to him now, hair blowing in her face. Bathers walked by looking at the ground for seashells.

"You think anybody followed you?"

"I don't know," Jackie said, "I don't do this too often."

Smelling of some kind of powder. Clean and healthy.

"You act like it, you cool."

"I don't think it matters if they followed me or not. They know what we're doing."

Ordell said, "How's that again?"

"I told them we'd be meeting."

"Wait a minute. You told them it's *me?*"

"They already know that. They know more about you than I do. The ATF guy kept talking about guns. I said I can't help you there. . . ."

"But you'd see what you could find out?"

She moved right up on him saying, "Look, the only way I can get permission to fly is if I agree to help them. I have to give them something. Or appear to. But it has to be something they can check, otherwise I could be blowing smoke. So the first thing I give them is what they already know. Do you understand that?"

"What was the next thing?"

"I told them you have money in Freeport and you want me to bring it here. A half million put away and more coming in."

"You told them all that?"

"It's true, isn't it?"

"What's that got to do with it?"

"Is it true or not?"

"I said around that amount."

"They know I was delivering for you," Jackie said. "I mentioned the half million—they're not that interested in the money, they want you with guns. I said, well, if you want proof he's getting paid for selling them, let me bring the money in. I'll make two deliveries, the first one with ten thousand, like a dry run. I said, you watch, see how it works. Then you set up for the next delivery, when I bring in the half million plus."

"How it works," Ordell said. "I come by your place and pick it up."

"I told them you're very careful. You send someone to meet me, and I never know who it is."

Ordell said, "That's an idea. You know it?"

"If you'll listen," Jackie said, "you'll see it's the whole idea. The first time I do it they're lurking about, they see me hand the ten thousand to someone."

"Who?"

"I don't know, one of your friends."

"A woman?"

"If you want."

"Yeah, I think a woman."

"The next trip, when I come with all the money, it'll look like I hand it to the same one I did before. . . ."

"But you don't."

"No, I give it to someone else, first."

"And they follow the wrong one," Ordell said, "thinking she's bringing it to me, huh?"

"That's the idea."

"So we need two people, two women."

Jackie nodded, looking as though she was thinking about it, or remembering what else she'd told them. The woman was cool.

"Where does this happen?"

"I don't know yet."

"You have two different flight bags and make a switch."

"I guess so."

"You *guess?*"

"I haven't worked it out yet."

"The woman they think has the money but don't, they gonna come down on."

"If she doesn't have it, what's the problem?"

"Has to be a woman won't open her mouth." Ordell paused to look at this idea. "They still know I'm the one it's coming to."

"Once you have the money," Jackie said, "that's your problem. You're on your own."

"You must see a piece of this for yourself."

"Ten percent. Plus, what we've already agreed to. A hundred thousand if I go to jail."

"But you helping them. They gonna let you off."

She turned to face the ocean, saying to him, "Maybe." Her eyes closed now, the breeze blowing her hair. Fine looking.

Ordell said, "If they say they gonna let the first run go through, why don't we bring the whole load in that time?"

She said, her eyes still closed, "I don't trust them all that much. Let's see how it goes." She pulled her T-shirt off over her head and shook her hair free.

Ordell saw what looked like a swimsuit bra covering her ninnies. Not much showing, but they looked to be fine ones. He said, "I have to do some thinking on this."

She said, "You should," and walked out to the hard-packed wet sand. Stood there and then looked around at him. "You know someone named Cujo?"

What was this now? Man, coming out of nowhere.

"What about him?"

"He's at Good Sam."

"What you talking about?"

She said, "He was shot yesterday," and started walking out in the ocean.

"Wait a minute!"

Ordell yelled it at her, but she kept going. He ran down to the hard-packed sand. "Who told you that?" She didn't hear him, so he moved toward her yelling, "Come back here!" and the surf came in over his alligators before he realized it. Shit. He watched her dive into a wave. Watched her come up and dive into another one, her butt in the white shorts mooning him.

Melanie had the vodka on the coffee table now, close by with a bowl of ice, while Louis finished up a cigar-size joint she'd rolled Jamaica-style, Louis sucking away in a cloud of white smoke. This guy appreciated everything you gave him. Five vodkas so far, with the dope, but very attentive. Head against the sofa cushion, staring at her through deep, dark enlarged pupils as she spoke about their pal Ordell:

How he'd looked at the cocaine business at one time and found it too competitive, all the corners taken; try to move on one you'd get shot. Guns, though, you didn't need a franchise, you could sell guns wherever there was a demand. She told how Ordell saw himself as an international arms dealer when, come on, the only people he sold to were dopers, Jamaican crazies, and now the cartel guys from Medellín.

"Making out though. He's doing all right," Louis said, raising his glass in slow motion.

"Well, so far he is," Melanie said, with some doubt in her tone. She had washed up and put a shirt on, the romance part over for the time being. She said, "You have to admit he's not too bright."

Louis said he wouldn't go so far as to say that.

Melanie said, "Louis," in her quietest serious tone, "he puts his fingers on the words when he reads. He moves his lips. Let's say he's streetwise. But that doesn't stop him from being a fuckup."

Louis said, "If you're talking about the kidnapping, I was in it too, you know."

"You weren't in Freeport," Melanie said, "were you, when my provider at the time was told to pay up or he'd never see his wife again? And he'd already filed for divorce, and if he *didn't* ever see her again it would save him a fortune?" Melanie smiled at Louis. "No, you weren't. They made a movie that was something like it. I've forgotten the title. Danny DeVito's the husband, Bette Midler gets kidnapped?"

Louis seemed to think about it and shook his head.

"We happened to see it on TV, not more than a month ago. Ordell's watching, he goes, 'What is this shit? You believe it?' I said, 'Hey, if it doesn't even work as a movie . . .' Now he's talking about it again—I mean the real kidnapping. You know why? Because of this Nazi freak he met."

"Big Guy," Louis said. "I saw him."

"At the white-power rally. That's why he brought you there," Melanie said, "to see him."

Louis nodded. " 'Cause he looks like Richard."

She kept staring at Louis until he said, "What?"

"I understand you and Richard didn't get along," Melanie said. "You wanted to kill him." She watched Louis shrug, it seemed with an effort. "Richard raped the woman you were holding. . . ."

"He tried to."

"You liked her, didn't you?"

"She was nice."

"You got her out before the cops landed on Richard. Took her to your apartment?" She waited but he didn't confirm or deny. "Ordell thought you had something going there."

Louis shook his head.

"It would've been pretty weird if you did." Melanie watched Louis sip his drink and lower the glass to rest on his thigh. "Well, Ordell has something going. He must've told you."

Louis said, "About fate bringing us all together?"

Melanie slid her shoulder along the sofa toward him. "Fate, my ass. He's bringing you in for one reason. When he goes after the Nazi freak and all his guns, somebody's gonna have to kill him. He wants you to do it."

Louis had his head turned, resting against the cushion, close enough to touch. He stared at her forever before he said, "Why?"

"Who does Big Guy look like? Richard. Someone you wanted to kill."

"I don't know."

"Ordell believes it, he told me. He goes, 'Louis, he get out there and see Big Guy, he gonna see Richard and want to shoot him when I say to.'" Louis smiled and she said, "Do I sound like him?"

"Yeah, that was good."

"If you go, don't turn your back on him," Melanie said, moving closer to him, staring into those giant pupils, "or he'll try to leave you there. I mean dead, Louis, the gun in your hand and he's off the hook."

"He told you that?"

"It's the way he thinks now, he's changed. The other night he killed a man who worked for him."

"Why?"

"Ask him."

"I ought to get out of here. Is that what you're saying?"

Melanie made a face, for a moment in pain. She said, "Oh, no . . . Baby, I want you to stick around. Use him before he uses you, and take what you want." She said, "I can't imagine a guy who robs banks having trouble with that."

She watched him grin, not sure what it meant until he said, "You're serious," and she grinned back at him, close enough to smell the weed on his breath.

"You bet I am. What's he ever done for us?"

Louis seemed to think about it a moment.

"I guess not much."

"Oh, man," Melanie said. "You know how long I've been waiting for this?"

———

15

Gallery Renee was located on the street level of The Gardens Mall, in a dim area between Sears and Bloomingdale's: a deep rectangular space, high ceiling, white walls and turquoise trim that picked up the mall's color motif.

Twelve thirty Sunday afternoon Max was looking through showroom glass at the gallery's bare walls, a few paintings on the floor against the walls, and at three black metal containers spaced down the length of the room. He thought of Grecian urns, then realized what they were: the eight hundred twenty dollars' worth of olive pots Renee had called about last Monday, wanting him to drop everything and bring a check. There they were, COD, so she'd paid for them. Black rusted metal jars about three feet high. One near the entrance. He moved that way and saw the sign on the glass, SORRY, CLOSED TODAY. Renee's work, the ornate capital letters, the words underlined three times. Closed—but when he pushed on the brass handle the door opened. Max entered, pausing to look in the olive pot standing close by. Cigarette butts, gum wrappers, a Styrofoam cup . . . A skinny young Latin-looking guy with hair to his shoulders was coming out from the back with a painting, a big one. He lowered it to lean against a library table in the middle of the floor and looked at Max.

"Can you read? We close today."

Now he was going back, through a hall at the rear to a door that was open and showed daylight.

Max walked up to the painting: six or seven feet by five and greenish, different shades of thick green paint with touches of red, yellowish tan, black . . . He had no idea what it was. Maybe a jungle and those were green figures coming out, emerging from the growth; it was hard to tell. More paintings were propped against the other side of the table. Paintings coming down, the ones on the floor, the new ones going up, Renee getting ready for one of her cheese-and-wine shows. She could be in back, in her office. Max looked that way and saw the young Latin guy coming with another canvas.

He said to Max, "I told you we close," and placed the canvas against the first one he'd brought out. Rising, he tossed his hair from his face. Stringy, still more than he needed. He looked familiar . . .

Saying to Max standing there, "What's your problem?"

And Max almost smiled. "I'm Renee's husband."

The guy said, "Yeah? . . ." and waited.

"Where is she, in back?"

"She getting me something to eat."

"You work here?"

Max could see the little asshole didn't like that. He said, "No, I don't *work* here." Turned and went back to the rear of the gallery.

Max walked around the table to find more green paintings. He stooped to look at the signature, a black scrawl.

David de la Villa.

The guy had to be Da-veed, the Cuban busboy from Chuck and Harold's Renee had said weeks ago was about to be discovered. Coming back now with another canvas . . .

About five nine and weighed maybe one thirty in his black T-shirt and skinny black jeans.

Max said, "You're David, huh?" with the right pronunciation. "I was wondering what this's supposed to be." Looking at the painting in front of him.

The Cuban busboy said, "It's what it *is*, not what it's supposed to be." He opened a drawer in the table, brought out sheets of paper with DAVID DE LA VILLA bold across the top, and handed one to Max. A press release. Name, born 1965 in Hialeah . . . He said, "If you don't know anything, read the part what the newspaper says, *The Post*."

Max found it, a quote underlined. He read aloud, "'. . . de la Villa has rendered a vivid collage of his life, albeit in metaphor . . . he paints with a wry and youthful gallantry.'" Max looked at the painting again. "Yeah, now I see the youthful gallantry. I wouldn't say it's especially wry though. What do you paint with, a shovel?"

"I see you don't know shit," the Cuban busboy said.

Max might admit that, but not today, pretty sure now why the busboy looked familiar. The diamond stud in his ear, his hair, his attitude, his little pussy mustache. Max said, "Those are people in there?"

"From my life," the busboy said, "looking for ways to escape."

Max moved in closer. "You have something pasted on there, huh? I thought it was all paint, it looks like leaves."

"From the sugar cane. I show life as a cane field that has trapped us and we have to break out."

"There's no cane in Hialeah I know of. If this is your life," Max said, looking from the canvas to the busboy, "how come I don't see anything about breaking *in?* Didn't I write you a bond a few years ago? You were up on a burglary charge?"

"You crazy."

"Aren't you David Ortega?"

"You see my name there, read it."

"What, de la Villa? That's your artsy name. You were David Ortega when I knew you. You copped to possession of stolen property and did about six months."

David Ortega de la Villa turned, started walking away.

Max said after him, "You sell any of this shit?"

The busboy stopped and turned around.

"Now I see why she leave you."

"You selling or not? I'd like to know how my wife's doing, if anything."

"Now I see why she don't talk to you. Already she sell five in like two weeks. *Treinta*—thirty-five hundred each one."

"You're kidding. What's Renee get?"

"That's her business, not yours."

Max kept his mouth shut. Her business but his money going into it to pay the rent, the phone—at least he hadn't paid for the olive jars, three-foot iron ashtrays it would take two guys to lift and empty. He wanted her to walk in right now with Da-veed's lunch—he'd march her into the office and tell her that was it, no more, she was on her own. He was quitting the bail-bond business and filing for divorce.

He looked at the painting in front of him.

Maybe not spring the divorce on her just yet.

But definitely tell her he wasn't paying any more of her bills.

Da-veed, the home-invading artist, said, "You see this one?" coming over to a canvas. "Look at it good. Tell me is someone in there you know."

"I don't see *any*body in there."

"In this part, right here."

Max stared and a figure began to appear. A boy? He moved closer, squinting. A boy's short hair but a woman, dots to indicate her exposed breasts, a tiny dark smudge that might be her bush. A pale-green woman in the dark-green leaves pasted down and painted over.

"Is that supposed to be Renee?"

"Man, you don't reco'nize your own wife? Yeah, she pose for me naked like that all the time."

It was hard to imagine. Renee used to go in the closet to put her nightgown on. How could this little asshole get her to take her clothes off? But wait a minute . . . Max said, "What's Renee doing in a cane field?"

"The field is a symbol of her oppression, what she desires to escape," the busboy said. "Her years of bondage to you. No life of her own."

Max said, "Bondage?"

And stopped. What was he going to do, rehash twenty-seven years of married life with this kid? He had a better idea and said, "Do me a favor, will you?"

The busboy said, "What?" suspicious.

"Put me in there, coming out of the cane."

Ordell loved this mall, the biggest, jazziest one he'd ever been in, done all modern with trees, with fountains, skylight domes way up there, the best stores. . . . They had Saks Fifth Avenue, where Ordell liked to buy his clothes; Macy's; Bloomie's; Burdine's; Sears, where Louis should go. They had up on the second level all different ethnic café counters where you ordered your food and brought it out to an area where you could sit down if you could find a place. Crowded every day now in the season. Jackie said it might be the place to make the delivery. Maybe even make the switch *and* the delivery right there; it was busy and confusing enough the way the area was laid out, Jackie said like a maze.

She was still at the table having some kind of Greek shit in that pita bread. He hadn't seen anything he wanted to eat and they'd finished their business, so he was leaving—once he called the hospital, learn how Cujo was doing. The boy didn't have a phone in his room, you had to ask about him and get somebody to tell you. The man that came on the phone yesterday kept wanting to know who this was calling; so he'd tried again last night and the nurse said Hulon was doing fine—who?—and going home, it looked like, in a few days. She said "home" but meant jail, or else didn't know any better. In the paper it said Hulon Miller, Jr., had "gunned down" the FDLE officer before he was "shot and apprehended" by a federal agent. The time and location told Ordell they were on his ass and now he'd have another one could be telling stories on him, Cujo looking to cop. What he needed to do was speak to Cujo before they rode him out to Gun Club. Make a visit to the hospital.

Ordell had a mall guide with a map in it that showed telephones on the lower level, back in a corner by Burdine's. He started across the big open area in the center of the mall, where you had a view of the fountain and the pools, headed for the down escalator, and stopped. Ordell turned around quick and crossed back to duck inside Barnie's Coffee & Tea Company.

Who was that coming off the up escalator but the bail bondsman, Max Cherry, Max heading toward the food counters now.

Ordell, watching from Barnie's, began to think: Wait now. Why had he ducked in here to hide from Max? It wasn't until this moment, stopping to look at what he was doing, he thought of the Rolex watch—that was it—and the possibility Max had found out what it was worth. It was instinct had made him duck in here. Something watching over his ass while his head was someplace else. He said to himself, You see that? Man, you have a gift.

Max walked past the food counters lined with customers: Olympus, Café Manet, Nate's Deli, China Town, the Italian Eatery, wondering which one would appeal to Renee, always a finicky eater. Didn't like anything to touch on her plate, not even peas and mashed potatoes. Chick-fil-A, Gourmet Grill, Nacos Tacos . . . that could be it, something spicy for the busboy. But she wasn't at Nacos Tacos or at Stuff 'N Turkey, not at any of the counters. Max turned to the eating area in the semicircle of cafés: rings of tables around and beneath an eight-pillared gazebo the size of a house with a fountain in the center. Areas were sectioned off by dividers and planters; aisles seemed to go around in circles. He moved a few steps in and began looking at one section at a time, his gaze inch-

ing along, thinking it was too crowded to pick anyone out. . . .

And saw her within a few seconds.

Renee sitting by herself: that skullcap of dark hair,
turquoise loop earrings, a dark blue dress off one
shoulder, Renee picking at a salad, taking dainty
bites, a carryout container on the table . . .

Close by, almost next to him, a woman's voice said,
"Max?" and he knew it was Jackie before he turned
and saw her looking up at him, Jackie with her cigarette and a cup of coffee, finished with her lunch. She
said, "What're you up to?" with that kind of shy
smile.

"I walked right past you."

"I know," Jackie said, "ignoring me. You were
looking for someone."

Not anymore. He did glance over as he sat down
and moved plastic lunch dishes aside to lean over his
arms on the table, Max out of Renee's line of sight if
she happened to look this way. He said, "You clean
your plate," and watched her raise her cigarette.
"How're you doing?"

"Not bad."

Moving her shoulders in the light cotton sweater
she wore without a blouse, the sleeves pushed up.

"What're you, a bag lady?"

On the bench next to her she had what looked like
an assortment of shopping bags folded and stuffed
inside a black Saks Fifth Avenue bag.

She said, "I go back to work tomorrow," as if that
explained the bags.

It didn't matter. He said, "You talked them into it."

"They seem to like the idea."

"Bring the money in and they follow it?"

"Yeah, but I'm going to dress it up. Put the money in a shopping bag and hand it to someone I meet here."

"You don't actually do it that way?"

"He always picked it up at my place," Jackie said. "But now with ATF involved I want to stage it, you know, make it look more intriguing, like we know what we're doing. Then it's up to Ray to follow the shopping bag. Nicolet, the ATF guy."

"Make the delivery," Max said, "somewhere in the mall?"

"I think right around here."

"Sit down, leave the bag under the table?"

"Something like that."

"Will Ordell go for it?"

"I'm helping him bring his money in," Jackie said. "He loves the idea."

With that gleam. Serious business but having fun. It was strange, both of them smiling a little, treating it lightly until Max said, "I heard about Tyler," and her expression changed. "I saw it in the paper and called a guy I know in the State Attorney's Office. He said he's gonna be okay."

"Yeah, Tyler's not a bad guy, I like him," Jackie said. "Only now I'm dealing strictly with Nicolet. He likes the idea of picking up the money, but says he has to get Ordell with guns."

"I won't say I told you," Max said.

"He says he doesn't care about the money, but I think he likes it more than he lets on—if you know what I mean."

He watched Jackie draw on her cigarette and let out a slow stream of smoke. As she raised her coffee cup Max leaned back to check on Renee—still there, nibbling—and came forward again to the table.

Jackie was watching him.

"You're meeting someone."

Max shook his head. "My wife's sitting over there."

"You were looking for her."

"Yeah, but I hadn't made plans to meet her."

Jackie leaned back against the bench, looking that way.

"Where is she?"

"Three tables over, in the blue dress."

He watched Jackie looking at his wife.

"She's quite petite."

"Yes, she is."

"Don't you want to talk to her?"

"It can wait." Jackie was looking at him again and he said, "I called you last night."

"I know, I got your message. Ray wanted to have dinner, to talk about the sting we're plotting. That's what he calls it, a sting. He's being nice to me," Jackie said, leaning in now to rest her arms on the table. "I can't help wondering if he's interested in the money for himself."

"Because he's nice to you?"

"Setting me up to make a proposition."

"Has he hinted around?"

"Not really."

"Then why do you think he might want it?"

"I knew a narcotics cop one time," Jackie said. "He told me that in a raid, 'the whole package never gets back to the station.' His exact words."

"You know some interesting people," Max said.

"I believe him, because later on he was suspended and forced to retire."

"Has Nicolet told you any stories like that?"

She shook her head. "He tries to act cool."

"There's no harm in that. He's a young guy, having fun being a cop. He might cut a few corners to get a conviction—from what I've heard about him—but I can't see him walking off with that kind of money, it's evidence."

She said, "What about you, Max, if you had the chance?"

"If I was in Nicolet's place?"

She might've meant that and changed her mind, shaking her head. "No, I mean *you*, right now. Not if you were someone else."

"If I saw a way to walk off with a shopping bag full of money, would I take it?"

She said, "You know where it came from. It's not like it's someone's life savings. It wouldn't even be missed."

Watching him, waiting for an answer.

She was serious.

"I might be tempted," Max said. "Especially now, since I'm getting out of the bail-bond business."

That stopped her, no question about it.

"I have to stand behind all my active bonds, but I'm not writing any new ones."

She eased back against the bench. "Why?"

"I'm tired of doing it. . . . I'm in a bad situation with the insurance company I represent. The only way to get out of it is quit the business."

"When did you decide?"

"It's been coming. I finally made up my mind—I guess it was Thursday."

"The day you got me out of jail."

"That night I went to pick up a guy. Sat there in the dark with a stun gun, the place smelling of mildew . . ."

"After we were together," Jackie said.

Max paused. "Yeah . . . I thought, What am I doing here? Nineteen years of this. I made up my mind to quit the business. And while I was at it, file for divorce."

She was staring at him but didn't seem surprised now.

"All of a sudden, after twenty-seven years?"

"You look back," Max said, "you can't believe that much time went by. You look ahead and you think, shit, if it goes that fast I better do something with it."

"Have you told Renee?"

"That's why I came here."

Jackie looked over that way. "She's leaving."

"I'll get to it," Max said. He saw Renee in her off-one-shoulder dark blue gown that reached almost to the floor standing by the table, picking up her bag and the carryout container for the busboy.

"She looks good," Jackie said. "How old is she?"

"Fifty-three."

"Stays in shape."

"She's her main concern," Max said.

"Seems very confident. The way she walks, holds her head."

"Is she gone?"

Jackie turned to him again, nodding. "You're afraid of her, aren't you?"

"I think it's more, I never really got to know her. We didn't talk much, all those years. You know when you're with someone and you have to try and think of something to say?" Jackie was nodding. "That's how it was. What she's doing now, age fifty-three, Renee poses nude for a Cuban busboy who paints cane fields and she sells them for thirty-five hundred a copy. So she's all set."

"Which bothers you more," Jackie said, "her posing nude or making money?"

"The guy bothers me, the painter," Max said. "He irritates the hell out of me, but so what? I outweigh him fifty pounds, I hit him it's assault with intent, a three-thousand-dollar bond. Renee, what she's doing I think is great. She's finally got something going and I don't have to feel guilty trying to understand her."

"You don't have to support her either," Jackie said.

"There's that too. She's working and I'm not."

"Then why don't you sound happy about it?"

"Right now I'm relieved, that's enough."

Jackie lit a cigarette before she looked at him again. "I'm not sure you answered my question."

"Which one?"

"If you had the chance, unemployed now, to walk off with a half million plus, would you do it?"

"I said I'd be tempted." She kept staring at him and he said, "You know I was kidding."

"Were you?"

Max said, "Don't even think about it, okay? You could get killed, you could get sent to prison. . . ."

He stopped because she had that look in her eyes again, that gleam with the smile in it that turned him on.

She said, "But what if there was a way to do it?"

They had told Ordell on the phone, third floor east wing and the room number. Half-past eleven Sunday night, all he had to do was wait in the stairwell for the deputy to get tired sitting by himself in the hall and go up to the nurse's counter to stretch his legs and visit. That's how easy it was to get to see Cujo. Ordell walked into the semidark room wearing a dark suit and necktie, carrying a box of peanut brittle he set on the bedside stand. He pulled the pillow out from under Cujo's head, not wasting any time.

Cujo said, "Hey, shit," coming awake cranky and with bad breath.

Ordell said, "Hey, my man," laying the pillow on Cujo's chest, "how you doing? You making it? They treating you all right?"

Cujo said, "What you want?" squinting and scowling at him, mean and grouchy waking up from his sleep.

Ordell said, "Man, they ought to give you something for your breath," moving the pillow up to Cujo's chin. "Close your eyes, I be out of here in a minute." Ordell took a good hold on the pillow with both hands, started to lift it, and the overhead light came on in the room.

Now a fat nurse helper was right there at the foot of the bed saying, "What're you doing in here?"

Ordell glanced around to see the deputy in here too, an older guy but big, with a belly on him.

"I was fixing his pillow," Ordell said, "fluffin' it for him so he be comfortable. Turning it to the cool side."

The fat nurse helper said, "You're not supposed to be in here. It's way past visiting hours." The fat deputy next to her now, watching him with that dumb-eyed no-shit deputy look.

Ordell held his hands out to the sides, resigned.

"I told his mama I'd come visit. She use to keep house for my mama 'fore my mama passed on. But see, I'm Seven-Day Adventis' and I was out door-to-door collecting for the church all day. You know, for the poor people ain't got nothing to eat?"

The fat nurse helper said, "Well, you're not suppose to be in here."

And the fat deputy said, "Get your ass out, now."

So Ordell wasn't able to settle his mind about Cujo. Shit. He left knowing he had a problem on his hands.

16

Sunday evening, early, Ordell had brought Louis to his house on 30th Street in West Palm, introduced him to Simone, telling her to take good care of Louis, he would be staying here a few days. Ordell showed Louis the guest room, the Beretta nine in the bureau drawer he was to bring along tomorrow, and left saying he had to visit a friend in the hospital, "See you in the morning."

That Sunday evening was an experience.

Louis thought the colored woman might be Ordell's aunt. Simone asked could she fix him something to eat. Louis said no thanks. She went in her room and Louis sat down to watch *Murder, She Wrote* thinking Simone was in there for the night, older people generally going to bed early. A Movie of the Week came on next.

About half-past nine a different woman came out

of the bedroom. The one who'd gone in looked like Aunt Jemima in an old housecoat and a scarf tied around her head. The one that came out was twenty years younger, had shiny black hair done in a swirl, dangle earrings, blue around her eyes and big fake lashes, a skintight silver dress and backless heels to match. She said to Louis she understood he was from Detroit. She said she used to know plenty of white boys there she'd meet at the Flame Showbar, at Sportrees, later on at the Watts Club Mozambique, and take them to after-hours places after. She said to Louis, "You do any of that?" He said sometimes he did, he had met Ordell at the Watts Club. Simone said, "Baby, I'm gonna take you home." The Movie of the Week went off and Motown came on.

Monday morning Louis left the house early, before Simone was up, and had his breakfast at a Denny's. They were meeting in the parking lot of the Hilton on Southern Boulevard just off the Interstate. Louis arrived to see Ordell in blue coveralls standing by a van parked next to his Mercedes, having a smoke. Melanie was in there listening to the radio, moving her head to the beat. Ordell came over to Louis's car saying, "Lemme see what you have you so proud of."

Louis opened the trunk and showed Ordell his shiny guns, the Colt Python and the Mossberg 500 with the laser scope. The Beretta from the bureau drawer was in there too. Ordell said, "Bring it." Louis took the Beretta and stuck it in his waist, under his sport shirt hanging out.

"And that Star Trek shotgun," Ordell said. "Big Guy gets a kick out of that kind of shit."

Louis brought it out in a fold of newspaper, closed the trunk, and followed Ordell over to the back of the van. Ordell turned to him saying, "Simone get you to bone her?"

Innocent, then starting to grin, and Louis knew he'd been waiting all that time looking at guns to ask the question.

"She put on a show," Louis said.

"Yes, she does."

"Did 'Baby Love' with all the gestures."

"The choreography," Ordell said. "You swear it's the Supremes, huh?"

"It *was* the Supremes, on the record."

"I mean the way the woman moves."

"She did 'Stop! In the Name of Love.'"

"'Before you break my heart,'" Ordell said.

"She did Gladys Knight."

"With the Pips or without? She does it both ways."

"With the Pips."

"She do Syreeta Wright?"

"I don't know. She did some I never heard of."

"Syreeta was married to Stevie Wonder."

"She was great," Louis said. "I mean she had every little move down."

"She get you to bone her?"

"She wanted me to come in her room."

"Yeah?"

"Said she needed her back rubbed, from all that moving around."

"She like her feet rubbed too."

"I told her, man, I was worn out and had a headache."

"Yeah?"

"Middle of the night I wake up? Simone's in bed with me. She says, 'How's your headache, baby? Is it gone?'"

Ordell said, "You boned her, didn't you?"

The rear door of the van came open and a black kid wearing a black bandanna stuck his head out saying, "Bread, we sitting here—man, we going or not?"

"Right now," Ordell said. "Get back in there," and opened the door enough for Louis to see three black kids crouched in there with guns—AK-47s, they looked like—staring back at him. Ordell said, "This is Louis, the famous bank robber from Detroit I mention to you? Louis, these two cats are Sweatman and Snow, and the mean-looking motherfucker that can't wait is Zulu. They call me Bread, huh? Short for Whitebread. Hey, you all think up a name for my man Louis here," Ordell said and slammed the door closed. He said to Louis, "They love me. You know why? 'Cause I'm from Dee-troit and that is a no-shit recommendation, man. You from there with these homeboys, you *it*."

Melanie came out of the Mercedes in her cutoffs and a halter top, a frayed knit bag hanging from her shoulder. She said, "Hi, Louis," without making eye contact and stood with her arms folded while Ordell said he and Louis would go in the van with the jackboys and Melanie would follow them in Louis's

Toyota. Louis asked why his car? Ordell said, for coming back. Like that explained it. Louis said, "Whatever you say."

On the way out Southern Boulevard toward Loxahatchee, Ordell talked about the jackboys loud enough for them to hear him in back, calling them crazy motherfuckers and asking if they had ever heard of *pistolocos?* They were the jackboys of Colombia. Ordell looked at the rearview mirror telling them, "You get two million pesos to shoot a government man down there in Medellín, the drug capital of the world. That's two hundred grand American the druggies pay you. Get you high on some mean shit they call *basuco*, made from coke but takes hold of you worse. You think two hundred thousand, man, you can buy your mother a condo on the fucking beach. Do another government man and buy yourself a car like mine and all the clothes you want. Only you know what you got down there besides the druggies and the *pistolocos?* You got all kind of hoods and punks shooting each other. You got terrorists—you know what I'm saying, terrorists? You got them and the others I mentioned and you got death-squad guys too, all going around killing each other. You know how many got shot dead or died of a violent death in that one town last year, Medellín? Over five thousand and most of them guys your age, just starting their young life. You hear what I'm saying? That's ten times more even than get taken out in Detroit any given year—tell you the kind of place it is. You see how lucky you are to live here in the U.S.A.?"

Louis would glance over his shoulder at the jack-boys, three big kids, their heads and shoulders moving with the motion of the van. Quiet, serious in the gloom back there. Like migrants being taken to work, except for the Chinese machine guns they held.

Ordell didn't say a word about their business this morning until, a few miles past the Loxahatchee Road Prison, he turned off Southern to head through open scrub and they were by themselves out here. A dark line way off marked the beginning of the cane fields, a half million acres from here down into the Everglades. Ordell looked at his rearview mirror.

"We getting close now. Turn on this dirt road. . . . The man don't make it easy to get to his place."

A road lined with shaggy Australian pines on the other side of a worn-out canal. A few miles of dust and stones hitting the underside of the van and Louis could see a farm layout through the trees: neat-looking red-brick ranch, barn with pens and a tractor shed to one side, a Quonset hut off on the other side of the house. Louis hung on tight as Ordell cranked the wheel hard and the van bounced in and out of the ruts.

"You see that turtle? Shit, I missed him," Ordell said and glanced at his mirror. "You all take a look right now quick, see what we coming to. We cross the bridge we on the man's property."

The van rumbled over loose planks spanning the canal and Ordell looked at the mirror again.

"See that big tin building? That's call a Quonset, where the man keeps all his guns and military shit. Has a M-60 machine gun in there mounted on a jeep we gonna tear off. Has hand grenades. Has what they call a L-A-W rocket launcher, has a bunch of them. It stands for Light Antitank Weapon. Has the rocket already inside and the instructions printed on how to shoot it and then throw it away, it's a disposable weapon. Government man comes driving along in his car down in Medellín—*bam*, he's gone."

Ordell said, "I expect we gonna find the man by hisself. His wife, I heard she got tired standing inspection, dusting all his guns and shit, and left him." Turning into a gravel drive then, Ordell said, "No, it looks like the man's got company this morning. Couple of bikes . . ."

Parked behind a pickup truck in the drive, the bikes becoming Harleys as the van crept up behind them.

"They over at the gun range," Ordell said. "See? Up back of the tin building?"

A long counter with a flat roof over it, about fifty yards from the house. Two men stood there. Off beyond them were targets on posts and a high ridge of earth, like a levee.

"Couple of Bikers for Racism," Ordell said, "practicing up to shoot us African-Americans when we go to move in their neighborhood and take our pleasure with their women. You all get down now. Me and Louis, once we get out you gonna be quiet as mice, you dig? No looking out the window. You hear us in the house commence to shoot, that's your signal. You go take out the bikers straightaway. That's your assignment on this operation, the Turkey Shoot, huh? Listen."

They could hear gunfire now coming from the range, thin popping sounds in the open, shots spaced apart.

"Firing pistols," Ordell said. "They have these targets with ugly-looking Neegroes painted on them they shoot at. Nigger coming at them with a machete —you *know* this brother's gonna get shot. Don't have a gun on him, he deserves to, being that dumb."

Louis looked over his shoulder again. The jackboys were doing coke now, digging it from a baggie with teaspoons, each one with his own, sniffing and wiping their noses on their sleeves.

"Got our own *pistolocos,*" Ordell said, glancing at the mirror again, then reached over to take what looked like an Army Colt .45 automatic from the glove box. He racked the slide and stuck the gun inside his coveralls, saying to Louis, "You ready? Let's shake and bake."

Louis got out with the Mossberg in the fold of newspaper. He adjusted the Beretta, digging into his groin, then pulled it out of his waist—the hell with it —laid it on the seat, and closed the door. Louis walked around the front of the van to join Ordell. He glanced back to see Melanie getting out of the Toyota parked behind them, hanging the knit bag from her shoulder. Melanie coming up to them now, not looking too happy.

"There he is," Ordell said.

He raised his hand to wave and Louis looked toward the house.

"How you doing, Big Guy?"

Still grinning, Ordell lowered his voice to say, "Look at the motherfucker. Thinks he's A-dolf Hitler."

The man stood on his stoop across half the front yard from them, dressed in tan Desert Storm camouflage pants and a GI khaki T-shirt, paratrooper boots planted two feet apart, hands on his hips.

Melanie said, "If you think I'm gonna fuck that bozo, you're out of your mind."

Ordell turned his head. "Be cool. Just bring the man on's all you have to do."

Then turned his head back saying, "Look who I brought to see you, Gerald. 'Member I told you about Melanie? Here she is, man."

Gerald had animal heads with horns and antlers mounted on his knotty pine walls. He had framed color prints of different fish. He had brown leather furniture, a wagon-wheel chandelier, crossed muskets over his fireplace, trophies sitting on glass-front gun cabinets, a rack of shotguns . . . Nothing in the room with a woman's touch.

Ordell was telling Gerald how anxious his friends were to see his place, hoping he didn't mind their dropping in like this, while Melanie poked around looking at things, bending over, sticking her butt out, and Gerald's eyes would follow her cutoffs.

Louis stood holding the Mossberg in the fold of newspaper, looking around, then moved to a window to check on the two bikers. Still out there making popping sounds.

Gerald got rid of the cigar stuck in the corner of his mouth, dropping it in an ashtray made from a shell casing, sucked in his gut, and strolled over to tell Melanie about the fish prints. All the different kinds you could take out of Lake Okeechobee. Bullhead, bluegill, channel cat . . . Gerald taking peeks at Melanie's bare shoulder and down the front of her halter, his hands shoved into his back pockets, as if to keep them from touching her. Timid, Louis thought, for a man his size. Gerald turned to Ordell saying they were going out to the kitchen. "You and him make yourselves at home."

Ordell picked up a hand grenade that was now a cigarette lighter and came over to Louis flicking it at him.

"Big Guy's something, huh?"

Louis turned from the window. "What'd you tell him about Melanie?"

"I said she gets off looking at guns. It's the truth."

"So he'll try and nail her."

"I 'magine. You want to protect her, go in there and shoot him."

They were eye to eye.

Louis said, "You know you're gonna have to."

Ordell said, "Somebody is."

They came back in the room, Melanie holding a mug of coffee, the knit bag still hanging from her shoulder. Gerald said, "Why don't you boys go out to the range? I'll loan you a couple pistols."

Ordell said to Louis, "Show Big Guy your piece."

Louis took the Mossberg from the fold of newspaper and held it out. He watched Gerald looking at it, not too impressed.

"It's got a laser scope on it," Ordell said.

Gerald came over to take the gun from Louis and walked back with it to where Melanie stood with her coffee. He said to her, "Can I be frank? I wouldn't hang this in my toilet," checking it out now, racking the pump. He aimed, squeezed the grip, and put the red laser dot between the eyes of a white-tailed buck on his wall. "You still have to hold your weapon against recoil. That red dot don't mean shit, if you'll pardon my French," he said to Melanie. "I'll go against him with an old single-shot Remington I got as a kid and outscore him any time he wants. Put some cash on the line, make it interesting." He tossed the Mossberg back to Louis saying, "Careful now, you got a load in the chamber." Shaking his head then to say, "What's a weapon like that for, all chromed up? I sure as hell wouldn't take it into combat."

Louis said, "It ain't bad for holding up liquor stores."

Melanie rolled her eyes at him.

Gerald shrugged. "That's about its speed."

Louis, at first, had thought the guy was suspicious, even the way he looked at Melanie. What were these people doing here? Or he was annoyed for the same reason and because of it barely opened his mouth. The way Louis saw him now, the guy liked being on the muscle; he had to be challenged in some way to get his head to work. Gerald was about fifty or so; he could suck in his stomach but not that big butt on him. He believed no doubt he looked slick in his Desert Storm camies and was too confident to know he had a narrow brain in his crew-cut head. This type pissed Louis off. The convict in him liked the feeling of heat he got looking at the guy, knowing he could control it and mess with him.

Louis, figuring the guy's age, said, "Gerald, you ever been to war?"

"I been to tactical encampments," Gerald said, "in Georgia and here in Florida. Going way back, I trained for the Bay of Pigs and just missed it."

"Have you ever looked death in the face?"

"Meaning what?"

"Combat—what did you think?"

"I've taken part in combat exercises with live ammo," Gerald said, "put on by former recon marines. Don't kid yourself, I know what a fire fight is like."

Louis had never been in combat either. No, but he'd seen two men shot—one running from a work gang at Huntsville, another climbing the fence at Starke—and had seen a man stabbed to death, a man set on fire, a man right after he had been strangled with a coat hanger, and believed these counted for something. So he said to Gerald, "Bullshit. That ain't looking death in the face, that's playing. That's what kids do." Louis taking it to this asshole standing there in his combat boots in a roomful of guns. Louis working himself up for what he knew was coming.

Ordell moved away from the window as he started in, saying, "Big Guy's been training, getting ready for the black revolution." Ordell playing with the zipper tab on his coveralls, zipping it up, zipping it down. "He hears us saying we shall overcome and knows it's gonna happen."

Louis had looked over his shoulder at the window. He heard Ordell, but not that popping sound outside. It had stopped. He saw the two bikers by the gun-range counter, maybe reloading.

Ordell saying, "It won't be like the A-rab war out in the desert. Unh-unh, the nigger war's gonna be in the streets. Gonna be a job stopping us natives, huh, man?" Ordell provoking the guy, saying, "You think you and your racist brothers can handle it?"

Gerald said, "You talking to me like that in my *home*?" Lines in his face drawn tight. Fired up now. "Why'd you come here, bringing your whore? To get your black ass whipped? I'll do it for you, you want."

Ordell had his coveralls zipped down to his waist, his hand going inside. It was about to happen. Ordell was going to shoot the guy. Louis felt it and wanted him to come on, hurry up if he was going to do it. Louis anxious—he had to look out the window again, quick, check on the bikers.

They were leaving the gun range: two heavyset guys coming with pistols and rifles.

Louis turned from the window. He said, "Those

guys are coming," trying to be cool about it, wanting Ordell to know without throwing him off.

But it did, it stopped Ordell and he looked over, his hand still inside his coveralls.

In that moment Melanie yelled, "Shoot him!"

Louis saw her pulling the knit bag from her shoulder, that much, before he swung the Mossberg at Gerald, putting it on him as the man got to Ordell and slammed a fist into him. It drove Ordell back to land hard in a leather chair, the Colt auto cleared, in his hand, and Gerald took it away from him: punched him in the mouth, twisted the gun from his hand, and threw it over on the sofa, out of the way. He got into a crouch then and hooked his fist into Ordell's face, then threw the other hand, bouncing Ordell's head against the brown leather cushion.

Melanie yelled it again, "Shoot him!" and Gerald paused, sinking to one knee as if to rest, then to look over his shoulder.

At Melanie, Louis thought. But the man was looking this way, right at him, staring. Louis squeezed the grip and saw the red laser dot appear on Gerald's forehead. Gerald grinned at him.

"You got the nerve? Asking have I ever looked death in the face. Shit, you ain't ever seen any combat, have you?"

Melanie's voice said, "What're you waiting for?"

Gerald turned enough to look at her. "He's got buckshot in there, honey. How's he gonna get me without hitting his nigger friend?" He said to Louis, "Am I right? Shit, you don't have the nerve anyway."

Louis went for him, raising the Mossberg to lay it across his head, aiming at that crew cut, and caught the man's shoulder. Gerald rose up in his GI T-shirt, all arms, grabbed the barrel and gave it a twist, and Louis, hanging on, was thrown against the chair on top of Ordell. Louis slid off, scrambled out of the man's reach to have room to move. Got to his feet . . . Gerald was standing with his back to him.

Gerald, and now Louis, watching as Melanie's hand came out of her knit bag with a stubby bluesteel automatic. Gerald said, "Now what is that you have, some kind of low-cal pussy gun?"

Melanie was holding it in both hands now, arms extended, aimed at Gerald.

He tossed the shotgun to land on the sofa, looked at Melanie and said, "Okay, now you put that down, honey, and I won't press charges against you." Confident about it, as though it would settle the matter.

Melanie didn't say anything. She shot him.

Louis felt himself jump—the sound was so loud in that closed room. He looked at Gerald. The man hadn't moved; he stood there.

Melanie said, "I'm not a whore, you bozo."

Christ, and shot him again.

Louis saw Gerald grab his side this time as if he'd been stung.

She shot him again and his hands went to his chest and his knees started to buckle as he moved toward her and she shot him again: the sound ringing and ringing in this room full of guns and animal heads, until it faded away and the man was lying on the floor.

Ordell said through his bloody mouth, barely moving it, "Is he dead?"

Melanie said, "You bet he is."

Ordell said to Louis, "They coming?" And to Melanie, "Girl, where'd you get that gun?"

Louis was at the window now.

He saw the two bikers standing in kind of a crouch with their rifles, shoulders hunched, looking this way, nearer the house now than the gun range. He saw them out there in the open, cautious. Saw them both look toward the driveway at the same time and start to turn in that direction, raising their rifles. Louis heard the sound of automatic weapons, not as loud as he heard them in Ordell's gun movie or in any movie he had ever seen, and watched the two bikers drop where they were standing, seem to collapse, fall without firing a shot, the sound of the automatic weapons continuing until finally it stopped. Pretty soon the jackboys appeared, the kids with their Chinese guns, curved banana clips, looking at the men on the ground and then toward the house.

Louis wondered if combat was like that. If you had a seat and could watch it.

He heard Ordell say, "They get 'em?"

Louis nodded. He said, "Yeah."

And heard Ordell say, "Man, my mouth is *sore*. I think I'm gonna have to go the dentist."

Heard him say, "Now I have to get those boys to load up the van. We going home in Louis's car, if it makes it." Heard him say, "You ever shoot anybody before?"

And heard Melanie say, "Hardly."

He watched the jackboys poke at the bikers with the muzzles of their guns. Now Ordell appeared, walking up to them, and it surprised Louis; he hadn't heard Ordell leave the room. Louis turned from the window to see Melanie on the sofa, still holding the pistol.

She said, "Why didn't you shoot him?"

Louis said, "You did all right."

Melanie looked at Gerald on the floor. She said, "I don't mean him."

17

Jackie didn't see Ray Nicolet until she came off the elevator in the airport parking structure, Tuesday afternoon. He said, "We have to stop meeting like this," deadpan, posed against the front fender of a Rolls.

She was supposed to smile, so she did; because he was young, he was having fun being a cop, and because she had to be nice to him. She could smile, too, at his swagger, coming to take the wheels from her in his cowboy boots, a gun beneath that light jacket, stuck in his jeans.

"I thought you'd be waiting in Customs."

"We don't need to bring them in," Nicolet said. "This is ATF business. How was your flight?"

"Smooth, all the way."

"I imagine you're glad to be working again."

"You'll never know," Jackie said, walking with him now along the row of cars.

"We have the money here?"

"Ten thousand."

"Anything else? Weed, coke?"

"No, but I can get you some."

"I'll toke once in a while if it's there," Nicolet said. "You know, like at a party. But I won't buy it, it's against the law."

He placed the wheels in the trunk of the Honda and brought the flight bag in the front seat with him. Jackie slipped in behind the wheel. Opening the bag he said, "Three-ten PM," and gave the date and location, where they were. "I'm now taking a manila envelope from the subject's flight bag. The envelope contains currency . . . all the same denomination, one-hundred-dollar bills. Now I'm counting it."

Jackie said, "What're you doing?"

He showed her the mike hooked to his lapel, then pressed the palm of his hand over it. "I'm recording."

"You said you were letting this one go through."

"I am. Don't worry about it."

"Then why're you being so official?"

"I don't want any surprises. Every step of this goes in my report."

She watched him count the bills, dab each one with a green felt-tipped pen, and describe where he was putting the mark, ". . . on the first zero of the numeral one hundred in the upper left corner." He finished and said, "I'm putting the currency back in the envelope, ten thousand dollars. The subject will deliver the money in . . ."

Jackie said, "A Saks Fifth Avenue shopping bag," smoking a cigarette now.

"A Saks Fifth Avenue shopping bag."

She gestured to several bags on the back seat.

"A large black bag with handles and red lettering," Nicolet said, took the recorder from his coat pocket, and turned it off. "Okay, we can go."

"You're not coming with me, are you?"

"I'll be along," Nicolet said. "What time you have to be there?"

"Four thirty. I'm meeting a woman."

"What's her name?"

"He wouldn't tell me. Will you be alone?"

"Don't worry about it. The woman leaves, somebody'll be on her."

"But you're not going to stop her," Jackie said.

Nicolet had the door open and was getting out.

"Are you?"

He stuck his head back in. "Why would I do that?"

Max got to the mall at four, parked by Sears, and went in through the store. He'd stop and see Renee, talk to her, get that over with. Tell her he had to leave if she started one of her monologues. All that time he could never think of anything to say to her, she never had trouble talking to him. Always about herself.

Jackie had said four thirty. Watch the way it works. A woman would come up to her table or sit at the one next to it. There would be lots of people, she said, the café area busy from noon on. If he came early, look for her at Saks.

The sign on the showroom glass said DAVID DE LA VILLA in dark green, with dates.

A white cloth covered the library table in the center of the gallery, the walls hung with green paintings, the busboy's cane fields, Renee peering naked from one. . . .

Too small to see from the entrance, through the showroom glass, but that's where she was—on the wall to the right, the third canvas. Max entered. The olive pot just inside seemed to hold the same cigarette butts, gum wrappers, the Styrofoam cup—no more, no less. He saw Renee.

Coming out from the back with a tray full of cheese and crackers. She looked up and saw him and looked down again.

He said, "Renee?"

She said, "Oh, it's you," placing the tray on the table, centering it.

He wondered how he could be anyone else standing here.

"It's nice to see you too."

She avoided looking at him now. "I have an exhibit opening at five." Getting that tray exactly in the center, an inch this way.

"I know," Max said, "but I'd like to talk to you."

"You can't see I'm busy?"

"With the cheese and crackers," Max said. "I know they're an important part of your life."

"What do you want?"

He hesitated. The busboy was coming with a silver tray and a coat over his arm. Max waited, looking at Renee waiting for the busboy. Renee wearing a gauzy white gown to the floor he thought of as a flower-child dress, or the kind women dancing around Stonehenge in the moonlight wore. Renee making up for lost time. Max thinking, Like all of us. Now David de la Villa arrived with a tray of raw vegetables surrounding some kind of creamy dip. He placed the tray on the table and put on the coat, a tux jacket, an old one, over a yellow tank top he was wearing with jeans frayed at the knees. He said to Renee, "Is he bothering you?"

Nothing here made sense. What if he *was* bothering her? What could this guy do about it?

"We're talking," Max said.

Renee shook her head. "No, we're not." And her pert little cap of black hair moved, a sprig of earth-mother green in it, no strands of gray showing, they were gone. She turned to leave, green loop earrings swinging. "I told him we're busy."

"You heard her," the busboy said.

Max stood there puzzled, staring at this freak in the tux staring back at him, but aware of Renee leaving them and he said after her, "It's important."

She paused long enough to look back and tell him, "So is my show."

Familiar? I'm working. Well, I'm working too. I'd like to talk to you. I'm busy. I'm filing for divorce. . . . That might get her attention. He turned to the

busboy, who irritated him more than anyone he
could think of in recent memory.

"You know what you look like?"

"Yeah, what?"

The guy standing hip cocked, waiting.

Max hesitated. Because the guy could look whatever way he wanted, he was the show, he was putting
the art lovers on and making out. . . . *Or,* the guy
had talent, he knew how to paint, and Max, in his
seersucker jacket and wing-tips, didn't know shit.
That was a possibility Max could look at like a big
boy and admit. Even somewhat proud of himself. So
he said, "Never mind," and turned to leave.

"I see you around here again I'm gonna call security," Max heard that irritating fucking busboy say
and almost stopped. "Have them throw you out."
But he kept going. The bond for first-degree murder,
if you could get one, was fifty thousand.

Four thirty on the dot, Jackie picked up a couple of
egg rolls and an iced tea at China Town and walked
past the semicircle of café counters with her Saks
bag, on display in her Islands Air uniform. Next, she
moved through the maze of aisles in the center area,
beneath the giant gazebo, before choosing a table
and slipped in behind it to sit against a planter, able
to see what was going on around her. She thought
she might spot Nicolet; Max, if he was able to make
it; but didn't count on picking out any ATF agents,
assuming Nicolet had people with him. She didn't
put a lot of trust in anything he told her. He did say

someone would follow whoever picked up the money. But that didn't mean another ATF agent. Jackie had a hunch Ordell would send the woman he lived with, the one who answered the phone, said he wasn't there, and hung up. Fifteen minutes passed. Jackie finished her egg rolls and lit a cigarette.

A slender young black woman holding a full tray and a Saks bag hanging from her hand said, "This seat taken?"

Jackie told her no, sit down, and watched her unload the tray. Tacos, enchiladas, refried beans, a large-size Coke, napkins, plastic utensils . . . "You're hungry," Jackie said.

The slender young woman, dark and quite pretty, said, "Yes'm." She couldn't be more than twenty.

Jackie said, "Put your bag on the floor, okay? Under the table. We might as well make it look good." She watched the young woman, who hadn't looked right at her since sitting down, bend sideways to glance under the table.

"Right next to mine. Then when I leave," Jackie said, "well, you know. What's your name?"

She did look up saying, "Sheronda?" and down again at her tray.

"Go ahead and start. I think I spoke to you on the phone one time," Jackie said, "when I was in jail and called Ordell. Wasn't that you?"

She said, "I think it was."

"I told you my name? Jackie?"

Sheronda said, "Yes'm," and sat waiting.

"Really, start eating. I won't bother you anymore."

Jackie watched her begin, Sheronda hunching close to the tray. "I just want to ask you one question. Are you and Ordell married?"

"He say we like the same thing as married," Sheronda said, without raising her head.

"Did you drive here?"

"Yes'm, he got a car for me to use."

"You do live together," Jackie said.

Sheronda hesitated and Jackie didn't think she was going to answer. When she did, she said, "Most of the times," still not raising her head.

Jackie said, "Not every day?"

"Sometime every day, for a while."

"Then you don't see him for a few days."

"Yes'm."

"You know what's in the bag you're taking?"

"He say is a surprise."

Jackie stubbed out her cigarette. She said, "Well, it was nice talking to you," picked up Sheronda's bag, and left.

Max could see them from the Cappuccino Bar. He watched Jackie coming away from the table and told the girl behind the counter not to take his coffee, he'd be right back. Jackie didn't see him, heading out with a certain amount of purpose. Max's idea was to tag along, not catch up with her until they were well away from here. That plan changed as he saw the guy step out of Barnie's Coffee & Tea Company and Jackie stopped. Max did too. He watched the young guy in a sport coat and jeans, cowboy boots, take the

Saks bag from her and reach into it, looking at her as he did. The guy would be Ray Nicolet, Max decided, making sure she wasn't walking off with the ten thousand. Max, the former cop, thinking for Nicolet: You can't trust anyone, can you? Especially a confidential informant. They talked for a minute. Not, it would seem, about anything too serious. Jackie nodded, listened to Nicolet, nodded again, turned and walked off. A few strides and she was around the corner, gone, and Nicolet was looking toward the seating area talking to himself now, or into a radio mike he had on him. Max returned to the Cappuccino Bar to finish his coffee.

He had recognized the young black woman with Jackie, the same one who lived in the house on 31st Street and he had spoken to Friday morning looking for Ordell. Still trying to find him, five days now with the fake Rolex that wasn't bad-looking, kept the right time, but still wasn't worth a thousand bucks. He'd had it appraised at a jewelry store and Winston was right, the watch sold for about two fifty.

The young woman was still working her way through that pile of Mexican food, not looking up. Now she did. Turning her head to a woman at the next table. An older black woman.

Max watched.

The older woman said something. Now the younger woman picked up the ashtray Jackie had used and handed it to the older woman. They exchanged a few words. Then didn't say anything for a minute or so, the older woman smoking a cigarette now. Jackie had talked to the younger woman the whole time they were together, not at all sly about it, right out in front. The older woman had a cup of coffee in front of her, nothing to eat. Now she said something again to the younger woman, only this time without looking at her. The younger woman paused, then began eating again in a hurry.

Max's cappuccino was cold.

As he finished it the younger woman was getting up from the table. He watched her stoop to get the Saks shopping bag, straighten her slim body, look around, and come out of the seating area. He watched her walk past the Café Manet, past Barnie's Coffee & Tea, and turn the corner before the cowboy stepped out. He watched Nicolet allow the young woman to get some distance on him before he spoke to his radio mike and followed after her, around the corner. Max turned to see the older woman putting out her cigarette.

She sat there another couple of minutes before picking up—how about that—a Saks Fifth Avenue shopping bag and walking away from the table, toward the café counters on the other side of the seating area.

This one was not in the scenario Jackie had described. It didn't matter. Even if she was carrying some other store's shopping bag Max would have still followed her: down the escalator and along the lower level of the mall to Burdine's, through the store, outside and down an aisle in the parking area to a Mercury sedan, a big tan one, an older model. He knew who the younger woman was and where she lived. But nothing about this one, getting in the car with her shopping bag and driving off.

Max wrote the license number in his notebook and went back inside to find a pay phone. His old pal from the Sheriff's office, Harry Boland, head of the TAC unit, would be home now having a bourbon. They'd talk—Max would ask him to have someone call him at the office, later, with the name and address.

Ordell said, "It was like that monster in the movie *Alien*, the one ate people? He's looking at Sigourney Weaver in her underwear and it don't mean shit to him. You want to yell at him, 'That's Sigourney Weaver in her underwear, man. What's wrong with you?' "

Louis said, "Gerald reminded you of that?"

"The way he didn't take Melanie out and jump on her. They go in the kitchen, he fixes her a cup of coffee."

"It worked out," Louis said, committed now, no getting off.

"Yeah, old Melanie."

"Would you have shot him?"

"If I had to."

"If you *had* to—the guy's beating the shit out of you. . . . You mean if you got mad?"

Talking the way they used to a long time ago. Ordell grinning at him. In the Mercedes on the way to Simone's house, early Tuesday evening. Louis knowing why Ordell had him staying there now. Not to be entertained. The main reason, to keep an eye on the cash Simone was bringing home. Ordell getting him more and more involved in his business.

Monday night, late, Ordell had taken him to the self-service storage place off Australian Avenue in a warehouse district, rows of garage doors, one after another: Ordell careful, making sure they weren't followed and there was no one around who might see them. He removed the padlock, raised the door of the space he'd rented, and there they were in his flashlight beam: all kinds of assault weapons converted to full automatic, boxes of silencers that reminded Louis of parts in a factory bin, the M-60 machine gun and LAW rocket launchers they'd taken from Gerald's place that day. Ordell said tomorrow night or the next, all this shit would be packed, loaded in the van, and driven down to Islamorada in the Keys, put on Mr. Walker's boat and taken over to the Bahamas. Mr. Walker would make the delivery to the middleman who bought the stuff for the Colombian druggies and get paid. A good two hundred thousand worth of weapons here, less expenses, would bring his total up close to a million in the bank over there.

Telling all this to Louis in the dark, confiding.

Even giving him the key to the padlock, so he could bring over a few guns, TEC-9s, still at Simone's house.

Louis hearing the familiar voice of his old buddy,

certain now it wasn't Ordell trying to use him, it was Melanie.

Ordell saying, "You appreciate this kind of situation, Louis. It can make you rich, yeah, but you see some fun in the idea too, huh? You see funny kind of things that happen nobody else sees. You know what I'm saying? You the only white guy I ever met understands what the fuck I'm ever talking about. Melanie don't. Melanie can say funny things without knowing it. But when she thinks she's funny, she ain't. Like we in the car coming home from Gerald's? You hear her? She says, 'You two guys are still a couple of fuckups.' See, she thinks she can say that after shooting the man. Like she's kidding and I'm not gonna say nothing."

"You didn't," Louis said.

"No, but I remember it. See, she disses you and thinks it's funny. I don't like to be dissed in a kidding way less it's somebody I respect."

Louis said, "You trust her?"

"I never have," Ordell said, "from the minute I first met her laying in the sun. I keep an eye on her, she can still surprise me, like having that gun. Little Walther .32—you believe how loud it was? She must've stole it off me and I didn't even know she had it. Where else she gonna get a pistol like that cost eight hundred? She ain't gonna buy it."

Louis said, "I'd keep both eyes on her."

Ordell's gaze moved from the road, Windsor Avenue, to Louis. "She trying to work you against me? . . . You don't have to say, I know the woman.

She gonna look at every angle, make sure she lands on her feet. She shot Big Guy five times, didn't she?"

"Four," Louis said.

"Okay, four. The piece holds seven loads. How come if she wants me out of this, she didn't do it when she had the chance? You know why? 'Cause she ain't sure you can take it all the way. You could've shot me and Big Guy at the same time, but you didn't do it. Melanie's thinking hey, shit, 'cause he don't have the nerve? She's the kind, wants to know who's gonna win 'fore she puts her money down."

"Why do you keep her around?"

Ordell grinned at him. "She's my fine big girl, man. Now I got you watching my back. . . ."

"You take too many chances," Louis said. "You expose yourself. Too many people know what you're doing."

"High profit," Ordell said, "high risk. I need the people till this's done. I know who I can trust and who I can't. The only one worries me right now is Cujo, I mentioned to you. They got him up at Gun Club. I called, they don't have a bond set on him yet. I'd like to get him out of there and send him on his way, only I'm afraid the bond's gonna be too high to get him one without the cash, and I don't have it right now. I *don't* think they'll get him to talk about me right away. He'll act tough for a while, and all I need is a couple more days. Get my ass out of here."

They turned off Windsor onto 30th Street and pulled up in front of Simone's stucco Spanish-looking house, Ordell saying, "You take those TEC-9s over to storage?"

"I'll do it tonight."

Ordell saying, "You never told me, you bone that old woman or not?"

18

Nicolet stopped in during prime time Tuesday evening, showed his ID, shook hands with Max, shook hands with Winston, and said, "Winston Willie Powell—I was a kid my dad used to take me to the fights at the Convention Center in Miami? I saw you beat up on Tommy Laglesia and a guy named Jesus Diaz, Hey-*soos*. I remember thinking, A name like that, he'll never make it. You won thirty-nine professional fights, lost only a couple on decisions?"

"Something like that," Winston said.

"It's a pleasure to shake your hand," Nicolet said and sat down next to Max's desk, his back to Winston. "It's a pleasure meeting you too," he said to Max. "All the stories I've heard about you, I mean when you were with PBSO, closing homicides in two, three days."

"You better," Max said, "or you're in trouble."

"I know what you mean," Nicolet said. "The longer a case sits there, nothing happening . . ." The phone rang and he paused until Winston picked it up. "I have kind of a problem I think you could help me with, Max. Having been in law enforcement, you know the airtight case we have to have to get a conviction."

"All I know about Ordell Robbie," Max said, "is where he lives, and I'm not absolutely sure of that."

Nicolet grinned. "How'd you know it was about him?"

"I've been waiting for you to stop by."

"It's about him indirectly," Nicolet said. "You know the guy that shot the FDLE agent, Tyler? We're convinced he works for Ordell."

"Hulon Miller, Jr.," Max said. "I've written him several times going back to when he was sixteen years old."

Nicolet said, "Is that right?" squinting at Max to show how interested he was, laying it on.

This had to be a big favor the guy wanted.

"Seventeen arrests, I think nine or ten convictions," Nicolet said, "this is a tough kid, knows the system intimately. We got him with a stolen gun, a stolen car. . . . We *saw* him at Ordell's house. In fact it was right after we saw you stop by there."

"Last Friday," Max said. "You also have him for attempted murder, assaulting a federal officer, concealed weapon, discharging a firearm . . ." The phone rang. Max looked over as Winston picked it up again. "What else?"

"He knows he's in deep shit," Nicolet said, "but now he's a star 'cause he shot a cop. I mean out at the jail. Limps around there—I put a nine through him that almost took his dick off, I wish it had. It was those fucking smoke-glass windows in the car, I had to fire at him blind."

"So he won't talk to you," Max said.

"He gives me dirty looks."

"You have enough to threaten him with."

"He knows all that. I try a different approach, I tell him, 'Cujo, my man, I could've killed you; you owe me one. Let's talk about Ordell Robbie.' He goes, 'Who?' 'Tell me what you know about him.' 'Who?' I go, 'Man, you sound like a fucking owl.' So he's in there, no bond . . . I get an idea, go see him. 'How about if I get you bonded out, man? Would you like that?' Now I've gotten his attention. I tell him, 'You only have to do one thing for me. No snitching, only this one thing. Introduce me to Ordell. Tell him I came to you before, weeks ago, looking for guns. That's all you have to do, I take it from there.'"

Max waited. He said, "Yeah?"

"That's it. I get next to Ordell, smile a lot, kiss his ass, and he shows me his machine guns."

"You just said there's no bond."

"That's right, but I can get the federal magistrate to set one."

"How much?"

"Twenty-five thousand. But, see, it's only if you'll write it, to help us out."

"Who puts up the collateral?"

"There isn't any. No money changes hands. That's why I say you'd be helping us out."

Max smiled. He looked over at Winston, off the phone now. "You have to hear this. He wants us to write a twenty-five-thousand-dollar bond with no premium, no collateral, on a guy who's been arrested seventeen times and shot a cop."

Now Winston was smiling.

Nicolet glanced over his shoulder at him.

"As a favor. What's wrong with that?"

"You're talking about a guy," Max said, "who's the highest kind of risk that he'll take off, who's a threat to the community . . . He shoots somebody, another cop, he runs and we're holding his paper."

Nicolet was shaking his head. "Wait, okay? I guarantee the guy won't be out of my sight. But even if he does run, you won't be out the twenty-five, I promise. I got the magistrate's word on it. She knows exactly what we're doing, that it's not the ordinary kind of bond situation."

"What if she dies, retires, gets transferred, hit by lightning—come on," Max said, "you think I'm crazy? I'm gonna sign my name to a promissory note for twenty-five grand on your word that it'll never be called for payment?" He looked over at Winston. "You ever hear of anything like this?"

"Yeah, I have. I know a bondsman in Miami done it," Winston said. "Was ten grand. The case got shifted to another court after the guy ran? The new judge says he'd never approve this kind of bullshit in the first place, made the bondsman pay up."

"I'll get it in writing," Nicolet said.

Winston shook his head.

Max said, "Have the magistrate sign a statement saying it's a phony bond? It's hard enough getting them to sign warrants." Max paused. "Against my better judgment I'll go along with you partway. We won't charge the ten percent fee if you can get someone to put up the collateral. How about yourself? You have a house?"

"My ex-wife's got it," Nicolet said.

"It's just as well," Max said. "Another reason it won't work, everybody on the street will know Hulon cut a deal. He might as well wear a sign, 'I fink for ATF.' Most likely if he doesn't run, he's dead."

Nicolet had that squinty look again. "I thought you'd go for this."

"Why?"

"You were a cop, you know what it's like. You'd see it as worth a try."

"You have my sympathy," Max said. "How's that?"

"I guess you have your problems too," Nicolet said. "Like you write a bond on a guy and he disappears? . . ."

"We go get him," Max said.

"But you can't find this one 'cause he's hidden away in the Federal Witness Security program? You have any high-bond defendants might disappear on you like that?"

Max looked at Winston. "Now he's threatening us."

"Ask him," Winston said, "he's ever had his head punched off his shoulders?"

Nicolet looked around to give Winston a grin. "Hey, I was putting you on. We're on the same side, man."

Winston said, "Long as you don't step over the line."

Nicolet looked at Max and raised his eyebrows, innocent. "I was kidding, okay?"

Max nodded. Maybe he was, maybe he wasn't. The guy was young, aggressive, dying to make a collar, put Ordell Robbie away. Max was all for that. He said, "Check out a guy named Louis Gara, released from Starke, I don't know, a couple of months ago. Check with Glades Mutual in Miami. Get next to him, I think he can take you to Ordell."

They talked about Louis Gara for a few minutes and Nicolet left.

Winston said, "One of the calls was for you. Gave me a name . . ." Winston looked at his notepad. "Simone Harrison, lives on 30th Street?"

Max shook his head. "Never heard of her."

"Drives a '85 Mercury?"

Simone did Martha and the Vandellas doing "Heat Wave" and then "Quicksand" for Louis, Louis nodding his head almost in time, drinking rum this evening, her drink. He started clapping his hands and Simone had to tell him, "No, baby, like this," show him where the beat was. The rum helped loosen him. She did Mary Wells doing "My Guy." Did Mary Wells and Marvin Gaye doing "What's the Matter with You, Baby," and held her hands out for Louis to join her, do the Marvin Gaye part. Louis said he didn't know the words. Actually he didn't know shit but was a big fella with muscle on him, big hard bones, a lot of black hair on his white body. She said, "Listen to the words, sugar. It's how you learn them." Told him, "Here, do this," showing him how to hold his hands limp and move his hips sloooow, see? Simone giving him a dreamy look to quiet him down and quit watching his feet, saying, "It's up here, baby, in the center of you," hand on her tummy, "not down there on the floor."

He took hold of her, still moving.

"Let's go in the bedroom."

"We can't dance in there, baby."

When he started moving his hands over her and got one up underneath her skirt Simone said, "What you looking for in there?"

"I found it."

"Yeah, I think you have."

"Let's go in the bedroom."

"Baby, don't tear my underwear. They brand new today."

"I could, easy."

The new undies reminded her of the mall, meeting the girl she was supposed to meet, and she said, "We have to put the money away. Can't leave it sitting out."

"I will."

"Have to hide it."

"I'm gonna hide the weenie."

They said cute things like that, white boys did. Even big middle-age jailbirds.

"You are, huh? You feeling good, baby? Yeaaaah . . . But don't tear my underwear, okay, sugar? You like to tear underwear, lemme put on an old pair for you."

Max rang the bell and waited, hearing the faint sound of music he gradually identified as vintage Motown, the sound familiar, but couldn't name the vocal group or the number they were doing. He rang the bell and waited again, close to a minute, before a woman's voice said, "What you want?"

"Ordell," Max said, staring at the peephole. Too dark for the woman to see him unless she turned the porch light on.

"He ain't here."

"I'm supposed to meet him."

"Where?"

"Here. He said nine o'clock." It was about ten to.

"Wait a minute."

He could hear children playing across the street, little black kids, Max thinking it was past their bedtime, they should be inside.

A man's voice said, "What do you want?"

"I already told the lady, I'm meeting Ordell."

There was a silence.

"Are you a cop?"

"I'm a bail bondsman. Turn the porch light on, I'll show you my ID."

The man's voice said, "I thought it was you."

Sounding confident now.

The door opened. Max saw Louis Gara standing there in a pair of pants, no shirt, fingering the thick mat of hair on his chest. Max took a moment to make the connection: both friends of Ordell's, it could explain Louis being here but not what he was doing with the woman.

Louis said, "You aren't meeting Ordell. He would've told me."

"So you're working for him," Max said. "Well, I'm looking for both of you, so it's not like I'm wasting my time."

He walked in brushing Louis with a shoulder that turned him off balance to hit the door, banging it against the wall. Max glanced at him.

"You okay?"

The woman said, "I don't want no rough stuff."

She stood holding her housecoat closed, barefoot but wearing makeup, her face highlighted blue and red, her hair done up for a party. What was going on here? Both of them half undressed, Puerto Rican rum and Coke bottles on the coffee table but no glasses, the Motown sound filling the room. Max said, "Ms. Harrison, what group is that?"

"The Marvelettes," Simone said, " 'Too Many Fish in the Sea.' Like it's getting in here." She walked over to the stereo and turned it off.

Max watched her. "Does this guy live here?"

Louis was standing by the coffee table now. The woman walked past him, touching his bare arm, to sit down in a deep-cushioned rocker and cross her legs, showing Max some thigh. She said, "You want to know anything about Louis, why don't you ask him? He standing right there."

"I'm sorry to bother you," Max said. "He and I can step outside to talk."

"No, it's all right." Simone leaned over to pick up a Coca-Cola bottle, some left in it. "Long as you behave yourselves."

This woman was going to watch.

It was hard to tell her age with all that makeup and the way her hair was piled on her head and what looked like a strand of pearls running through the hairdo.

"Louis used to work for me."

The woman said, "Oh, is that right?"

"When he left he busted the front door of my office and took a couple of guns."

Louis said, "What ones?" with a straight face. "You mean the Mossberg and the Python?"

Max saw four years of state prison in Louis's pose, hands on his hips showing his muscle. What he didn't see was the dead stare, that convict look in Louis's eyes, more glazed now than threatening, Louis too drunk to pull it off.

Max said, "Louis, you're never gonna make it."

The guy didn't know what he was doing.

"Where're the guns?"

Louis shrugged his shoulders, or flexed them.

"In your car?"

"He loan it to somebody," Simone said. "His car

ain't here, or any guns. You gonna search my house, see if I'm lying?"

"He can't," Louis said.

Max turned to him. "You want to call the cops?"

"You try looking around, I'll stop you," Louis said.

Max wished he had his stun gun with him. He brought the Browning auto out of his jacket, the inside pocket, and put it on Louis. "Sit down, okay? If you come at me, I'll shoot you. It won't kill you but it'll hurt like hell and you'll limp for the rest of your life." He glanced at the woman. "It might even save his life."

She nodded, sitting in her rocker. "It might."

"Guy gets out of prison, he does everything he can to go back."

"He can't help it," Simone said. "You know the story, the scorpion ast the turtle could he ride on him acrost a stream?"

"I don't think so."

"This scorpion ast a turtle could he ride on him acrost a stream. The turtle says, 'No way, and let you sting me?' The scorpion says, 'I do that we both'd drown. You think I want to kill myself?' Turtle says okay. They get out in the middle of the stream? The scorpion stings him. Now they drowning and the turtle says, 'You crazy? Why'd you do that?' The scorpion says, 'I can't help it, man, it's my nature. It's the way I am.'"

Max nodded. "That's a good story."

"Scorpion says, 'It's the way I am,'" Simone said.

"It's the way he is too, and every one of them I ever met that come out. They can't wait to go back."

"I'm going to look around your house," Max said.

"You ain't asking, are you?"

Max shook his head.

"You know what your guns look like? You can identify them?"

"Shotgun and a revolver."

"All right, go ahead," Simone said. "You find any other guns, or you find something else and you take it? The man's gonna come after you. Understand? Man that has more guns'n you ever saw in your life."

Louis sat erect gripping the arms of his chair, looking at it step by step, thinking, Wait a minute, what happened here? The woman's riding him on the bed, he's about to let go and bounce her off the ceiling, and now this guy's going around searching the house?

The doorbell rings. She gets up saying it must be Ordell wanting something, rings the bell 'stead of walking in on them. Comes back in the room, it ain't Ordell, some man. Puts his pants on, goes to the door. Jesus Christ, it's Max Cherry. So, what's the problem? How does Max know about this place if Ordell didn't tell him? Lying about meeting Ordell, but maybe he isn't. So let him in. You can take him. He mentions the guns, shove it in his face. Oh, you mean the Mossberg and the Python? Deadpan, no expression. If he doesn't think it's funny, fuck him. What can he do? He can't prove anything.

But it wasn't like that. It happened too fast and he wasn't ready. He should have thought about it some more before letting him in. Comes in and he's *in*, he takes over.

He said to Simone, "I'm not in shape."

"You look fine to me, baby."

"I thought I was yesterday, but I'm not. I don't feel that edge. You know, *ready*."

"You talking crazy now. You have the man's guns?"

"Not here."

"Then what you worried about? He ain't the police."

"What if he was?"

"Well, you wouldn't have let him in, would you? Baby, you just messed up in the head a little from being in stir. I seen it do that to people."

"That's what I'm saying. Inside, I was in shape. I come out—you can lose the edge fast, your sense of . . . you know."

She sighed. "Yeah, I know, baby." Looked up to see Max and said, "Uh-oh."

Max coming out of the hallway with a Saks Fifth Avenue shopping bag, the pistol stuck in his waist.

"That's the something else I mentioned you best not take," Simone said, and looked over at Louis. "You see what's happening? You my witness I didn't take it. Was this man here you used to work for."

Louis waited for Max to say something about his guns, but he was speaking to Simone.

"Tell Ordell we're even. I left something in the bedroom for him."

"What," Simone said, "a receipt?"

Max gave her a smile and Louis wondered if he'd missed something, if the two of them knew each other. Max was speaking to her again saying, "I'd have Ordell pick up those machine guns you have in your closet, tonight, or as soon as possible. The police find them here, you could lose your house."

Max was leaving now. Simone raised her hand and waved it at him, like waving him off.

Louis watched her, thinking about the TEC-9s in the closet he was supposed to take out to the storage place. He turned his head to see Max open the door and walk out with the shopping bag. Louis continued to stare at the door.

Simone got up and headed for the bedroom.

Louis was thinking he should not drink rum. Or he should find a glass and have another one. "Rum and Coca-Cola," the Andrew Sisters. He had started this afternoon in the bar at Ocean Mall, Casey's, hiding out from Melanie, thinking of her as a female cannibal. Bourbon this afternoon, rum this evening, nothing to eat in between . . . You had to be in shape for this, the same as you had to be at Starke to get through each day. It took a lot of effort.

Simone came in the living room holding a wad of bills in one hand and a gold wristwatch in the other. She said, "That man works? Has a job?"

Louis watched her sit down at the coffee table and begin counting hundred-dollar bills.

"He's a bail bondsman."

"I wondered," Simone said, " 'cause he don't know shit about robbing people."

19

"You brought me a present."

That was the first thing Jackie said, looking at the shopping bag: taking a guess but not too happy about it, no gleam of fun in those green eyes. Max shook his head, holding the bag out to her.

"Take it."

She wouldn't, she slipped her hands into the back pockets of her jeans and he had to smile.

"It's yours. The same one you gave the young girl and she turned around and gave to a woman, I bet anything, wasn't part of your plan. It turns out she's a friend of a guy named Louis Gara, an ex-con who used to work for me and now, it looks like, works for Ordell. You going to ask me in for a drink or not?"

He watched her stare at the Saks bag another few moments, trying to figure it out for herself, then turned and went into the kitchen. Max closed the door and followed her; he set the shopping bag on the kitchen table. She didn't ask him one question getting ice from the refrigerator, making drinks, so he started telling her about it: how he got the woman's name and address and went there, ran into Louis Gara, who had stolen guns from the office. . . . Jackie handed him his drink. She listened, but didn't look that interested. He took a sip and told her about searching the woman's house for his guns and finding the Saks bag in the bedroom closet, ten thousand dollars in it. Jackie was watching him now. He reached into the bag, brought out ten one hundred-dollar bills, and spread them on the table saying all of them were marked, right there.

Now she was interested.

"You took his money."

That was the second thing Jackie said.

Max said, "He owed it to me," and explained that part of it, the thousand representing the premium on her bond, as a matter of fact, and how he left the watch and the rest of the money, nine thousand, with the woman.

"But you took a thousand."

"I knew it was his. . . ."

"Was it easy?"

"You mean did they give me any trouble?"

She motioned, tilting her head to the side, and he followed her white T-shirt, her hips moving in the jeans, through the living room in lamplight and out onto the balcony to stand in the dark by the metal rail.

"I mean, was it easy to pick up his money and walk out with it?"

"I took what he owed me, that's all."

"You're sure it's his money."

"I know it's what you delivered, it's marked."

"So it was okay to take it from the woman's house."

Jackie quietly playing with him three floors above dark shapes down in the yard, trees, shrubs, dots of orange light lining a walk, high enough for Max to feel alone with her in the night. He knew what she was doing.

"Ordinarily I wouldn't."

"This was different."

"Considering the kind of guy he is."

"And how he came by the money?"

"Not so much that."

"You know he won't call the police."

"That occurred to me."

"It made it easier."

"In a way."

"So it didn't bother you, to take it."

She was close enough to touch. He said, "There's a difference." She waited and he said, "I don't see what I did anything at all like walking off with a half million."

"You could if you tried," Jackie said. "We know he won't call the police. . . ."

"No, he'll come after you himself."

"He'll be in jail."

Max watched her raise her glass and then glance into the living room and saw light reflected in her eyes for a moment. He wanted to touch her face.

She said, "Think of it as money that shouldn't even be here, the way it was made. I mean, does anyone have a legal right to it?"

"The feds," Max said, "it's evidence."

"It may be evidence if they get their hands on it," Jackie said, "but right now it's just money. They want Ordell. They're not interested in the money, because they don't need it to convict him. They'll look for it—it's gone, misplaced? . . . What is it they say, the whole package never gets to the station?"

"You're rationalizing."

"It's what you do, Max, to go through with it once you start. Not have any lingering doubts that might trip you up. You're looking for work, aren't you?" In her quiet tone. "I know you're looking for something you don't seem to have."

He touched her face. Saw her expression, waiting.

He kissed her, moving his hand over her hair, and had to look at her face again, pale in the dark, her eyes not leaving his as she reached out and dropped her glass over the rail. There was no sound. He felt her hands slip inside his jacket and around him, her fingers on his body. Now Max reached out over the rail and let his glass fall.

* * *

In the moment she looked at him and said, "You took his money," he knew they would be in this bed before too long and that his life was about to change.

They made love in the dark, on the sheets with the spread pulled down. Took off their clothes and made love. She left and returned still naked with cigarettes and drinks. There were so many things he wanted to say to her, but she was quiet now, so he was quiet. He would tell her later to give them Louis Gara; it would get her points. She reached over and put her hand on him.

They made love again with the lamp on and this time he knew his life had already changed.

She said, "We're alike. We weren't before, you were holding back, but now we are. You and I." She said, "Could you pass out complimentary tropical punch in little plastic cups? That's my alternative and it's unacceptable."

He looked at her lying naked against the headboard with her drink and a cigarette.

"So the money's a way out."

She looked at him with that gleam in her eyes.

"I'm not saying it wouldn't be fun to have."

He thought about it and said, "Or, we're taking it so the bad guys won't get it."

"If you like that one," Jackie said, "use it."

He nodded, giving it some more thought.

"Hold on to the money and see what happens. It's not worth going to prison over. But if the feds, as you say, don't care about it . . . I mean if it's not there and they don't see it as that big a deal . . . Or they don't have time to count it at the airport, when you come in, and they get some of it . . ."

"But not the whole package," Jackie said.

Those eyes smiling at him as she drew on her cigarette and he said, "Let me try one of those."

20

Ordell asked Jackie to come to the apartment in Palm Beach Shores Wednesday, after her flight was in, for what he called the Pay Day meeting.

Tonight, the weapons would be taken down to Islamorada and put on Mr. Walker's boat. He'd make delivery tomorrow and get paid and the next day, Friday, Jackie would bring all his cash over from Freeport.

Louis arrived. He said Simone was getting dressed still; told him to say she'd be a little late. Ordell said you can't enter that woman's house and not get taken to bed, can you? Louis wasn't saying. Ordell asked had he moved the TEC-9s to the storage place. Louis said early this morning and gave Ordell the padlock key. Outside of that Louis wasn't saying much; acting strange.

Jackie arrived. He introduced her to Louis, his old

buddy, said, "This is Melanie," and was surprised the two women looked about the same age and wore the same kind of blue jeans. The difference in them, Melanie's were cut off at her butt, she was messier-looking and had those huge titties. Jackie had that fine slim body on her and Melanie, you could tell the way she looked at Jackie, wished she had one like it.

The first thing Jackie did, she took him out on the balcony and said, "I don't want any more surprises. We do it the way I lay it out or no Pay Day."

Ordell said he didn't know what she was talking about. What kind of surprises?

"The woman I gave the money to passing it on to someone else." Her saying it surprised Ordell.

"How you know she did that?"

"I was there, I saw it."

"Well, you weren't sup*pose* to be there."

"I hung around," Jackie said, "thinking you might pull something like that."

Ordell told her it was his money, he could do what he wanted with it. And Jackie said not if she was going to stick her neck out; it had to be done her way or not at all. So then Ordell explained how he'd wanted Simone there to see how it worked, account of Simone would be the one receiving the money from her on Pay Day. Simone, he said, ought to be here any minute. Nice woman, Jackie would like her.

They went in the living room and he said for Louis to call Simone, tell her to get her tail over here, they were waiting on her. Louis didn't know the number, the place he was staying, and it irritated Ordell. He picked up the phone from the counter and called her himself. Let it ring and ring. No answer.

"She's on her way," Ordell said and looked at Melanie, now that she'd served drinks, resting her big butt on the sofa. He said, "Leave us now, would you please?" in a nice tone of voice.

Melanie hauled herself off the sofa and came past him into the kitchen. Ordell turned at the counter.

"Girl, I said leave us. Go on outside and play in the sand." His tone cool now.

She didn't say a word, went past everybody into the bedroom. "Now she gonna pout," Ordell said. "Fix her hair, have to find her sandals, find her bag, her sunglasses . . ." They waited. When she came out Ordell said, "You have a nice time, hear? . . . And don't slam the door."

She did, though, slammed it hard.

Ordell shook his head. Louis was giving him a look. So was Jackie. Neither of them saying anything till Jackie glanced at her watch and said she had to go in a minute.

"Where?"

"I have to meet the ATF guy."

"That works on my nerves, you talking to him."

"If I didn't, *this* wouldn't work," Jackie said. "I'll tell him Friday's the day. He'll stop me at the airport, mark the bills . . ."

Ordell shook his head. "Man, I don't like that part."

"It washes off," Louis said.

"I'll tell him we're doing it the same way as before," Jackie said. "They'll follow Sheronda. . . . I hate to leave her holding the bag, so to speak."

"She come home that time and look in the bag?" Ordell said. "Love the underwear Simone gave her. Sheronda don't know nothing about the money. She thinks it's some kind of game we rich folks play, exchanging gifts."

"I got potholders," Jackie said.

"See, that's how the woman thinks."

"Tell her I could use a blouse," Jackie said, "size six, something simple."

Ordell said, "You giving her a Macy bag this time?"

"The one Simone gives me. Right, we'll make the switch at Macy's," Jackie said. "Simone knows what I look like, doesn't she?"

"She saw you with Sheronda."

"So if she doesn't come soon . . ."

"Lemme be sure of this," Ordell said. "Simone goes to the dress department with her Macy bag. . . ."

"Designer clothes."

"She waits for you to go in the place where you try things on."

"The fitting room. There's a sign over the door."

"Why we doing it in there?"

"I have a hunch they'll be watching me. We can't risk switching bags out in the open, or even in the dining area. You're sure about Simone? You can trust her?"

"She like a big sister to me."

"It has to be a woman who comes in."

"She'll do fine," Ordell said. "You come out with her Macy bag and go meet Sheronda. Simone peeks out, waits for Louis to give her the sign nobody's watching. She leaves the store, gets in her car, and I follow her here. Make sure nothing happens to her."

Jackie was anxious now to leave, not wanting the ATF man upset with her. Ordell walked her down the hall to the elevator and pressed the button. She said to him, "Once I deliver, I'll have to trust you."

"Meaning the deal we have," Ordell said. "I been trusting you all this time, haven't I? We agreed on ten percent of what you bring in and that's what you gonna get."

"And a hundred thousand if I go to jail."

"Yeah, that too. But you haven't told me where I put it for you."

The elevator came and the door slid open. She held it, looking at him. "Give it to the bail bondsman, Max Cherry. He'll take care of it."

Ordell squinted his eyes saying, "Max Cherry?" Surprised and wanting to think about this. "You and him friends now? You told him the deal?"

She got on the elevator still holding the door and turned to him shaking her head. "He won't know where it came from, only that it's my money."

Ordell said, "Max Cherry? You know what you doing?" The door slid closed as he was saying, "Don't you know bail bondsmen are crooks?"

Ordell stood there a few moments. He knew he wasn't ever going to pay Jackie her cut or for going to jail. That didn't bother him. What did was her be-

---

ing tight with Max Cherry. That might be something to think about.

Back in the apartment, he and Louis alone now, Ordell said, "Tell me what's bothering you."

Louis said, "Max Cherry."

And there he was again, springing up. Max Cherry. "You ran into him?"

"He ran into me," Louis said. "He knew where to find me."

Jackie stopped at Ocean Mall to try Ray Nicolet again, to tell him about Louis. Show what a good girl she was, cooperating. Max had said last night not to waste time; he'd already called Nicolet and told him where Louis was staying. This morning she had tried Ray's beeper number before flying out and again when she got back. She would use the phone in Casey's, check her messages before trying his beeper again; it was too late to get him at the office. Jackie walked in the entrance off the mall.

There was a crowd in here already. The phone in use. A fat guy lounged against the wall with the receiver wedged between his shoulder and his chins, nearly hidden. She turned away and saw Melanie sitting near the end of the bar, Melanie swiveled around on her stool watching her, motioning now to come over. She raised her glass.

"Have a drink."

"I'm waiting for the phone."

"Good luck, that guy's been on it a half hour."

Jackie said, "I'll find another one. See you."

Turned to leave and Melanie said, "I know what this gig's about, the whole thing, what you've been doing for him. Have one with me, I'll tell you a secret."

Melanie was drinking rum and Coke, she said for the past hour with guys hitting on her, creeps in tourist outfits. Jackie ordered a beer, took a sip, and a guy put his hands on their shoulders. Would they like to come over to the table, "join me and my buddy for a refreshment?" Without looking at him Melanie told him to fuck off, and rolled her eyes at Jackie.

"That's what we need, some bright conversation. Where you from? . . . Oh, really? Where are *you* from? . . . Ohio, huh? No shit."

Jackie said, "How long have you been with Ordell?"

"This time? Almost a year. I've known him forever."

"Why did he make you leave?"

"So you wouldn't be nervous. He wants you to think I'm only there to give him blow jobs, obviously not a security risk." Melanie laid her arms on the curved edge of the bar and her cheek against her shoulder, looking at Jackie on the stool next to her. "The day before yesterday I saved his fucking life. This Nazi was about to beat him to death and I shot the guy four times, in the heart. Today he tells me to go play in the fucking sand."

Jackie sipped her beer. "You shot a Nazi."

"One of those white-supremacy geeks. We were out there to rip off all this military stuff he's got. You know, army weapons? I was supposed to get Gerald naked so Ordell'd be sure the guy wasn't armed when he shot him. Once in a while Ordell gets into the rough stuff, but usually he plays it safe, has these crazy black kids that work for him do the heavy shit. They killed two other guys that happened to be there.''

Jackie said, "Where was this?"

"At Gerald's. Out by Loxahatchee. You know Mr. Walker?''

Jackie nodded.

"Ask him about Ordell, he'll tell you. Mr. Walker's my buddy, he sends me good stuff.''

"That was your coke," Jackie said.

Melanie made a face to show pain. "Oh, man, listen, I'm sorry about that. I hope they don't come down on you, Jesus, on my account. Ordell should've told you it was in your bag. You know, or at least asked if you'd mind bringing it. That wasn't right.''

"He said he didn't know about it.''

"You believe that? Yeah, well, I guess you have to trust him. If you're in it, well, what're you gonna do, you're fucking in it, you just have to hope for the best. I'd have second thoughts, but then I know him. You get busted, they'll come down on you a lot harder than on the dope thing. I mean, forty-two grams compared to all those fucking machine guns and rockets? Come on . . . And all that cash?" Melanie raised her head enough to sip her drink, then laid her cheek against her shoulder again, her eyes not leaving Jackie's. "Having that money in your flight bag, even ten thousand, must be tempting. Fifty thousand the time you were busted?"

Jackie nodded.

"He fucks up, which he's been known to do," Melanie said, "and they get the cash, they get my dope, and they've got you hanging. It's a shame, you know it? Your next trip, you're gonna have over half a million in your flight bag." Melanie's eyes softened and so did her voice. "If you've thought of cutting Ordell out of this one, I sure wouldn't blame you."

Jackie smiled.

"You think I'm kidding," Melanie said.

"Dreaming," Jackie said.

"You know how easy it would be? Because he trusts you," Melanie said, "and won't be anywhere near that mall? Pull one more switch, up front. That's it. Listen, if you're interested and you need help . . ."

"Keep it between us girls?" Jackie said.

"Why not? What's that son of a bitch ever done for us?"

"But he'll know."

"By the time he figures it out, you're gone, on your way to California, Mexico, shit, anywhere, Alaska, just go. Get someplace and then decide what to do. You don't want to think too much first and talk yourself out of it. You know, allow it to work on your nerves."

"You've done this before," Jackie said.

Melanie turned her head, as if to check if anyone was listening, and looked at Jackie again. "I've scored cash, dope, jewelry, a painting once that was supposed to be priceless and turned out to be a fake. Cars now and then—ninety miles an hour out of there one time in this asshole's Mercedes I dropped at the airport in Key West. Get clear and then take off, like to Spain. No backpacks, they'll check you for drugs. You're too old for a backpack anyway. Wear a dress, good shoes, you'll walk through Customs in almost any civilized country except here and Israel. You don't want to go to Israel anyway, it isn't safe."

Jackie said, "That's it?"

"How it's done," Melanie said.

Jackie said, "Thanks," and slid off the stool.

Melanie's head came up in a hurry. "Where you going?"

"Find a telephone," Jackie said.

It was close to seven by the time she got the message Nicolet had left on her machine, ran home to change, and arrived at Good Samaritan in a print dress and earrings. Nicolet brought a chair over as she spoke to Tyler, smiling, working up to touching his hair and giving him a pat on the head. Not exactly in a motherly way, though he looked about seventeen sitting up in bed with a can of beer. There were flowers on every surface that would hold them and get-well cards upright on the windowsill. Nicolet got her seated. She brought out a cigarette and lit it.

"I have something to report," Jackie said. "Two things. I deliver the money the day after tomorrow.

Same arrangement, four thirty at The Gardens Mall.
I'll be meeting Sheronda."

"The one lives on Thirty-first Street," Nicolet said
to Tyler.

Tyler nodded. "She married to Ordell?"

"They live together," Jackie said, "but he's not
there all the time. Sheronda has no idea what's going
on. She's nice, I hope you don't have to arrest her."

Nicolet said, "What kind of deal can she offer?"

"She was too scared to open the door," Tyler said.
"She gives you Ordell as the man the money's for,
that ought to get her off." He said to Jackie, "What's
the other thing you have for us?"

"Ordell has a guy working for him named Louis
Gara."

She saw Tyler look at Nicolet and she turned to
him, next to her, as he said, "Have you met him?"

"This afternoon, at an apartment in Palm Beach
Shores. I don't think Gara lives there, but I can probably find out."

Nicolet reached down to lift a grocery sack from
the floor to his lap. "You talk to him?"

"Not really."

"What's he do for Ordell?"

"I don't know yet. I suppose I could ask."

"You want a beer?"

"I'd love one."

Nicolet reached in the sack, twisted a can from a
six-pack, popped it open, and handed Jackie the can,
wet, ice-cold. She took a sip.

"I know he just got out of prison. They seem to be pretty close for a white guy and a black guy."

Tyler was grinning at her. "You're doing all right."

"Enough to get me off?"

"We know about Louis Gara," Nicolet said, "he's a bank robber. Late last night we put the house where he's staying on Thirtieth Street, West Palm, under surveillance. This morning about five thirty he comes out, walks over to a house on Thirty-first where Sheronda lives, gets car keys from her, and takes off in a Toyota parked in the drive. The car's registered to him. He's followed to a self-service storage place off Australian Avenue in Riviera Beach. You've seen them, they look like rows of garages?" Nicolet looked at Tyler. "That must've been where Cujo was going."

Tyler, nodding, said, "I know, to drop off the piece. And we thought it was the bump shop."

That went by Jackie; she let it go.

"He opened one of the doors," Nicolet said to her, "brought a cardboard box out of the trunk of his car, and put it inside. He comes out and returns to the house on Thirtieth. Three thirty this afternoon he drove to the apartment you mentioned in Palm Beach Shores."

It surprised her. "Then you must've seen me go in."

"I wasn't there," Nicolet said. "I was at the storage place with a search warrant and a locksmith. We enter—it's full of guns, all kinds, even military weapons. . . . Some of the stuff we know was taken from that farm out by Loxahatchee, where the triple homicide took place on Monday.''

"One of them," Jackie said, "a white supremacist named Gerald something?''

"Yeah, it was on the news yesterday, front page of the paper. This morning too.''

"I didn't see it," Jackie said. "A woman named Melanie, Ordell's girlfriend, told me she shot Gerald four times in the heart. Is that right?''

They were both staring at her. Nicolet said, "Four, yeah, but not in the heart.''

"I didn't think so.''

"She told you she did it? When was this?''

"About an hour and a half ago at Casey's, right after I left the apartment. That's where she lives. She said some, quote, 'crazy young black kids' who work for Ordell killed the other two.''

Tyler and Nicolet looked at each other again and Nicolet said, "She tell you their names?''

Jackie shook her head, drawing on her cigarette. She said, "I don't even know Melanie's last name," and saw Nicolet look at Tyler again.

"You know a Melanie?''

"I don't think so," Tyler said. "What's she look like?''

Jackie said, "Well, she has very large tits. . . .''

Tyler said, "Yeah?''

"A lot of blond hair. She's about thirty but looks much older.''

Nicolet said, "Why'd she tell you about it?''

"Because she's pissed at Ordell. She shoots a guy

who's beating him up and he won't let her sit in on the Pay Day meeting," Jackie said. "Pay Day is what happens Friday. He likes to use code names. Rum Punch is his deal with the Colombians."

Nicolet said, "We used that once, Rumpunch, one word, rounding up Jamaican posses. So we can put Ordell at the scene. What about Louis, was he there?"

"She didn't say."

Nicolet was quiet for a moment.

"If Melanie's pissed off enough at Ordell . . ."

"She won't leave," Jackie said. "I'm sure of it."

Nicolet looked at Tyler. "You know what they say, once they've had a black guy. . . . But I want him more than I bet she does. There's gonna be a fistfight," Nicolet said to Jackie, "over who gets him now, ATF or Faron's people and the Sheriff's office. You said there's one more arms delivery coming up?"

Jackie nodded. "That's what he told me."

"They've got enough there, it could go down anytime. My beeper goes off, man, I'm out of here."

Jackie said, "What if Ordell's not with them?"

"I don't care if he is or not, I know it's his dump," Nicolet said. "We can show weapons there were lifted from Gerald's place and take Ordell on the homicides *and* the guns. It's better than what we had going before, I love it. Get him sent to Marion, that would be beautiful. You're in lockdown there twenty-two hours a day."

Jackie put her beer can on the floor; got up, crossed to the lavatory, and dropped her cigarette in the toilet. She came out and stood by the door to the hall.

"When am I off the hook?"

"When it's over," Nicolet said.

She looked at Tyler. "I'm your case, not his."

"That's right," Tyler said, "and I'm calling the state attorney tomorrow, get him to agree on a no-file."

Jackie said, "An A-99?"

Tyler smiled at her. "Why don't you stay a while? We'll get rid of Ray . . ."

Louis turned off Windsor Avenue to Thirtieth Street and Ordell, riding with him, said, "Keep going. I don't like that Chevy back there. Guy sitting in it."

"I didn't notice him," Louis said, looking at his mirror. "Was he black or white?"

"How do I know he's black or white in the dark?"

"It's a black neighborhood," Louis said.

"I *know* that. But they got brothers are cops too, if you never heard of it. Look, no lights on. Too early for her to be in bed. Go 'round the block."

Louis turned on South Terrace and then on 29th and came around again to Simone's street. Now they came past the Chevy and Ordell looked back at it.

"Shit, I can't tell. Go on to Sheronda's, see what it looks like over there, Thirty-first Street."

"I know where it is."

"Man, they make it hard for you. No, forget going over there. Turn around up here at the corner and go back. Man, I have to find out right now. The house's dark . . . Guy in the Chevy could be staking out anybody. Or it's some man thinks his woman's running around on him. The cops don't know you, so how could they know you staying there?"

"Max Cherry knows."

"Hey, fuck him. We going in the house."

They parked in the drive and entered through the side door. "Not one light on in here. This ain't like her," Ordell said in the kitchen. "Well, we only have to look one place, where she keeps her Motown records. If they gone, she's gone."

Louis said from the living room in the dark, "They're gone."

Ordell said, "Shit. Well, let's look for the money."

Louis said, "You know if she's gone the money's gone. It's *why* she's gone."

"What? You saying nine thousand dollars gonna make her run off, leave her home? Man, that hurts me. I was gonna give her two for helping me out."

"She left your watch," Louis said.

"It has something to do with Max Cherry," Ordell said. "Comes in her house, it scared her."

"It scared me," Louis said. "How'd he find out I was here?"

"Man, this shit works on my nerves," Ordell said. "Tells me I should change the plans around. First thing, I have to find somebody to take Simone's place."

"Don't look at me," Louis said.

"I'm not looking at you, I'm thinking who I can use."

"You're looking at me," Louis said in the dark.

"You could do it."

"Walk in the women's fitting room? How would I work that?"

"Shit," Ordell said. "Lemme think."

Max didn't touch the phone: on the table with the lamp and digital clock, next to Jackie's side of the queen-size bed. It rang while she was in the kitchen, three times and stopped. She would have picked it up standing by the counter in a man's dress shirt she put on leaving the bedroom, nothing under it, lighting a cigarette now, talking to Ordell or Ray Nicolet about Friday, the clock reading 10:37, while she finished making their drinks. Max got a cigarette from the table on his side.

Five left in the pack he'd bought this morning before seeing the lawyer about filing, the lawyer suggesting he and Renee sell the house, divide their assets, and that should do it. Then in the kitchen before coming to bed Jackie saying, "This is all you have to do," describing his part in making off with a half million or so. "Okay?"

Nothing to it. If changing your life was this simple, why was he ever concerned about the everyday stuff, writing fifteen thousand criminal offenders? He said to Jackie, "Okay," and was committed, more certain of his part in this than hers. Until she stood close to him in the kitchen and he lifted the skirt up over her thighs, looking at this girl in a summer dress, fun in her eyes, and knew they were in it together. He did. And was sure of it when they made love, again looking at her eyes.

The times he had doubts, he was alone. Wondering if she was using him and he would never see her again once it was done.

It was 10:45.

He used to think that with the name Max Cherry he should be a character. Max the legendary bail bondsman who told wild stories about skip-tracing, collaring felons on the run, to the patrons of the Helen Wilkes bar. He did tell one—how he drove all the way to Van Horn, Texas, to return a defendant who'd skipped on a five-hundred-dollar bond—and they didn't get it, failed to understand the street value of what that kind of dedication meant. He settled for being a man of his word instead of a character, and that could be why he was here.

Jackie came in with their drinks, the man's dress shirt hanging open. "That was Faron." She handed Max his glass and moved around to her side of the bed. It was 10:51.

"You have a nice chat?"

"Ray just got word they're moving the guns, three guys, and left. So I called Ordell hoping to God he wasn't one of them. We don't want to lose him now, after all this."

Max watched her place her drink on the night table and light a cigarette before slipping into bed, propping her pillows against the headboard.

"He must've been home," Max said.

"At the apartment. I told him he was about to go out of business and he carried on for a while. That's what took so long, getting him calmed down. I told him we'd better bring the money in tomorrow. He said Mr. Walker was in Islamorada, he'd have to get in touch with him. I said, drive down and get him. Take him to Miami and put him on a plane to Freeport, he has to be there to meet my flight. I told him if he wanted his money he'd better get it out of there quick. He said okay, Mr. Walker would take his cut and put exactly five hundred and fifty thousand in my bag. Now I have to get in touch with Ray before I leave in the morning."

So calm about it. Max said, "Why?"

"Tell him it's tomorrow."

"If he's not at the mall, so much the better."

"I *want* him to be there, that's part of it. Let him search me and see I'm clean."

"You're starting to sound like people I know."

Jackie said, "I'm going to tell Ray that Ordell changed his mind. With what's happened he's afraid to bring in all of his money, but will need about fifty thousand for bail, in case he's picked up."

"He'll need more than that."

"Don't be so literal. This is what I tell Ray."

"But you show him the money at the airport."

"Well, you know I'm not going to show him the whole amount. He'll see fifty thousand."

"Where's the rest of it?"

"In the bag, underneath."

"What if he looks through it?"

"He won't. He'll be expecting fifty thousand and there it is, on top. He didn't search my bag the last time."

"You're taking an awful chance."

"If he finds it, I say Mr. Walker put the money in and I didn't know it was there, like the coke."

"Then you're out, you get nothing."

"Right, but I tried and I'm not in jail."

"Keep it simple, huh?"

"Exactly." She said, "Oh," thinking of something else. "Is tomorrow okay?"

He had to smile. "I'll try to be there."

Jackie was quiet for several moments smoking her cigarette, staring off.

"It's pretty much the same plan. Your part doesn't change."

"You're gonna have surveillance all over you."

"I know. That's why you don't make a move till I come out of the fitting room."

"In a dress."

"Well, a suit, an Isani I've had my eye on. The only thing I don't like about it now," Jackie said, "Simone's disappeared, and guess who's taking her place. Melanie."

21

The three jackboys in the self-service storage unit, Sweatman, Snow, and Zulu wearing his black bandanna and sunglasses, had brought cardboard boxes to load the different weapons in, wrapping each piece in newspaper. The guns didn't have to be packed too good going from here in the van to halfway down in the Keys and put on a boat. It got so hot with the door closed using flashlights, Zulu turned the van around, drove it partway in, and put on the headlights. There wasn't anybody outside from here to Australian Avenue so what was the difference? When they finished packing the boxes he'd turn the van around again and they'd load it through the rear. When they heard the voice outside they thought it was somebody's radio. When they stopped to listen and heard the voice again they knew what it was, shit, a bullhorn, police telling them, "Come out with your hands up!"

The voice said something about they were federal officers and to lay their guns down and come out one at a time with their hands in the air.

Sweatman said, "How they gonna shoot us, they down the street? They have to be right there in front to do it."

Snow said, "Shit, we got all the guns we need."

Zulu said, "Sweat, get in the van and take a look out the back. See where they at."

He had pulled the van far enough into the unit that they could open the doors and get in without being seen. Zulu started looking through boxes, saying to Snow, "Where those throwaway rocket shooters we got out at Big Guy's?"

Sweatman came back and said they had both ends of this street blocked with green and whites and were some of them up on the roof too, laying down up there right across the street. Zulu turned to him with an olive-colored LAW rocket launcher in his hands, a tube twenty-four inches long with a grip, a trigger, sights, and writing on it with pictographs. "How to fire the motherfucker," Zulu said. "Each of us take one and get in the van."

Snow said, "I want my AK."

Zulu said, "We bringing AKs, but this the mother-fucker gonna set us free. See, here the instructions."

They all wore flak jackets with identifying letters on the back. Nicolet, ATF, huddled behind the radio cars with an agent from FDLE and an older guy named Boland who commanded the Sheriff's Office TAC unit. They stared at the lighted street of garage doors on both sides to the back end of a van sticking out of one of the units. The surveillance team said there were three of them, young black guys. Two jumped out when the van arrived; the driver backed it in first, then turned it around. Beyond the van, at the opposite end of the street, sets of blue gum balls were flashing. There were about fifty law enforcement officers on the scene.

"If they're all young guys," Nicolet said, "the one I want isn't there, so I'll need to take prisoners. The only problem I see, they have about a hundred and fifty machine guns, a big M-60, grenades, and half a dozen rocket launchers. It could drag on. These guys have more firepower than we do."

The TAC guy said, "But can they shoot?"

"I don't want to find out," Nicolet said. "Before they start firing rockets at us, I thought I'd go up there and toss in a flash-bang."

"The van's in the way," the TAC guy said.

"It's my cover," Nicolet said. "Bounce it in there off the roof of the van. The concussion knocks them on their ass and we'd have about seven seconds to get the drop on them. I need those guys alive."

Zulu had his sunglasses off to read the pictographs printed on the side of the LAW rocket launcher, holding the weapon in the van's headlight beam. " 'Pull pin,' " Zulu said. " 'Re-move . . . rear . . . cov-er and . . .' "

" 'Strap,' " Snow said. "Say remove the rear cover and that strap there."

Zulu said, "Yeah, this thing," and began reading again. "Now. 'Pull o-pen un-til . . .' Shit."

"Say to pull the motherfucker open," Sweatman said.

"It's what I'm doing," Zulu said. "You pull open your own one. Hey, like this."

His LAW rocket launcher was now thirty-six inches long.

Zulu said, " 'Re- . . .' The fuck is that word there?"

Snow said, " 'Re- . . . *lease*.' Yeah, it say to re-lease the . . . something. 'Release the safe-ty.' Yeah, that thing right there. Release it."

Zulu said, "Push it?"

Snow said, "Release the motherfucker however you suppose to release it. I think, yeah, you push it. Then the next word it say to aim. You ready to shoot."

Zulu said, "I am? What's this next one say?"

Snow said, " 'Squee- . . .' I think it say 'Squeeze.' "

Sweatman said, "What's it say on top there? That 'Danger'?"

Snow said, "Lemme see. Yeah, it say 'Danger . . . rear blast . . .' "

Something hit the top of the van. They heard it and then saw it, a round kind of long thing like a stick of dynamite, bounce past over their heads to land among cardboard boxes. They heard a sound like *poof.* For maybe two seconds they stood frozen before the concussion grenade exploded with a flash of blinding light and a bang so loud it slammed all three of them against the front of the van.

They were on the pavement now with their rocket launchers and machine guns, dazed, blinking their eyes in the dust clouding the headlight beam, looking up at flak jackets and shotguns.

Nicolet hunched down next to Zulu. He picked up a rocket launcher, glanced at the instructions, and laid the weapon across the jackboy's chest.

"Couldn't read it, could you? You dumb fuck—we wondered what you were doing. See?" Nicolet said, "You should never've dropped out of school."

Ordell had Louis meet him at a bar on Broadway in Riviera Beach, all black in here, Louis looking over his shoulder sitting at the bar, Ordell telling him, "You all right, you with me." Ordell was edgy too, in his mind, anxious and smoking cigarettes with his rum drink: wanting to drive by the storage place, see what it looked like, and having to drive down to Islamorada tonight, pick up Mr. Walker, and get him on a plane to Freeport. Everything at once. It would be good, though, to get out of town this evening and not show himself too much tomorrow either.

He said to Louis, "The main thing I want to tell you: Melanie goes in the place where they try on clothes."

"The fitting room," Louis said. "I make sure no suits are around before she comes out."

"Do that," Ordell said. "But then don't leave. You do, she gonna walk with the Macy bag. You know what I'm saying? Take the bag from her and split, don't wait. She give you any trouble, punch her in the mouth. What I mean, you have to take it from her, dig? Else Melanie's gone and *it's* gone. All of it. Five hundred and fifty thousand, man."

22

Thursday, on the Freeport to West Palm flight, Jackie spent fifteen minutes in the lavatory rearranging her bag. The five hundred thousand she put in first took nearly half the space. She tucked lingerie around the edges, covered the money with blouses and two skirts and tied it all down, tight. The remaining fifty thousand went in last, across the top.

When she came out, a guy who'd been to Freeport to gamble said, "I'm waiting for a drink and you spend half the flight in the can. Soon as we land I'm making a formal complaint."

Jackie said, "Because I was airsick?"

"How can you be a stew if you get airsick?"

"That's why I'm quitting."

"I'm still gonna make the complaint."

"Because I was airsick," Jackie said, "or because I called you an asshole?"

It confused him. He said, "You didn't call me that."

Jackie said, "I didn't? Okay, you're an asshole."

It was her last flight.

Ray Nicolet was waiting on the top floor of the parking structure. He took the wheels from her saying, "We have to stop meeting like this."

"You said that the last time."

"So? It's true, isn't it? We could meet someplace else when this's buttoned up. What do you think?"

"We could, if I'm not in jail."

"Faron called the State Attorney's Office. You were no-filed this morning in circuit court."

Like that—hearing it in a dim parking structure among empty cars. She stopped and waited for Nicolet to look back and pause. "Are you saying I'm off the hook?"

"Free as a bird. I expect you to deliver the goods though, finish the job. How much you have this time?"

"What I told you," Jackie said, "fifty thousand. He's pretty sure he's going to need bail money."

"If a bond is set, which I doubt," Nicolet said. They reached Jackie's Honda. As she unlocked the trunk he said, "Last night we scored what would bring him another two hundred grand, easy, and took three of his boys without firing a shot."

Jackie raised the trunk lid. "But you didn't get Ordell."

"Not yet. One of 'em will give him up. Or the guy you met in the hospital, he's ready to flip." Nicolet placed the wheels in Jackie's trunk and got in the car with the flight bag. It was on his lap unzipped and open by the time Jackie slid in behind the wheel.

He said, "That's fifty thousand, huh?" looking at the packets of hundred-dollar bills, each bound with a rubber band. "It doesn't look like that much."

"I was told ten thousand in each pack."

"You didn't count it?"

"I never have. It's not my money."

"He might've slipped some coke in here. Did you check?"

She watched Nicolet's hand feel through the packets of currency and into the folds of a skirt.

"Mr. Walker promised he'd never do that again."

"Where your curlers?"

"I didn't bring them."

She watched his hand move to a pair of black heels wedged into one side. His fingers touched the shoes, then moved again to pick up one of the packets. He held it close to his ear and riffled the bills with his thumb.

"Ten thousand, right."

Nicolet rubbed the bills between his fingers and handed the packet to Jackie. "There's coke dust on it. You feel it? Half the money in Florida, I think if you tested it you'd find dust."

Jackie fingered the bills. Ten thousand in her hand. She smiled, saying, "Are you tempted?"

Nicolet looked at her. "What, to put one of these in my pocket? If I did, I'd have to let you have one too, wouldn't I? Or we could take what we want, there's no receipt with it. Nobody knows how much is here but us." He took the packet from her and dropped it in the flight bag. "I've seen more money sitting on tables in dope houses, in cardboard boxes in property rooms. I've seen all kinds of dirty money lying around, and I've never been tempted to take any. How about you?"

Jackie said, "You're kidding."

"No, I'm not."

"Try to skim off Ordell?"

"Or me," Nicolet said. "Once I mark it, this fifty grand belongs to ATF."

"How would I take any of it," Jackie said, "if I'm being watched every second?"

"That's what I want you to understand, you'd be dumb to try. You put this fifty in your shopping bag, it's what I expect to find when I look in Sheronda's. You going with Saks bags again?"

"Macy's this time."

"Why?"

"Ask Ordell."

"I can hardly wait," Nicolet said.

What do you wear to walk off with a half million bucks? Go casual, with running shoes, or dress up? Max gave it some thought and put on his tan poplin suit with a blue shirt and navy tie. His instructions were to hang around the Anne Klein display on Macy's second level, women's clothes, and watch for Jackie to walk out of the fitting room at approximately four thirty. Give whatever surveillance they had on her time to clear out. Then approach a salesclerk and tell her his wife thinks she left a shopping bag in one of the dressing rooms. With beach towels in it.

He had read that a prompt man was a lonely man, and it seemed to be true: now a few minutes past four standing outside Gallery Renee, a newspaper under his arm, looking in at green paintings, no sign of Renee—until he heard her voice.

"Max?"

Sad, or maybe uncertain. She was behind him, standing in the middle of the concourse, Renee holding one of the busboy's paintings upright on the floor.

"It came this morning," Renee said. "A process server delivered it, like a court summons."

"That's what it is," Max said.

She seemed so small holding on to that big canvas, unaware of shoppers walking around her. It was a trait of hers, being unaware: stopping to talk in the middle of traffic, in doorways of public places, in a parking lot, a car waiting to take the space where she stood.

"I was sadly disappointed," Renee said. "I thought you might show more class than have a stranger inform me. After twenty-seven years, Max, do you think that's fair?"

He said, "Why don't you come over here out of the way?" Shoppers were looking at Renee, then turning as they went by to glance at him. "Here, let me help you."

She walked into her gallery, Renee wearing a baggy, Arab-looking outfit, layers of material in tan and white, black stripes running through it. Max followed, stopping to catch the glass door swinging at him. He got the painting inside and leaned it against the table in the center, ready for more of Renee, her tiny head with its cap of dark hair sticking out of the Arab outfit, eyes brightly made up. Renee looking at the canvas now.

"I was positive Ralph Lauren would buy one, after I schlepped it all the way over there. I said, 'Hang something that has some life in it, energy, instead of those stupid English horse prints.'"

"What do they know," Max said, for some reason sympathizing with her. She was looking at him now, her expression telling him she was still sadly disappointed.

"You could have come to me, Max, told me what you planned to do."

"I did come to you. You were busy with your cheese and crackers."

"I sold three of David's paintings at the reception. Another one yesterday."

"You're doing all right."

"Twenty-seven years," Renee said, "as if they never happened."

He was thinking, No, they happened, they must have. But didn't say anything. Why start? Get her to accept the fact and leave. It was ten after.

Renee was looking at the painting again, the cane field, with kind of a lost expression, or vacant. She said, "We've had our differences. We've grown apart, there's no getting around that. I have my art. You have . . . I suppose your business." She looked at him now. "But we had some good times too, didn't we, Max?"

Was that from a song?

Good times too, didn't we?

He tried to think of one in particular. There was that period in the beginning when he couldn't keep his hands off of her and he thought she would get to like it, way back, before he had given up trying to think of things to talk about. Maybe there weren't any, at least not memorable ones, the entire twenty-seven years but not counting the periods of separation. Those weren't bad. The times with Cricket singing country to him, Cricket in what passed for moonlight . . . It was funny, he liked waitresses. Jackie was different. Intelligent but horny, in a quiet, unhurried way—reaching into his pants on the balcony and dropping her glass over the side, taking hold of him. He would never get tired of being with her. . . . He said to Renee, "Yeah, there were times," and saw her chin quiver.

She could do that, make it quiver anytime she wanted, and it seemed to always work; he'd feel guilty or sorry for her without knowing why.

She looked at the cane field again saying, "What's the use talking about it, you've made up your mind." Renee sighed. "If this is what you want . . ."

"Don't you think it makes sense?"

"I suppose." She raised her head to look at him

again, the chin no longer quivering. "But that doesn't mean it isn't going to cost you."

Max said, "Renee, you never came cheap."

Frieda, the saleswoman in the fitting room with Jackie, stood in a fashion-model slouch, hand on her kidney with fingers pointing to her spine. She said, "The Isani's absolutely darling on you."

Jackie looked over her shoulder at the mirror. "I'm used to a narrower skirt."

"Your figure," Frieda said, "you can go straight or fluid and swingy. You're traveling abroad?"

"I thought I'd start out in Paris, drive through the wine country."

"Oh, you're going by yourself?"

"I may," Jackie said. "I'm not sure."

"Mix and match with separates, that silk jersey I showed you? It travels beautifully." Frieda picked up several dresses from the back of a chair. "You like a narrow skirt, why don't you try on that Zang Toi, with the off-center slit?"

Jackie glanced at her watch. "Okay. I know I want the suit. In fact I think I'll wear it—get out of this uniform."

"The black silk, it's a knockout on you," Frieda said, and walked out.

Louis and Melanie were by the Donna Karan New York display, Louis watching the opening in the paneled wall that said FITTING ROOM over it, down at the far end of the designer section. Jackie had said at the meeting to wait here and not come in before twenty-five after. It was getting onto that now. He was pretty sure he'd have a better view of the fitting room over by the Dana Buchman display. Once Melanie went in, he wanted to be sure he saw her when she came out. Women shoppers would creep by and he'd feel them looking at him. Like what was he doing here? Melanie kept busy. She'd hold up a blouse to look it over and then throw it back on the shelf. She never folded anything up again. She was all butt in her white tube skirt and denim jacket, but didn't look too bad. He was surprised she was interested in clothes, because she didn't seem to have many, always wearing those cutoffs. Louis was holding the Macy's shopping bag they'd exchange for the one Jackie had. He was afraid if Melanie carried it she'd be shoplifting, stuffing things in the bag. They didn't need mall security on them, guys in green sport coats and peach-colored ties. At least they didn't pack. Louis had on his new light-blue sport coat. He wished this was over. Melanie made him nervous.

He said, "Come on," motioning to her, and crossed the aisle to the Dana Buchman display. He looked back, motioning to her again, and bumped into a woman as he turned to look toward the fitting room. Louis said, "I beg your pardon," saw the woman's lifeless eyes, and realized, Christ, it was a manne-quin. Melanie came up to him saying, "You talking to yourself, Louis?"

He thought this would give them a straight-on view of the fitting room, but there was another display between it and them, mannequins standing around in poses. They did look real. Louis nudged Melanie and said, "Come on."

She said, "What're we waiting for? Why don't I just do it?"

"She said four twenty-five."

"It's almost that now."

Louis motioned to her and she followed him to a section that said MICHI MOON on a display board. Melanie, looking at the clothes, said, "Far out."

"Get ready," Louis said, handing her the Macy's bag, beach towels in it Jackie had told him to buy. Now he saw a woman with dresses over her arm come out of the fitting room and start hanging the dresses on different racks. There were a few women in the area prowling through the racks, only one guy; he was sitting in a chair over by Ellen Tracy reading a newspaper. He looked up, toward the rear area, and Louis said, "Jesus Christ, it's Max."

Melanie turned from Michi Moon saying, "Who?"

"That's the guy I used to work for, Max Cherry. What's he doing here?"

"I don't know," Melanie said. "Is he a cross-dresser? Ask him."

"He's married, he could be here with his wife," Louis said, and remembered that Max didn't live with his wife, they were separated. Or he was here with his girlfriend, that could be. Louis glanced toward Melanie. She was gone, walking toward the fitting room. He looked at Max again, about fifty feet away, Max strolling off too, over to the Anne Klein section. Dressed up in a suit and tie, he had to be with some woman. Louis stepped to one end of the Michi Moon display. Melanie was already in the fitting room.

"That's cute. What's the top, cotton?"

"Linen," Jackie said. "The skirt's sand-washed silk."

"It's nice, and I don't usually go for a full skirt."

"This's the look," Jackie said, "fluid and swingy."

"It's okay on you. How much?"

"Five fifty for the jacket . . ."

"Christ."

"Two sixty-eight for the skirt."

"I guess you can afford it," Melanie said, handing Jackie her shopping bag. "We could've worked this. You know that, don't you? You would've made out a lot better than you're going to, believe me."

Jackie pushed open the louvered door to a dressing room, went in with Melanie's shopping bag, and came out with her own.

"That's the same one," Melanie said, "the same towel? Are you putting me on or what?"

Jackie's hand went inside the bag, dug beneath the towels, and came out with a packet of hundred-dollar bills she held in Melanie's face, letting her stare for a moment before shoving the money down in the bag again. Jackie didn't say a word.

Neither did Melanie. She took the bag and left.

In the dressing room again with the door closed, Jackie transferred the five hundred thousand from her flight bag to the shopping bag Melanie had brought. Packed her uniform in the flight bag. Put on the nifty black silk. . . . She'd have to pass on the Zang Toi with the off-center slit; no time to try it on. Pay for the suit and the Isani separates, which she'd take with her. But ask to leave her flight bag at the cashier's counter, pick it up later.

Okay, then as she's walking out say to Frieda, "Oh. Someone left a shopping bag in there. Looks like beach towels." She exits. A minute or so later Max enters, he's looking for a shopping bag his wife thinks she left in a dressing room. Beach towels in it.

Once she was out on the floor in plain sight she would have to appear anxious, helpless, and run off looking for Nicolet, *some*one, to tell what happened. How Melanie, just a minute ago, barged into the fitting room, grabbed the money, and took off. Melanie, the one who shot the guy—Jackie sounding a little frantic by then. Nicolet would go into action, do whatever they did, and when he got back to her with or without Melanie there would be questions, all kinds, but none, Jackie believed, she couldn't handle. The only real problem she saw down the road was Max.

Melanie had come out of the fitting room and moved through racks of clothes heading for the aisle. She caught a glimpse of Louis still at the Michi Moon display. He saw her and she saw him cutting across the floor now past Dana Buchman to head her off. They met in the aisle at Donna Karan New York.

"What're you doing?"

He said it with kind of a strung-out, spacy look that scared her for a moment.

"I'm getting out of here. What do you think?"

"Lemme have the bag."

"Fuck you. I can carry it."

She tried to push past him and he caught her by the arm to pull her around.

"Goddamn it, gimme the bag."

"What're you gonna do, hit me?"

"If I have to."

He was ready, his fist cocked close to his shoulder. He grabbed the open edge of the bag and when she tried to pull it away, holding on to the loop handles, the bag started to tear open at the seam—not much, but enough that she let go saying, "Okay, okay, take it, Jesus, what's wrong with you?"

He said, "I'm carrying it."

She said, "All right. You've got it. What'd you think I was gonna do, run off with it?"

He said, "If you had half a chance," holding the bag in his arm now, all that money crushed against his cheap sport coat. He turned and walked off. She followed him down the down escalator staring at his hair, at his scalp beginning to show through at the crown; followed him off on the main floor past girls offering perfume samples and out into the mall. Louis stopped.

Melanie said, "Remember where we came in?"

He looked up at palm trees, at turquoise structural

beams and the skylight ceiling way up there. He started off in the direction of Sears.

Melanie said, "The other way, Louis," and he stopped. "We came in through Burdine's, remember? Where you do your shopping?"

Louis didn't say anything. He wasn't strung out; maybe hung over. Definitely scared, Melanie decided, out of his element, the ex-con in a crowd of civilians he didn't know or trust, holding the shopping bag against his body.

She said, "Let's try to act like we're just plain folks, Louis. What do you say? Turn around. That's it, now put one foot in front of the other and we'll stroll down to Burdine's. Pick up a snappy straw hat to go with your snappy jacket. Would you like that?"

Max watched the fitting room from the Anne Klein display. He saw a woman who had to be Melanie, a lot of hair and a big can, duck in and come out again, gone, as he concentrated on the fitting room. The salesclerk went in, stayed a few minutes, and came out to the cashier's counter with clothes over her arm. No sign of Jackie yet. The clerk was ringing up the sale now, folding the clothes in boxes, two of them, and slipping the boxes into a shopping bag. There she was, finally. Jackie in a neat, short-sleeved black suit. With her flight bag. She placed it on the floor behind the counter, came up, and began looking around then, going into her act: agitated, distracted as she spoke to the clerk, paid for the clothes with cash and took the shopping bag from the counter. Max had spotted a young woman earlier who seemed to be hanging around and could be working surveillance, but didn't see her now; and none of the women shoppers poking through the racks would qualify for law enforcement. Jackie was walking away now, still looking around, anxious, the clerk saying something after her. Jackie kept going. Max watched her until she was out of sight down the aisle, heading for the mall. He waited. No one followed her. The salesclerk was alone now by the cashier's counter.

It was Max's turn.

Nineteen years dealing with people who took incredible risks. If he walked over to that counter he'd find out what it was like.

After, he was to go home and wait for Jackie's call. She'd come to the house or he'd meet her somewhere. Or he might not hear from her right away. Nicolet could be into it and she'd have to face him, tell her story, and stick to it. She said, "If you come through, I can handle it." And after that they would sort of drift away, disappear.

Apart or together. She didn't say and he didn't ask. And then what? She said, "Let's see what happens."

The one thing Max was sure of, standing by Anne Klein designs, he was in love with her and wanted to be with her, and if he had to suspend his judgment to do it, he would, with his eyes wide open. If he saw she was using him . . . He didn't think so, but if she was . . . Well, he would have to handle that, wouldn't he?

At the moment, walking away from Anne Klein toward the salesclerk at the cashier's counter, he was changing his life for good.

"You don't want a snappy straw? Hey, a pair of jams. Or what about a Hawaiian shirt? Louis, look."

Driving him nuts.

Melanie right behind him all the way through Burdine's poking at his arm, telling him to look at hats, shirts, bathing suits. He pushed through the door and was outside, for a few moments with a sense of relief, facing the aisles of empty cars in late sunlight. Shit, but then he couldn't remember where they'd parked. Melanie would pick up on it any second now. It wasn't this aisle right in front of the entrance, it was two or three over, he was pretty sure. To the left. When they came in the mall Louis was thinking of why they were here, not memorizing where they'd parked. Come out the wrong door you were in trouble. People lost their cars at malls all the time. It was why they had security guys driving around in those white utility cars, GMC Jimmys, to help you out. He could wait for Melanie to walk off.

But she didn't, she was waiting for him. She said, "You have no idea where we parked, do you? Jesus, but if you two aren't the biggest fuckups I've ever met in my life . . . How did you ever rob a bank? You come out and have to look for your car? You better give me the bag, Louis, before you lose it."

He didn't say anything.

"I'll hold it and you go get the car." She said, "No, that won't work. You don't know where it is."

He thought of hitting her.

"Or I get the car," Melanie said, running the words together, "we drive off, split the money, and each go our separate way. Fuck Ordell."

Punch her right in the mouth.

She said, "Okay, come on. It's this way, Lou-is. Here, give me your hand."

She stuck hers out, waiting. When he didn't take it she walked off and he followed after her, over to the second aisle and then cut between cars to the next one. She walked along the parked cars a little way and stopped.

"Is it in this aisle?"

"Yeah, down the end."

"You sure?"

He started off that way.

She said, "Lou-is," turned, and cut between cars to the next aisle.

He followed her. Sometimes when he was living in South Beach and drinking a lot he'd forget where he parked and have to roam up and down the streets. He'd had a few pops this afternoon before he picked her up. Melanie stopped.

She said, "Louis, I feel sorry for you, I really do." She said, "You need somebody to take care of you," and walked off swinging her can at him in that tight white tube skirt. She stopped, about to cut between the cars again, and turned to look at him.

"Is it this aisle or the next one over?"

————

He said, "This one," not caring if it was or not. He wasn't taking any more of this.

She said, "You sure?"

He said, "Don't say anything else, okay? I'm telling you, keep your mouth shut."

She seemed surprised, but then got her smirky look back, was about to speak, and Louis put his hand up, quick.

"I mean it. Don't say one fucking word."

Melanie said, "Okay, Lou-is . . ."

And told him he'd be walking around here all night looking for his car—got to say all that while he was reaching inside his jacket for the Beretta Ordell had given him. Once she saw it she shut up. Her face went blank. But then, Christ, she started talking again. Louis didn't hear what she said because right then he shot her. *Bam.* And saw her bounce off one of the cars. *Bam.* Shot her again to make sure and because it felt good. And that was that. He went down the aisle to his Toyota, where he'd said it was, got in with the shopping bag, and drove back this way. Coming to Melanie's tan legs sticking out from between the cars, Louis rolled his window down. He said to her, "Hey, look, I found it," and got out of there. One of those white Jimmys was coming up the next aisle.

Jackie hurried along the mall's upper level, breathless for the benefit of surveillance. (In actual fact anxious to put it on Melanie. That change in the plan, Melanie for Simone, was working out better than she'd expected.) Jackie headed straight for Barnie's Coffee & Tea Company on the edge of the café area, where Nicolet had hung out the time before.

He wasn't there.

She came out and two mall security guys in their green blazers almost ran her down, both with hand radios, dodged around her, and kept going. Coming away from Macy's she had noticed another security guy running toward Burdine's.

Jackie imagined Nicolet and his people, in contact by radio, were passing her along, telling one another: *Standing in front of Barnie's looking around. Moving into the table area now, she's all yours. Ten four, over and out.* Or whatever they said on police radios. Jackie still had her concerned look in place, a puzzled frown, when her gaze came to Sheronda with a tray from Stuff 'N Turkey and stopped.

Sheronda's eyes, above a large-size Coca Cola, watched as Jackie came over to the table and sat down, shoving her Macy's bag underneath.

"How're you doing?"

Sheronda put her Coke down and sat up straight, saying she was just fine. Jackie lit a cigarette.

She said, "The last time we exchanged gifts, a woman came by after I left and you swapped with her?"

"Simone," Sheronda said. "Nice lady, say she was Ordell's aunty. Yeah, she took the bag you put here and gave me the one she had."

"You know why we're doing this?"

"He say is like a game, you get surprises. Like the other time was nice underwear."

"The potholders are great," Jackie said.

"I didn't know what to get."

"I needed them—thanks."

"Ordell say this time we all bringing the same thing?"

"Towels," Jackie said.

Sheronda nodded. She smiled at Jackie watching her and lowered her eyes, innocent, no idea she was being used.

"But, you might be surprised," Jackie said and stubbed out her cigarette. "I have to go."

"Simone coming this time?"

"I don't know," Jackie said, "maybe. Take your time. Have something else if you want, there's no hurry." She took Sheronda's shopping bag from under the table and left.

Max came out of Macy's lower level to the mall's center-court pools and palm trees and headed off toward Sears, where he was parked outside. He passed the entrance to Bloomingdale's and came to the Gallery Renee.

There she was, standing by the table with the busboy, Da-veed showing her something in a magazine. The busboy looked up, saw Max, and paused. He said something to Renee and she was looking this way now. Max shifted the Macy's bag holding a half-million dollars to his right hand, away from the showroom window, and gave them a friendly wave as he passed. The busboy raised his hand, no finger, just a fist: a tough kid making out. Renee turned away.

The woman had no imagination.

A living mannequin stood posed in front of a ladies' apparel shop: a young woman with blond hair in gray jeans, a sequined cowboy shirt, and white fringed boots. She seemed poised to run. Or the way her hands were raised, to fend off something coming at her; though she would never see it with that blank stare, head cocked slightly to one side. A little girl stopped to touch the mannequin's fingers, touched, and pulled her hand back and ran to catch up to her mother.

Jackie, coming away from the café area, had paused to watch, waiting for the living mannequin to move. There was something familiar about the girl. Jackie, with her shopping bag, walked up to her and said, "How long do you have to do this?"

The girl didn't answer, her gaze leveled at Jackie's shoulder without expression, unblinking. For several moments Jackie stared at her with the feeling she was looking at herself. Blond hair and green eyes in a much younger version, but there she was, poised, ready to run or somehow defend herself. The one big difference, Jackie's eyes were focused. She saw rough times ahead she would have to feel and talk her way through. Face Nicolet, there was no chance of avoiding that. Maybe see Ordell again, it was possible. And finally come to a decision about Max.

That would be a tough one, because they were

alike, she felt good with him and knew he was doing this for her, not the money. She saw it in his eyes when she brought him along with her own eyes and could tell he knew she was playing with him, so it was okay. And yet he was his own person, a very decent guy, even if he was a bail bondsman—and had to smile thinking that, wondering if she sounded like his arty little wife. He was tender and he was rough too, in a good way that left her sore after. She said to him, "I don't think I can walk," and he said, "Then come back to bed." She would have to decide in the next day or so and she hadn't been that good at picking guys. When she told him, "Let's see what happens," she meant it. She liked him a lot. Maybe loved him. But didn't want to run off with him and learn too late it was a mistake. But how else did you find out? She needed to have the money in her hands to make an honest decision. And at the moment Max had it. She hoped.

The living mannequin changed her pose: came around to stand with her back to Jackie, fringed boots planted wide, fists on her hips, head cocked to stare dull-eyed over her shoulder, defiant. Without moving her mouth she said, "Will you get out of here?"

The poor girl trying to make a living. There were all kinds of ways. Jackie said, "You can do better than this," and walked away.

She didn't get far.

A guy with a hand radio was coming along the concourse toward her, noticeable in his suit among vacation outfits, casual wear. Jackie saw two more suits now and a young woman in a skirt and jacket carrying a shoulder bag, the suits spreading out as they approached, and now she saw Nicolet coming with a radio. Jackie waited.

When he was close enough she said, "Try to find a cop when you need one," and got ready for a rough time.

23

All Ordell wanted to know was, "Did you get it?"

No, Louis had to tell him how he's driving up to the apartment and sees two guys sitting in a car on Atlantic he's sure are watching the building and thinks they saw him go by. So he kept going around the block and now he was at Casey's, calling from there.

Ordell believed having a few pops, too, for his nerves. He tried to be patient with the man, saying, "I felt they was watching me, Louis; that's why I said to check. Now did you get it or didn't you?"

"I got it," Louis said. "Listen, there's something else I have to tell you."

"After I see the money," Ordell said, and told Louis how they'd work it. He'd get in his Mercedes like he was going out for cigarettes or a six-pack, just in his shirt-sleeves, an old pair of pants. Drive up to Ocean

Mall with the two guys following him. Park in back. Walk through Casey's and Louis would be waiting in his car, in front. They'd go someplace. . . . Ordell said he'd think of where and let him know. He asked Louis, "You count the money?"

Louis said he hadn't even looked at it yet; it was still in the shopping bag.

Ordell said, "Melanie must be dying to see it."

There was a silence on the line.

Ordell said, "Louis?"

"That's what I want to talk to you about," Louis said. "Melanie was giving me a hard time . . ."

"Not now," Ordell said. "I'll meet you in five minutes. Have your motor running."

As soon as he was in the car, Ordell reached around and got the Macy's bag from the back seat and held it on his lap with his arms around it, going "Hee hee hee," like a kid. When they were still on the Riviera bridge he said, "Go on up to Northlake, where all the car dealers are? We gonna leave this heap in a parking lot and get us one the police don't know about." When they were turning north on Broadway he said, "Hey, where's Melanie?" and looked around, like she might've been in back and he'd missed seeing her. "Where's my big girl at?"

"She bugged me," Louis said, "the whole time. Got nasty on me 'cause I wouldn't let her carry the bag. Started mouthing off . . . I couldn't remember right away when we came out where the car was parked, so then she got on me about that. 'Is it in this aisle, Lou-is? Is it in that one?' Man, she drove me fucking crazy the way she kept on.''

"So you left her there," Ordell said.

"I shot her," Louis said.

Ordell turned his head to look at him.

Louis could feel it. "I expect she's dead."

Ordell didn't say anything.

It was quiet in the car going up Broadway, Louis looking at black people on the sidewalks hanging out. He didn't know what Ordell was going to do.

"She wanted to split the money right there," Louis said. "Each of us go our separate ways and never come back."

Ordell didn't say anything.

Louis kept quiet, letting him think about it. Everything he'd said was true and he wasn't going to apologize for it. He had never shot anyone before and had thought about it all the way from The Gardens Mall down to Palm Beach Shores where he saw the two guys in the unmarked car. He would think of something else for a moment or so and then it would come into his mind all of a sudden—seeing her can in the tight skirt, seeing the look on her face, seeing her legs on the pavement—and for a second there he couldn't believe he had done it; but he had. He knew guys at Starke who'd shot people during arguments over practically nothing. A guy looking at another guy's girlfriend. Just looking. Maybe listening to their stories it had come to seem common to him. Being among bad influences.

He didn't feel too good.

Ordell said, "You shot her?"

"Twice," Louis said. "In the parking lot."

"Couldn't talk to her."

"You know how she is."

"You could've hit her."

"I thought of that."

Ordell was quiet for a minute.

"You expect she's dead, huh?"

"I'm pretty sure."

"Well, if you had to do it then you had to," Ordell said. "What we don't want is her surviving on us. Man, anybody else but that woman."

They were on Northlake Boulevard now, a big busy street full of car dealers and strip malls. Ordell said, "Pull over at that Ford place. On the street, don't drive in." He wanted to look at the money without taking it out of the Macy's bag. Give Louis ten grand to get a good used car for the time being, nothing that would attract attention.

Louis asked what kind. He was acting strange. Like coming out of being in shock.

"Just get a regular car," Ordell said. "You understand? Like the common folk drive. We have to do some slipping around here before we pull out tonight. I need my car. See if I can get a jackboy to pick it up and put a different plate on it. I left the keys. I want to see about getting some of my clothes too, at Sheronda's. Send somebody over there. I should've dressed when I come, 'stead of running out. I might have to sell the car—I don't know. But right now, my man, let's see what we have here."

Ordell pulled out a beach towel and threw it on the back seat. Pulled out another one saying, "They pretty, huh?" He threw it in back and looked in the bag. "All that money, it sure don't take up much space." Man, another towel inside. Ordell felt under it with his hand. Counted one, two, three packets with rubber bands, four, five . . . He ripped that next towel out of there, looked in the bag and felt his stomach drop, felt panic about to set in, and had to hold on tight and take a breath and let it out, telling himself to be cool, find out what was going on here, instead of taking Louis's head and putting it through the fucking windshield. He said, "Louis?"

If Louis did the rip-off he'd be ready for this moment, wouldn't he? Louis said, "What?"

"Where's the rest of it?"

Louis had a surprised look on his face now, or was acting dumb. He said, "How much is in there?"

"Maybe fifty," Ordell said. "Maybe not that much."

"You said five *hun*dred and fifty."

"I did, didn't I? So we light, huh, a half million."

"She came out with that bag," Louis said. "Never even put her hand in it and I didn't either."

"Came out of where?"

"The fitting room. It went down exactly the way it was suppose to."

"How long was Melanie in there?"

"Maybe a minute. She came right out."

"Louis, you telling me the truth?"

"Swear to God, she came out with the bag and I took it from her."

"Then what?"

"We left. Went out to the parking lot."

"Where you shot her."

"That's right."

"She ain't waiting somewhere with the half million I worked my ass off to earn?"

Louis said, "Jesus Christ."

"And you giving me this as my cut?"

Louis was shaking his head now, as if he couldn't believe what he was hearing.

"What'd you shoot her with?"

"It's in there," Louis said.

Ordell opened the glove box and brought out the Beretta. He smelled the barrel. It didn't tell him anything. He released the magazine and emptied it, one hollow point at a time, counting them, as they dropped into the Macy's bag. Two were gone out of a full load.

"Maybe I took two out," Louis said. "You fuck, I thought you trusted me. Now you'll have to wait, see if it's on the news."

Ordell kept looking at him, thinking as he stared. He said, "Okay, so it was Jackie Burke. I trusted her too."

"If she's got it," Louis said, "why didn't she take it all?"

Ordell nodded. "I have to think about that one. Then, I suppose, have to ask her." He reached into the bag, brought out a few hollow points, and began snapping them into the magazine. "See, if there was nothing in here but towels, then maybe she didn't have a chance to take it from her suitcase and ATF got it, or she hid it someplace in that mall. See, she had to show ATF the money at the airport. Okay, then the idea is it disappears and nobody knows where it went. Jackie, nobody. But her giving me this fifty— it's like she's telling me she took the rest of it. You know what I'm saying? Like she wants me to know it and is rubbing it in my face."

"I don't know," Louis said. "Either she has it or the feds."

"Or . . ." Ordell paused. "She gave it to somebody else first, before Melanie went in the dressing room."

It was quiet in the car.

Maybe a minute went by before Louis said, "Jesus Christ," in a quiet tone of voice.

Ordell, loading bullets in the magazine, looked up at him. "What?"

The man thinking of something that must've slipped his mind.

"You know who I saw there in the dress department?"

"Tell me," Ordell said.

"Sitting there reading a newspaper? I didn't think anything of it."

The man making excuses first, putting off saying it. Not wanting to sound dumb. Ordell waited.

"No—I did wonder what he was doing there, but didn't think it had anything to do with us. You know,

like maybe he was there with his wife or his girlfriend."

The man had to be out of excuses now. Ordell said,
"You gonna tell me who it was?"

"Max Cherry," Louis said.

Ordell looked out the windshield at traffic going
by, let his gaze move to look at the cars lining the
Ford dealer's lot, before turning to Louis again.

Louis was still there.

Something must've happened to him in prison.
Four years staring at the walls and drinking shine,
the man was burnt out, useless. Ordell said, "You see
Max Cherry in the dress department. We're about to
be handed half a million dollars—man, look at me
when I'm talking to you. And you don't think nothing
of him being there. Every time I ask you what's
wrong or what happened here, what would you tell
me?"

Louis frowned at him.

"Answer the question."

"I don't know what you mean."

Ordell shoved the magazine into the pistol, racked
the slide, and pressed the muzzle against Louis's
side.

"I said what would you tell me?"

Louis's eyes were wide open now.

"Yesterday I ask you, what's wrong, Louis? You say
it was Max Cherry knowing where you're staying. I
ask you what happened to Simone? You say Max
Cherry must've scared her. Say he scared you too.
Every time I turn around there's this Max Cherry the

bail bondsman. You worked for the man, you know he's a crook just like all of 'em. Money hungry, do anything to get it. You *saw* him, knowing what he is, and you let him take my fucking money right under your nose. Man, what *hap*pened to you?" Ordell pressed the barrel of the pistol as hard as he could into Louis's side, squeezed the trigger, and saw Louis jump with the blunt sound it made. Saw Louis's eyes open staring at him. He worked the barrel up higher on Louis's side, getting it under his arm, and shot him again, Louis pressed against the door. This time his head bounced off the window, fell forward with his chin against his chest, eyes open, and stayed that way.

Ordell said, "What's wrong with you, Louis?" He said, "Shit, you use to be a beautiful guy, you know it?"

Ordell left him there. He walked along Northlake Boulevard looking for the last car in the world anybody would expect to see him driving. He bought an '89 VW Golf with less than thirty thousand miles on it, maroon; paid fifty-two hundred for it out of the Macy bag.

Now he had to find a place to stay.

There was a woman in Riv'era Beach he used to see now and then. From the old school, did heroin 'stead of crack, hooked now and then. Yeah, saw her last night in the bar when he was talking to Louis and she kept looking at him. If he could remember her name . . .

24

They brought Jackie to the ATF office on South Dixie in West Palm. Nicolet removed a satchel charge from the chair by his desk so she could sit down. She asked him what it was. He said a bag of explosives and left her alone for about twenty minutes. To talk to his surveillance people, Jackie believed, and see if they had something to throw at her. While they were still at the mall she had told about Melanie coming into the fitting room and grabbing the money. They had her flight bag, so they must have spoken to Frieda, the saleswoman.

In the car coming here they told her Melanie was dead, shot twice, but no details. Nicolet, in the front seat of the ATF car, said, "You see what can happen?" Which meant he wasn't buying her story, or not all of it. The girl with the shoulder bag sitting next to her in back said, "That Unitel body mike isn't

worth shit in a mall. I couldn't hear anything but
Muzak.'' Nicolet glanced at her and the girl didn't
say another word. Jackie caught it. They had a hole
in their surveillance.

While Nicolet was away from the office Jackie
looked at photographs of weapons taken inside a
storage facility and thumbed through a copy of *Shotgun News*. No ashtrays, so she used someone's coffee
mug from this morning. The office, with two desks
pushed together, was smaller than Tyler's at FDLE,
messier, looking more lived in. There was a tagged
submachine gun on the other desk Jackie assumed
wasn't loaded.

Nicolet brought her a mug of coffee without asking
if she wanted one. A good sign. He had his coat and
tie off and didn't appear to be armed. Sitting down at
the desk he said, ''You didn't tell me you're gonna do
some shopping.''

''I thought I did, at the airport.''

Nicolet shook his head. ''I would think, this delivery on your mind, you'd wait till after.''

''I've had my eye on this suit,'' Jackie said, ''and I
was afraid it might be gone.''

''Why'd you leave your flight bag?''

''Well, first of all, I brought it to put my uniform in
and whatever else I bought I wasn't going to wear.''

''But you didn't.''

''No, because when I came out . . . Wait, let's
start over. The idea was, I'd leave whatever I bought
in the flight bag, not have to carry it around, and

meet Sheronda with the bag that had the fifty thousand in it."

He said it again, staring at her, "But you didn't."

"Because I didn't *have* it. Ray, I swear, Melanie came in and grabbed it." Subdued then: "And someone killed her for it?"

He took a few moments to stare.

"Where's the bag she gave you?"

"She didn't *give* me one. I tried to tell you before," Jackie said, "Melanie wasn't part of the plan. Ordell must've told her to do it. She comes in, grabs the shopping bag, and runs. I'm standing there in my underwear. What am I supposed to do, go after her? I had to get dressed. And by the time I came out, the saleswoman already had the things I'd bought in boxes, putting them in a bag."

"You took time to pay her."

"I had to."

"You could've left your purchases."

"Weren't you or someone there watching me?"

Nicolet didn't answer.

"I was frantic. I didn't know what to do."

"So you took the shopping bag with your purchases and went to meet Sheronda."

"After I looked for you. I went straight to Barnie's, you weren't there. Was I being watched or not?"

"You were under surveillance, yeah."

"Ray, how am I supposed to get anyone's attention, let them know what happened? You didn't tell me how to do that, did you?"

Nicolet paused, but didn't answer. He said, "You

took Sheronda's bag and left the one with the new clothes."

"A skirt and jacket."

"You bought 'em for yourself, didn't you?"

"I felt sorry for her. I told you, she has no idea what this is about. You looked in the boxes—did you take the clothes?"

"We'll hold them for the time being."

"Did she tell you about the other time? The woman who came and switched bags with her after I left the ten thousand?"

Nicolet said, "Wait a minute."

"Ask her about it."

"You tell me."

"I just did."

"What's the woman's name?"

"I don't know. Sheronda said Ordell's aunty. He changed the plan that time and he did it again, or else Melanie was on her own."

"There was a guy with her."

"Not in the fitting room."

"Melanie was seen coming out," Nicolet said. "Our agent doesn't know who this is, but the bag's identical to the one you had. Our agent sees this guy tussle with her and take the shopping bag. He holds on to it like it's pretty valuable. So our agent follows them to see where they're going and make contact with other agents, alert them. . . ."

Jackie said, "This is the one who had trouble with her body mike?"

Nicolet stared, not saying a word.

"Got Muzak playing in her ear?"

"There was some interference, yeah. Soon as she located another agent he radioed a description. . . ."

"So she wasn't around when I came out of the fitting room," Jackie said, "looking all over for you."

"By the time you got to Barnie's we were on you again. Saw you come out and go meet Sheronda." He paused. "The guy with Melanie, that was Louis Gara?"

"I didn't see him," Jackie said. "I was in my underwear."

"A white guy."

"Probably Louis. He killed Melanie?"

"It's possible."

"And ran off with the money, or took it to Ordell?" Nicolet waited, giving her the stare again.

"I don't want to find out you were working something with Louis."

"Don't worry."

"You're saying you don't know what happened to that fifty thousand."

"I have no idea."

"You'll take a polygraph on it?"

"If it'll make you happy."

She watched him staring again in silence. It wasn't his best pose, the deadpan cop; it lacked confidence.

He said, "I hope you haven't done anything dumb. If Louis took the money, Ordell could come after you to find out what happened."

"Aren't you watching him?"

"I have those four kids ready to point him out in federal court, but I want him with the marked bills too."

He hadn't answered the question. Jackie said, "I have a feeling you don't know where he is."

"He isn't going anywhere," Nicolet said, "if he doesn't have the money."

"You do know that much," Jackie said, "it wasn't delivered to him. Or you don't think it was."

Nicolet's intercom buzzed.

He picked up his phone, said "Yeah," in a quiet tone, listened for a minute, hung up, and said to Jackie, "Excuse me." He put his hand on her shoulder as he walked out past her.

That was nice. Telling her they were still friends; nothing personal, just doing his job. Or he simply wanted to touch her. Either way, she took it as a good sign. He wanted to believe her story.

She wondered what Max was doing at this moment; if he'd already taken care of the money. When she asked where he was going to hide it Max said, "You don't hide a half million dollars, you put it in the bank. First Union, in a lockbox." She told him, "Don't have a heart attack, okay? I won't be able to get it out." Be honest with Max and he smiled.

Nicolet came back in the office. He sat down at the desk again to face her before he said, "Louis Gara's dead. Lake Park Police found him in his car, shot twice by someone who had to've been, in the consensus of opinion, a friend, huh?—who jammed the gun against his body and blew him away."

Jackie kept quiet.

"Ordell left his apartment at five twenty," Nicolet said. "He drove a few blocks up to the beach mall there, parked in back, and went in the bar. He never came out."

"You mean you lost him," Jackie said.

Nicolet's set expression didn't change. "Louis could've picked him up, he had time. They drive up to Northlake Boulevard together, where Louis was found. . . ."

Jackie waited.

"What would Louis be doing around there?"

"I have no idea," Jackie said.

"A bar, some joint Ordell liked to frequent?"

"I never met him in a bar."

"If he calls, you'll let me know?"

"Yeah, but I don't know why he would."

Nicolet said, "He still has money in Freeport, doesn't he? Or is it all here now? Maybe not half a million, but more than fifty grand?"

Jackie said, "Ray, you saw what I had."

"What you showed me."

"You think I took some of it?"

"I have no evidence of your taking *any*thing. You didn't pay for your new duds with marked bills; I was glad to see that. You've been helping us out, you gave us Melanie, Louis, so I have to believe your story. That is, as much as what you told me."

Jackie waited.

"I'll settle for Ordell with the marked bills. If you have something else going you haven't told me about, it's between you and him. All I'm gonna say is, I hope we find him before he finds you."

25

"You won't believe this," Ordell said to Mr. Walker on the phone.

"I just seen a palmetta bug walk up Raynelle's leg. She kind of lying on the sofa. The palmetta bug went up her leg, went under her dress, and she never moved. In her nod, today and all day yesterday. I got her a package of needles and enough shit for a week. Now she moved her knee, touched herself . . . Wait now. I hear the palmetta bug saying something. Yeah, saying, 'Ouuu, it's nice here. I don't believe this woman washes herself, yeah.' You see palmetta bugs on the stove. They climb up there, break their teeth, man, on the grease been there for years. Mr. Walker? You have to get me out of here, man. When you come get your boat, drive up to the Lake Worth Inlet."

Ordell waited, listening.

"No, not today. I won't be ready. I told you, I have

to see Jackie. Night before last I went in her apartment, she never came home. Watched her place all day yesterday—I'm gonna have to call this Max Cherry, I think that's where she's at, or in a motel someplace. See, I don't think she'd run this soon, get the feds suspicious of her."

Ordell listened again and said, "Maybe tomorrow, or Monday . . . I can't *do* it today. I ain't leaving here without my money. . . . Man, you hear yourself? Think about it. You wouldn't *have* the fucking boat it wasn't for me. Man, I am finding out real fast who my friends are. . . . Wait a minute now. I already told you, I didn't shoot her, Louis did and I done Louis, didn't I? What can I tell you? . . . Mr. Walker? . . ."

Ordell looked at the glassy-eyed woman on the sofa.

"You believe it? Hung up on me. Do things for people and that's how they treat you. Man has a boat thirty-six feet long and I'm stuck in this privy." He said, "Girl, how can you live like this?"

Raynelle said, "Like what?"

Ordell had Max Cherry's business card, GENTLEMEN PREFER BONDS written on it. He dialed the number. The voice that answered sounded like Winston's, telling him Max wasn't there.

"He leave town?"

"He's around."

"Give me his home number."

"I'll give you his beeper."

Ordell left the little stucco house that looked like it

was rusting out, the screens broken, walked two blocks east and around the corner to the bar on Broadway where he dialed Max Cherry's beeper number and left the number in the phone booth for him to call. Ordell had a rum collins while he waited. The bartender was the one he'd asked Thursday night what was the name of the woman came in here did heroin and tricks on the side. Was it Danielle? The bartender said heroin was the dope of choice again with many. This one, Ordell said, was kind of red-headed, tall, had real skinny legs. The bartender said, Raynelle? That was it, Raynelle. Ordell found her that same night, bought her rum collinses till 1:00 A.M.—the woman a disappointment, losing it fast, had that same rusted-out look as her house.

The phone rang in the booth.

Ordell went in and closed the door.

Max Cherry's voice said, "I've been looking for you."

The first thing Max did, after he looked at the number on his beeper, he called the Sheriff's office and spoke to a buddy of his named Wendy, who ran the Communications Section. Wendy put him on hold and was back in less than a minute. She told him the number belonged to Cecil's Bar, on Broadway in Riviera Beach.

The next thing Max did, at his desk in the office now, was ask Winston if he'd ever been to Cecil's. Winston said he'd picked up FTAs there; it was lowlife but sociable, they knew him. Why? Max asked him to wait.

He dialed the number, fairly sure it was Ordell who'd called. So when his voice came on the line Max said, "I've been looking for you."

"You know who this is?"

"Mr. Robbie, isn't it? I have that ten thousand you put up. Isn't that why you called?"

There was a silence on the line.

"The bond collateral on Beaumont Livingston you moved over to cover Ms. Burke. Remember?"

"She got off, huh?"

"They decided not to file. Tell me where you are and I'll bring you your money."

Silence again.

Max waited.

"You still there?"

"Let's cut to it," Ordell said. "I know you helped her and you know what I want. Jackie can tell me a story, why she had to hang on to the money. Understand? I'll listen. I'll tell her yeah, that's cool, now please hand it over while we still friends. That's all has to happen. Understand? She don't want to be friends—tell her to think of Louis, where he's at right now. Tell her, she turns me in, I'll put it on her she's my accessory and we'll go upstate, man, hand in hand cuffed together. Understand? That's how it is. Tell her that and I'll call you after a while."

Max sat back in his chair, Winston, hunched over his desk, watching him. "That was Ordell," Max said, "calling from Cecil's. You have time, you think you could find out for me where he's staying?"

"Cops can't locate him, huh?"

"They don't have your personality."

"If it's what you want," Winston said. "I don't have to know what you're doing, long as you know."

"I think I do," Max said. "Is that good enough?"

"You quit the business or not?"

"I'm giving that second thoughts."

Winston pushed up from his desk. Walking out he said, "You make up your mind, let me know."

Jackie said, "You know how to make a girl happy, don't you, Max?" slipping her arms around him and kissing him. He handed her the bottle of Scotch he'd brought and watched her walk over to the low dresser, where there were opened cans of Diet Coke and a plastic ice bucket, to make their drinks. He had felt her body in the T-shirt that hung loose covering her hips and a pair of white panties: nearly forty-eight hours in this room in a Holiday Inn, clothes and a towel on the double bed closer to the bathroom. On the phone a little while ago she'd said, "I'm going nuts," sounding tired, bored, until he told her Ordell had called and he'd be over.

Taking the chair by the window Max said, "I know where he is." She turned to look at him and he said, "All Winston had to do was ask around. Ordell's living in Riviera Beach with a woman, a junkie. He has a maroon Volkswagen parked in front of the house. It's his disguise." Max was seated in late afternoon

light, the draperies open enough to show the room.
Jackie came over with their drinks to sit on the edge
of the bed next to his chair, her bare legs in light. She
reached over to put her drink on the table and took a
cigarette from the pack lying there.

"How does Winston find him if ATF and all the
local police around here aren't able to?"

"People talk to Winston," Max said. "He's street,
the same as they are and they trust him. They get
busted, they know a guy who can bond them out."

"You haven't told anyone, have you, where he is?"

"The police? Not yet. I thought we should talk
about it first. What I might do is drop in on him,"
Max said. "He'll no doubt be surprised to see
me. . . ."

"He's liable to shoot you."

"On the phone I told him I owe him the ten he put
up for your bond. He'd forgotten about it, or had
something else on his mind. I could bring the money
and the papers for him to sign. . . ."

"Why do that?"

"I doubt if he'd come to the office."

"He might," Jackie said, and seemed to like the
idea.

Max wasn't sure why. He said, "The simplest way
to work it, I go see him with the bond refund. To
make sure he's there, that's the main reason. Come
out and call the Sheriff's Office. Or the TAC unit's
already standing by and they go in."

Jackie was shaking her head. "Ray wants him."

"Everybody wants him, he's a homicide suspect.

What you have to think about," Max said, "it doesn't matter who takes him, you could have a problem. As soon as he's brought up he's liable to name you as an accessory."

"I know that," Jackie said, "that's why I want ATF to make the case. I'm their witness, I've been helping them. They wouldn't *have* a case without me. If it's his word against mine, who're they going to believe?"

"It's not that simple."

"It never was, so I'm not going to start worrying about it now. Look, Ray's dying to be a hero. He'll do anything."

Max took one of her cigarettes and lit it, Jackie watching him, waiting.

"Okay, you want Nicolet to make the collar. How?"

"Get Ordell to come to your office."

"Set him up," Max said. "I tell him you want to see him?"

He saw that gleam in her eyes.

"I want to give him his money."

"Why?"

"I've chickened out. I'm afraid of him. He'll like that."

Max thought about it, smoking his cigarette.

"What do you tell Nicolet, why you're meeting Ordell?"

"I don't know—something to do with the bond refund." Jackie was quiet for several moments. She picked up her drink and took a sip. "That's why

Ordell's there, for the refund. I'll say he called me and said I have to sign something."

"You don't."

"But I don't know that. It's why I call an ATF agent. I'm suspicious—what does he want? And I'm scared."

"You think Ordell's gonna come out of hiding? Every cop in South Florida looking for him?"

"Max, he has to if he wants his money. If he didn't, he'd be gone by now."

"If he wants it that bad he's desperate."

"Of course he is."

"What if he wants to meet someplace else?"

"The money's in your office, in the safe. It's the only place I'll see him."

"What if you can't get hold of Nicolet?"

"I'll get him."

"What if he's out of town?"

"If you don't want to do it, Max, just tell me."

He let that go, looking at her without saying anything, thinking he could make sure Winston was there. "Let's say Ordell goes for it," Max said. "He'll decide when you meet, you know that."

"It'll be tonight," Jackie said, "he's not going to sit around wasting time. He'll have to let you call me. He'll probably want to talk. I can handle that. I'll tell him I wasn't holding out on him, I didn't trust Melanie. So I gave her towels. We have to have our stories straight if he asks me. And I didn't know how to get in touch with him till you helped me out."

"Why weren't you home, where he could find you?"

"I was afraid. I wasn't sure he'd give me a chance to explain."

Max watched her thinking about it, her face moving into the light as she reached over to roll the tip of her cigarette in the ashtray, staring at it, saying, "I should be there before he arrives."

Max said, "Why?"

She didn't look up. "That's where I've been hiding, in your office."

"Nicolet—is he already there, or does he come busting in while we're chatting?"

"He's already there."

"What if he hears something he's not supposed to?"

"We won't let that happen."

"You still have a gun?"

Jackie looked up now. "Yeah, why?"

"Don't bring it."

26

Ordell believed looking out the window would be a waste of time. If they knew he was here they'd come busting in with their sledgehammer, or that big crowbar from hell he'd seen SWAT teams use on TV, pry a door right off its hinges. They come in yelling down, down, down, screaming it at you, and the next thing you had was a shotgun against your head as you're saying what is this, man, what's going on here. Wasting your breath.

It was because he was pacing the room, Raynelle nodding on the sofa for what company she was, and happened to look outside as he came to the window, he saw Max Cherry on the sidewalk. Ordell looked out that front window good then, both ways up and down the street expecting to see one of those big vans with FDLE on the side, or some other initials. There was nothing suspicious going on out there, almost dark, some people down the street, but just people. Ordell quick went to the sofa and had to move Raynelle's skinny ass to get his pistol from under the cushion. Max Cherry knocking on the door now. Ordell stuck the Beretta in his waist, under his shirt hanging out, pulled the woman up by her arms, walked her into the bedroom, and dumped her on the bed. He had another pistol there under the pillow and one in the kitchen. Max Cherry knocking some more as Ordell tried to think how Max could've found him, Ordell telling himself it was okay, the man was a bail bondsman, so be cool, you hear? Be cool. You want to know, ask him.

Ordell let him in and closed the door.

He watched Max Cherry turn, his hand going inside his seersucker jacket as he glanced around the room, and Ordell pulled his Beretta and put it on him. Like that. Max said to him, "You want your money? Your bond refund?" His hand came out of the jacket holding a wad of bills in a rubber band, tossed it up, and Ordell swiped it out of the air with his free hand.

"This's all?"

"I have a receipt for you to sign."

"I said, 'This's all?' You know what I want. Did you speak to her?" Ordell moved to a front window saying it and looked out again.

"I didn't bring anybody," Max said. "She wants to give you the money. If she didn't, there'd be cops coming through the fucking door while you're asking me questions."

"Where's it at, in your car?"

"She wants to give it to you herself and collect her cut, her ten percent. She wants to explain why she held on to it."

"I like to hear that too."

"Why she didn't give it to Melanie."

"Turn around," Ordell said. He started patting Max down. "You tell me why."

"Jackie didn't trust her. Melanie'd already tried to get Jackie to go in with her, the two of them work it and split the half million. What she did was take quite a risk to see you get your money."

"Lift up your pant legs," Ordell said. "You helped her?"

"All I did was walk out with it."

"Put the bail-bondsman twist on it, huh? Smelling all that cash? And you telling me you want me to have it?"

"The only reason I'm here, I don't want to see Jackie get shot or busted."

"Protecting her," Ordell said. "I think you're pimping me is what you're doing."

"Then let's forget the whole thing," Max said. "Stay here with your junkie friend and your VW." He started for the door.

"Hey, man." Ordell waved the pistol at him and Max stopped. "Go on sit over there on the couch." He watched Max looking at the stained cushions. "Do like I say, man, sit down. It's dry, my friend hasn't thrown up on herself in two days. That's it. Now tell me where my money's at."

"My office," Max said.

"And where's Jackie?"

"She's been there since Thursday night."

"She wanted to see me, why wasn't she home?"

"She was afraid."

"I have to see that."

"She still is. She doesn't want to get shot before she can tell you what happened."

"Have her bring me the money here."

"It's in the safe. She can't get at it."

"Call her, tell her the combination."

"She won't leave there till you have the money and you're gone. I'll tell you that right now."

"But you expect me to walk in there."

"If I wanted to set you up," Max said, "I already told you, they'd have busted in by now. She knows if you get picked up you'll name her as an accessory. That scares her more than anything."

"It's why she's giving up my money, huh? Not that bullshit about Melanie. I didn't trust her either, but I knew how to handle her." Ordell moved to the window again. "She was my fine big girl." The street was quiet, dark out now. "I said to Louis, 'Man, you could've hit her.' Give her a punch in the mouth." He turned to Max. "Jackie wants her cut, huh?"

"Fifty grand."

"How 'bout the money she wants if she does time?"

"She got off."

"Yeah, I forgot. All right, I give her the fifty ATF

marked up, since she let them do it, and she gives me my money. Do it at your office, huh?"

"She's there now."

"How 'bout your man Winston?"

"He's out at the jail."

"I call your office, she better answer the phone, not somebody else."

Ordell took Max's business card from his shirt pocket and looked at it going over to the phone, on the floor next to a chair with a clear-plastic cover over it. He hated the chair, you stuck to it. He needed to get out of this place. He needed his clothes. He needed to get his hair done, his pigtail was coming loose from fooling with it. He needed his *car*. He could take the license plate off the VW and put it on the Mercedes. Stop on the way . . . Or have Jackie go pick it up right now, key under the front seat, and bring it to Max's office, have it there ready. If nobody had stole it. Put the money in the trunk and you're gone, man. Put all the money in the trunk. Five hundred and the marked-up fifty. Tell them, well, that's how it is.

Ordell laid the pistol on his lap, picked up the phone, and dialed the number. He waited. Then smiled saying, "Hey, baby, how you doing? You know who this is?"

Nicolet would watch Faron and his wife Cheryl, the way they acted when she came to visit, and he'd get an urge to see his ex, Anita. It didn't make sense, because he thought the way Faron and Cheryl talked to each other was stupid. Hi, hon. How're you feeling, hon? Not bad, hon. Both of them hon, no identity of their own when they were together. Like all fathers were dad or daddy to their kids. Nicolet could not see himself in this anonymous group. And yet almost every time he saw Faron and Cheryl hon-ing and touching each other, he'd miss Anita and get her to meet him for a drink. He'd say, "What're you gonna have, hon?" and watch her tighten her black eyebrows giving him a serious funny look. Cheryl was a homemaker, Anita an X-ray technician at Good Samaritan. They'd met when he was there for a physical. She gave him a barium enema and he asked her how she'd managed to get a job shooting white gunk into assholes all day. Anita said she guessed she was just lucky. They never called each other hon while they were married or knew what they would have for dinner, both of them working. He still considered scoring with Jackie. She was there. But so was Anita. He was seeing her more since Faron was in the hospital. Finally this evening Anita said okay when he suggested going back to her apartment.

His beeper went off on her nightstand.

Anita said, "Shit." Nicolet said, "Keep hold of it, hon, and we won't lose it." He dialed the number showing on his beeper and was surprised when Jackie Burke answered. He asked where she was and got another surprise.

"What're you doing there?"

"Ordell called and left a message on my machine.

He said I have to sign something so he can get his money back, for my bond."

"You don't sign anything."

"I didn't think so. I have a feeling he wants me to bring the rest of his money here, from Freeport. What do I do?"

"He's gonna be there?"

"He said about eight."

Nicolet glanced at the clock on the stand. "Why didn't you call me sooner?"

"I just found out. Will you come, please?"

Anita said, "Pleeease."

Jackie said, "What?"

"Is Max there?"

"No, but the other guy is."

"I'll be there right away. Hang on."

Jackie said, "Hurry."

Nicolet hung up the phone. "I have to be there and get some backup in the next fifteen minutes."

Anita said, "You might as well, hon. You're not doing much good here."

Ordell drove. He'd take this VW over to the beach mall after and put its license plate on the Mercedes. Get on the turnpike and head north into the night.

"All the time I've known her," he said to Max, big next to him in the little car, "I never heard her sound scared like that. Ordinarily, man, she's cool. All she had to do was take a taxicab to where my car's at and have it for me. She would *not* do it."

He felt like talking while Max Cherry wasn't saying

a thing. He did take a cigarette, asking for one as Ordell lit up.

"How come you have that sign in your office, no smoking, if you smoke?"

"I started again," Max said.

"Yeah, I remember you didn't have an ashtray for me that first time I come in. I told you I had cash to put up as collateral and you said oh, use that coffee mug there. I could've used anything I wanted. I said that time, you have ways to skim money, don't you? 'Cause you all crooks in that business. The woman tells you her scheme, man, your greedy eyes light up. You both of you plan to rip me off, I know that, and lost your nerve, huh? Gonna have to stay a bail bondsman, deal with the scum while you try to act respectable, huh? The rest of your life."

Max Cherry sat there dumb, the man knowing what he was.

They were approaching Banyan. Max said, "It's the next street."

Ordell said, "I know where it is."

Max said, "Turn left."

"I *know* where to turn."

They parked in the lot next door, the VW angled against the side of the storefront building. Max got out and stood by the trunk. He watched Ordell adjust the pistol stuck in his waist as he approached, pulling his shirt over it.

"What do you need that for?"

"You never know, do you?" Ordell started toward the front of the building.

Max waited. "What about the fifty thousand?"

"We leave it in the trunk," Ordell said, "till I see she has my money." He led the way around front to where MAX CHERRY BAIL BONDS was painted on the window. Ordell said, "Now I want you ahead of me."

Max opened the door covered with a sheet of plywood and crossed to the lighted doorway, Ordell behind him saying, "Easy now." Max walked in.

He saw Jackie seated at his desk holding a cigarette, her legs crossed. He stepped aside, toward Winston's desk, and saw her looking at Ordell. She wore a man's shirt, very little makeup.

Ordell said, "Girl, you not suppose to smoke in here. Don't you see the sign?"

Max watched Jackie swivel the chair slowly toward the door to the meeting room. It was closed. He saw her gaze raise to the sign.

He saw the door open and saw Ray Nicolet step out of the room and heard Ordell's voice.

Ordell saying, "What's this shit?"

Max turned to look at him and saw Jackie, still with the cigarette, begin to swivel back toward Ordell, Jackie saying, "Ray . . ." without changing her expression, but raising her voice now as she said, *He's got a gun!*

Max saw Ordell's face change. Saw his eyes come open wide with a look of surprise and then panic. Saw him pulling at his shirt to get to the pistol and did have it in his hand, cleared. But Nicolet beat him. Nicolet brought up the Beretta nine from against his leg and shot Ordell in the chest. Shot him three times there in barely more than a second and it was done.

It seemed so quiet after.

Nicolet walked over to Ordell, lying in the doorway to the front office. A Sheriff's deputy with a shotgun appeared out of the dark. Then another one. Nicolet looked at them. He stooped and touched Ordell's throat. Stood up and turned to look at Jackie. He didn't say anything. He looked at Winston, standing in the doorway to the meeting room now. Turned again, this time to Max.

"You were with him."

"I went to give him his refund, so he wouldn't have to come here."

"How'd you know where he was?"

"I found out."

"You didn't tell any police? Not even these people" —meaning the deputies—"where you used to work?"

Max said, "I thought you wanted him," and kept staring to hold his attention.

But Nicolet turned to look at Ordell again. Something going through his mind. He said, "We don't know who has his money, do we? The marked bills."

Max looked at Jackie. She drew on her cigarette. Neither of them spoke. Nicolet would look in Ordell's car soon enough.

He seemed to want to say something, but wasn't sure how to put it—staring at the man he'd killed.

"You told me," Jackie said to him, "you hoped you'd get him before he got me. Remember that?"

Nicolet turned, still holding the gun at his side. He nodded.

"Well, you did," Jackie said. "Thank you."

27

Jackie said, "You finally got the door fixed."

"Yeah. You like it?"

"I've driven by a few times."

Max, at his desk, didn't say anything, waiting.

"Since the package came," Jackie said.

She stood in the doorway where a man had been killed ten days ago. She looked clean and fresh in white slacks and a bright green shirt, dark sunglasses she removed now and he could see her eyes.

"The mailman usually leaves them downstairs by the elevator, but he brought this one up. Maybe he shook the box—you know, and thought there had to be at least a half million in it."

"Less ten percent," Max said.

"Yeah, your fee. I had to figure that out, since there wasn't a note, no explanation. Only this isn't a bail bond, Max."

"I hesitated taking that much."

"You worked for it—if that's all you want."

He felt awkward sitting here; he thought if he didn't say much he'd be okay. She'd realize he understood how it was. But she didn't make it easy the way she was looking at him, with that gleam in her eyes. She said, "I thought you were quitting the business," and he shrugged.

"I don't know."

"How old are you, Max?"

It surprised him, because she knew.

"Fifty-seven."

"And you don't know what you want?"

He could answer that, but he hesitated and she said, "I know what I want. I'm leaving, I have my things in the car. Why don't you walk out with me? I want to show you something." Still he hesitated and she said, "Come on, Max. I won't hurt you." She smiled.

So he smiled and got up from the desk. He didn't want to; he felt let down. Still, he'd prepared himself and was resigned, sensing all along and despite moments of optimism this was the way it would end, if it ever got this far. Or if in fact, thinking of Nicolet, they were all the way out of it.

She said, "I saw Ray at the hospital the other day, when I went to visit Faron."

It amazed him and made him think of the time she said they were alike. Their minds working the same way.

Jackie saying, as they walked through the front office and he held the door for her, "Ray's working in a new area, looking for all kinds of weapons the Desert Storm soldiers are bringing back as souvenirs, Russian AK-47s, he said even live hand grenades. They found four pounds of plastic explosive one of the guys shipped home to his wife and she showed it to a neighbor, not having any idea what it was."

They walked along the front of the building.

"And, he's after a guy who owns a gun shop he says is 'woefully and wantonly' selling assault rifles to minors. He actually used those words. He called the guy who owns the gun shop a 'whackjob' and said he's going to take him down if it's the last thing he does."

"Did you tell Ray you were leaving?"

"I told him I might. His ex-wife was with him. Anita. Attractive but, well, a little overdone."

Max had the feeling he'd missed something. Maybe they should sit down and talk and he'd ask her questions. But they came around the corner of the building to the lot and he was looking at a black Mercedes convertible with its top down. He said, "That's Ordell's."

"I'm borrowing it," Jackie said. "They confiscated his Volkswagen, with the money in it. This one's sort of left over, you might say. The registration's in the glove box." She looked at Max for a moment. "What's the matter? Haven't you ever borrowed someone's car?"

He said, "Not after they're dead."

She walked around to the other side and looked

across the low black Mercedes at him. "Come on, Max. I'll take you away from all this."

"Dealing with scum," Max said, "and trying to act respectable." He saw Jackie frown, her nice eyes narrowing for a moment. "That's how Ordell described my situation."

"And you like it?" Jackie said.

Max hesitated.

"Where would we go?"

"I don't know," Jackie said, and he saw her eyes begin to smile. "Does it matter?"

Special Advance Preview from
the new Elmore Leonard title

PRONTO

Available October 1993 from Delacorte Press

ONE

One evening, it was toward the end of October, Harry Arno said to the woman he'd been seeing on and off the past few years, "I've made a decision. I'm going to tell you something I've never told anyone before in my life."

Joyce said, "You mean something you did when you were in the war?"

It stopped him. "How'd you know that?"

"When you were in Italy and you shot the deserter?"

Harry didn't say anything, staring at her.

"You already told me about it."

"Come on. When?"

"We were having drinks at the Cardozo, outside, not long after we started seeing each other again. You said it the same way you did just now, like you're going to tell me a secret. That's why I knew. Only I don't think you said anything about making a decision."

Now he was confused.

"I wasn't drinking then, was I?"

"You quit before that." Joyce paused and said, "Wait a minute. You know what? That was the second time you told me about shooting the guy. At Pisa, right? You showed me the picture of you holding up the Leaning Tower."

"It wasn't at Pisa," Harry said. "Not where I shot the guy."

"No, but around there."

"You're sure I told you about it twice?"

"The first time, it was when I was working at the club and we went out a few times. You were still drinking then."

"That was what, six or seven years ago."

"I hate to say it, Harry, but it's more like ten. I know I was almost thirty when I quit dancing."

Harry said, "Jesus Christ," figuring that would be about right, if Joyce was around forty now. Getting up there. He remembered her white skin in the spotlight, dark hair and pure white skin, the only topless dancer he ever knew who wore glasses while she performed; not contacts, real glasses with round black rims. For her age Joyce still looked pretty good. Time went by so fast. Harry had turned sixty-six two weeks ago. He was the same age as Paul Newman.

"You ever hear me tell anyone else?"

Joyce said, "I don't think so." And said right away, "If you want to tell it again, fine. It's a wonderful story."

He said, "No, that's okay."

They were in Harry's apartment at the Della Robbia on Ocean Drive listening to Frank Sinatra, Frank and Nelson Riddle driving "I've Got You Under My Skin," Harry speaking quietly, Joyce looking distracted. Harry all set to tell her about the time in Italy forty-seven years ago and then ask—this was the decision he'd finally made —if she would like to go there with him the end of January. Right after the Super Bowl.

But now he wasn't sure he wanted to take her.

For as long as he'd known Joyce Patton—Joy, when she was dancing topless—he had always wondered if he shouldn't be doing better.

Harry Arno was grossing six to seven thousand a week running a sports book out of three locations in South Miami Beach. He had to split fifty-fifty with a guy named Jimmy Capotorto—Jimmy Cap, Jumbo—who had a piece of whatever was illegal in Dade County, except cocaine, and he had to take expenses out of his end: the phones, rent, his sheet writers, various incidentals. But that was okay. Harry Arno was skimming a thousand a week off the top and had been doing it for as long as he had wiseguys as silent partners, going back twenty years. Before Jumbo Jimmy Cap there was a guy named Ed Grossi and before Grossi, going all the way back forty years, Harry had worked for S & G Syndicate bookies as a runner.

The idea originally was to get out of the business at sixty-five, a million-plus socked away in a Swiss bank through its branch in the Bahamas. Then changed his mind when the time came and kept working. So he'd quit at sixty-six. Right now the football season was in full swing and his customers would rather bet the pros than any other sport except basketball. Put down anywhere from a few hundred to a few grand—he had some heavy players—and watch the games on TV that Sunday. So now he'd wait until after the Super Bowl, January 26, to take off. Three months from now. What was the difference, retire at sixty-five or sixty-six, no one knew how old he was anyway. Or his real name, for that matter.

Harry Arno believed he was a hip guy; he kept up, didn't feel anywhere near sixty-six, knew Vanilla Ice was a white guy; he still had his hair, parted it on the right side and had it touched up every other week where he got his hair cut, up on Arthur Godfrey Road. Joyce now and then would arch her back, look up at him, and say, "We're almost the same height, aren't we?" Or she'd say, "What are you, about five seven?" Harry would tell her he was the height of the average U.S. fighting man in World War Two, five nine. Maybe a little less than that now, but in fairly good shape after a near heart attack, a blocked artery they opened with angioplasty. He jogged up and down Lummus Park for most of an hour every morning, the Della Robbia and the rest of the renovated Art Deco hotels on one side of him, the beach and the Atlantic Ocean on the other, hardly anyone outside yet. Most of the old retired people were gone, the old Jewish ladies with their sun hats and nose shields, and the new inhabitants of South Beach, the trendies down from New York, the dress designers and models, the actors, the stylish gays, didn't appear on the street before noon.

One day pretty soon now his players would be making phone calls asking, "What happened to Harry Arno?" realizing they didn't know anything about him.

He'd disappear and start a new life, one that was waiting for him. No more pressure. No more working for people he didn't respect. Maybe have a drink now and then. Maybe even a cigarette in the evening looking out at the bay at sunset. Have Joyce there with him.

Well, maybe. It wasn't like there weren't any women where he was going. Maybe get there first and settle in and then, if he felt like it, send for her. Have her come for a visit.

He was ready. Had passports in two different names, just in case. Saw a clear field ahead, no problems. Until the afternoon Buck Torres told him he was in trouble. October 29, outside Wolfie's on Collins Avenue.

Wolfie's was the only restaurant Harry knew of that still served Jell-O. A friend of his at *The Miami Herald* said, "And with a straight face." There was a "Harry Arno" on the sandwich menu he couldn't eat anymore. Pastrami and mozzarella with tomatoes and onions, a splash of Italian dressing. Harry could eat deli and he could eat Cuban if he was careful, not load up on the black beans. What he couldn't get used to were all the new places that served tofu and polenta, pesto sauce on everything. Sun-dried cherries and walnuts on grouper, for Christ sake.

October 29 Harry would remember he had vegetable soup, a few crackers, iced tea, and the Jell-O, strawberry. Stepped out into the sunlight in his beige warm-ups with the red piping, his Reeboks, and there was Buck Torres standing by an unmarked car, a blue '91 Caprice. Harry had been arrested by Buck Torres a half-dozen times or so; they knew each other pretty well and were friends. Not socially, Harry had never met Buck's wife, but friends in the way they trusted one another and always had time to talk about other things than what they did for a living. Buck Torres had never asked Harry about his business with Jimmy Capotorto, trying to get to Jimmy Cap through Harry.

This time was different, this October 29 afternoon. Harry could feel it. Torres said, "Man, you're looking sporty as ever. Get in, I'll drive you home."

Harry told him he had his car.

"That's all right," Torres said. "Get in anyway, we'll drive around."

They started south on Collins and pretty soon turned west toward Washington, not much traffic yet. By December it would be bumper to bumper down here. There was a stale cigarette smell in the car. Harry opened his window.

"What I'd like you to do," Buck Torres said, "is happen to take a look at the papers on the seat."

Harry already had.

A stack of legal sheets with the heading:

Addressed to the Circuit Court, Criminal Division, of the 11th Judicial Circuit in and for the County of Dade, Florida. Below that was the name of a judge and below the judge Harry saw the wording become personal, requesting authorization to hang wires on the telephone numbers of his three sports-book locations, "subscribed to by HARRY JACK ARNO," his name in there big.

He said, "Why're you going to all this trouble? Everybody knows what I do."

"It's serious this time," Torres said. "We've had pen registers on your phones since the beginning of football season. We know what numbers've been calling you and who you've called, twenty-four hours a day. Look at page fourteen."

"I believe you," Harry said.

"Last Sunday your phones had like a hundred and eighty incoming calls during action time, right before the pro games got started."

"I have a lot of friends," Harry said.

"Use that in court," Torres said, "you get a laugh and maybe a five-hundred-dollar fine. This's different."

Harry was still looking down at the legal papers.

He said, "This judge bets college games through a buddy of his, a lawyer. All Southeast Conference. He lays it on the hot side, the favorites, every time. He'll pick Florida, Florida State, and Miami, no matter what the line is."

"Turn to page twenty-eight," Torres said. "Look at the date and the signature."

"You already have me tapped?"

"The wire was okayed weeks ago. Those three numbers but not your residence."

Harry said, "Don't you know I record all my transactions? I could've given you my tapes, saved you the expense."

Torres turned right on Washington to head north past white storefronts that looked closed in the sunlight. The pastel colors and neon kitsch taking over South Beach not up this far yet. "It's a Bureau operation," Torres said. "They want Jimmy Cap, like they do every year or so, make a lot of noise. We do the legwork and they take what we come up with to a federal grand jury."

"What you're telling me," Harry said, "I could go down with Jimmy on a racketeering charge?"

He saw Torres glance over, Torres serious, and that began to bother him.

"That's how it started out," Torres said. "You go down unless you testify, help them put Jumbo away on a RICO indictment. I said to the agent in charge of the investigation, 'How you going to turn Harry Arno, hold six months over his head? He doesn't cross state lines. What he does is a misdemeanor.' McCormick, the agent in charge, goes, 'Yeah, he'd have to be desperate, wouldn't he?' So he thinks about it and he says, 'Okay, what if this guy Arno believes Jumbo wants him taken out?'"

Harry frowned. "Why would he?"

"Keep you from putting something on him."

"What do I tell, the guy's a fucking gangster? Everybody knows it."

Torres said, "You think I'm kidding?" No, he was serious, he was anxious, but took time now to pull over to the curb and park. He turned enough in the seat to face Harry and lay it out.

"The idea is to set you up. You think Jumbo is going to have you whacked and you go running to the Justice Department for protection."

"What I've always wanted to be," Harry said, "a fink."

Torres said, "Listen to me. McCormick says, 'Or work it so Arno does get whacked and you bring Jumbo up on a homicide.' He says, 'What would be wrong with that?' He says after he was kidding, but I'm not sure. He thinks about it some more. Now the idea, he says, 'What if we put it in Jumbo's ear this guy Arno is skimming on him?'" Torres kept talking even though Harry was shaking his head. "'Jumbo makes a threatening move. Arno sees what's happening, he freaks and comes running to Uncle.'"

"Every wire room I know of," Harry said, "the guy operating it skims. It's expected, just don't be obvious about it. I can take a hundred a week off the top for expenses, Jimmy knows it. Long as he gets his cut he's not going to say a fucking word."

Torres said, "Yeah, but what McCormick is talking about, the idea, get Jumbo to think you're skimming on him big-time, big amounts." Harry was shaking his head again and Torres said, "You mentioned Jumbo's cut. What's that, half?"

"Right down the middle," Harry said.

"He knows how much you gross each week?"

"Sure he does."

"How's he know the exact figure?"

"I tell him," Harry said. "He doesn't believe me he can listen to the tapes any time he wants."

"Has he ever?"

"You kidding? He's too fucking lazy."

Torres said, "Well, McCormick's had people monitoring all your action-time bets and running totals."

"Come on, they're listening to all that?"

"McCormick wants to know if what you make and what you tell Jumbo you make are the same thing."

"Guy's out of his mind," Harry said. "What about what my runners bring in? Hardly any of that's recorded. Or some players that're friends and call me at home? What about the different ways people who've come here from other parts of the country, Jersey for instance, place their bets? The language they use. A guy calls, he says, 'I like the Vikings and six for five dimes.' Another guys calls. 'Harry, the Saints minus seven thirty times.' He loses, what's the juice, straight ten percent? If they forget the juice they won't even get close to the gross. I keep the tapes in case there any disagreements after, who owes who, or I go to collect and the guy claims he never made the bet. It rarely happens, because if there is any doubt about what the player is putting down I ask him. Guy calls up, he says, 'Harry, give me the Lions and the Niners twenty times reverse. Bears a nickel, Chargers a nickel. Giants five times,

New England ten times *if* the Rams ten.' That's twice a day Saturday and Sunday I get straight bets, parlays, round robins, over and under, we got the NBA going into action, listen, I even get some hockey. You're telling me this Bureau guy's people are going to get a read out of that?"

Torres said, "Harry, we hear you talking to Jumbo, telling him the totals for the week, how you made out, all that. This one time we hear the two of you talking, we hear Jumbo ask you about a guy, this black dude in a suit, gold chains, that came up to him in the lounge out at Calder? Jumbo's having a drink between races. The black dude says, 'Man, you killed me last week.' Says he dropped ten thousand and paid another grand for the vig. We hear Jumbo ask you about the guy. You recall that?"

Harry took his time. "I told Jimmy it was news to me, right? You heard that? The guy was mistaken, he laid it off somewhere else. I said to Jimmy if he wanted to check my tapes he could."

Torres was nodding. "Yeah, but the black guy, Jumbo says, told him he laid the bet with *you*, nobody else. Ran into you at Wolfie's and you wrote it down."

"It never happened," Harry said. "I told Jimmy, 'Find the guy. Let him tell me to my face I took his bet.' I don't do business like that, with people I don't know. A player has to be recommended." Harry felt himself getting hot again, the same way he did on the phone talking to Jimmy Cap, all that coming back to him and realizing now what it was about. "I told Jimmy, 'This guy's setting me up, that's all, and I don't even know why.' Well, I do now."

"The guy's under indictment on a drug bust," Torres said. "He does what McCormick tells him and gets the charge reduced from Intent to Distribute to Simple Possession. See how he's working it? You can't prove the guy didn't put the bet down with you, right? And now Jumbo's wondering how many payoffs you might've skimmed on him. Okay, then another phone conversation we heard, Jumbo's discussing it with one of his guys. He says if the jig had the nerve to come up to him it must be true and tells the guy to handle it. This was yesterday afternoon."

Harry said, "Handle it. That's all he said?"

"He didn't say how he wanted it done, no."

"Who was he talking to?"

"Couple of times he called the guy Tommy."

"Tommy Bucks," Harry said. "Dark-complected guy. He came over from Sicily ten twelve years ago he was Tommy Bitonti."

"That's who I thought it was, Tommy Bucks," Torres said, getting out his pocket notebook. "He gives you that look, Don't fuck with me. Yeah, dark complected, but the guy's a sharp dresser. Anytime I've ever seen him he has on a suit and tie."

"Like in the fifties," Harry said. "You went out at night to a club you wore a suit or a good-looking sports jacket. Tommy came over—the first thing he learned was how to dress. Always looks like a million bucks. That's where he got his name, Tommy Bucks, but he's still a greaseball."

Harry watched Torres enter the name in his notebook. Tommy, Jimmy, like they were talking about little kids. Harry thought of something and said, "You must've wired Jimmy's place, too, if you heard him talking to other people." And saw Torres look up and then smile for the first time.

"You know his house on Indian Creek? Almost right across from the Eden Roc," Torres said. "We've had him under surveillance from the hotel. We see Jumbo out on his patio, he's wearing this giant pair of shorts—what's he weigh, three hundred pounds?"

"At least," Harry said. "Maybe three and a half."

"We're watching him, we notice he's always talking on a cordless phone. So we put some people in a boat that's tied to that dock on the hotel side of the creek? They use a scanner, lock in on his signal, his frequency, and monitor the phone conversations, whoever he's talking to. Portable handset, you don't need a court order."

For a few moments it was quiet in the car.

"What you pick up is in the air," Torres said. "You know, radio waves, and they're free. That's why you don't need authorization."

Harry nodded and it was quiet again.

He said, "I appreciate your telling me what's going on. I know you're sticking your neck out."

"I don't want to see you hurt," Torres said, "on account of this asshole McCormick."

Harry said, "Well, I'm not going to worry about it. If it was ten or twelve years ago and Jimmy told Tommy Bucks in those words, 'Handle it,' that would be a different story. I mean back when he first came over," Harry said. "Tommy's a Zip. You know what I mean? One of those guys they used to import from Sicily to handle the rough stuff. Guy could be a peasant right out of the fucking Middle Ages, looks around and he's in Miami Beach. Can't believe it. They hand the Zip a gun and say, 'There, that guy.' And the Zip takes him out. You understand? They import the kind of guy likes to shoot. He's got no priors here; nobody gives a shit if he gets picked up, convicted, put away. If he does, you send for another Zip. Guy comes over from Sicily, he's got on a black suit, shirt buttoned up, no tie, and a cap sitting on top of his head. That was Tommy Bucks ten twelve years ago when he was Tomasino Bitonti."

"So you hope he's changed more than his suit," Torres said. He stared at Harry. "You don't look too worried."

"I can always leave town," Harry said.

Torres grinned. "You're a cool guy. I'll give you that."

Harry shrugged. Man, was he trying.